His Own Appointed Day

His Own
Appointed Day

D. M. DEVINE

WALKER AND COMPANY

New York

First published in the United States of America
in 1966 by Walker and Company, a division of
Publications Development Corporation.

Printed in the United States of America

The Boy

THE FAIR-HAIRED boy at the back of the class-room was writing. On the desk in front of him Virgil's Aeneid half concealed the page on which he wrote. His left hand casually shielded the rest.

It was like any other November afternoon. A little colder than most, perhaps. And darker. There would be fog again to-night.

McGregor's voice droned on, murdering the poetry with the deadly literalness of his translation. Bradley didn't interrupt, hardly seemed to listen. Bradley's cold was worse to-day. His face was pinched and drawn, and he had a hard, dry little cough.

Mechanically the fair-haired boy turned the page of his Virgil as thirty-two other pages rustled. He continued to write.

". . . sense of power which is *exhilarating*. A few more hours. I wonder what Mother will do. To hell with her! To hell with them all, the whole lousy rotten . . ."

"Pratt! Are you with us, Pratt?"

"Sir?" Swiftly the boy shut the diary and slid the Aeneid flat on top of it.

"I asked you, Pratt, if McGregor's rendering of that line met with your approval?"

"No, sir. It was way off the beam. What line was it, sir?"

The class guffawed. Bradley's face darkened. He walked slowly up between the rows of desks to where the boy sat.

"There are limits to the insolence that——" His voice broke off in a convulsive sneeze. The boy took a handkerchief from his pocket and delicately wiped his sleeve. There was a nervous titter from the class.

He had gone too far. Bradley's hand swooped, flung aside the Aeneid and seized on the book underneath.

"What have we here?" he said, holding it aloft. "Ah-ha. A diary!" He lowered his arm and began to riffle through the pages. "Perhaps we may all benefit from the pearls that our young friend——"

The boy was on his feet, his eyes blazing. "That's private, sir. You've no right to touch it." He must stop him. What a *fool* he had been to provoke this.

But the master was already turning away, the book held open in his hand while his eyes skimmed down a page.

The boy pushed roughly past, then turned and faced him, barring his way. "Give it back," he said fiercely.

For a moment they stood there, silent, staring angrily at each other. Then Bradley coughed, and a spasm of pain crossed his face. His shoulders sagged and he thrust the book wearily at Pratt. "Take your grubby little secrets, boy," he said.

A sigh rippled through the class. A sigh of released tension, part relief, part disappointment.

Back at his desk the fair-haired boy mopped his brow. What a bloody fool he had been! Vanity, that's what it was. Vanity. A cheap desire to score off old Bradley.

Mary Reilly was construing now, her eyes anxious behind her prim little spectacles; more fluent than McGregor but equally insensitive. In the seat behind her the Anderson girl inched her skirt fractionally higher and stole a glance across the room to see if Jim Makin's eye was on her. It was.

Pratt gazed round with contempt at heads industriously bent. Puppets learning to conform, lapping up the lies and the propaganda they were fed. There was Ringo Edwards, even, picking his teeth and frowning in concentration, embodiment of the black sheep reformed.

A girl looked up and caught his eye. She smiled. Pratt stared stonily until she flushed and turned away. A stab of guilt shot through him. Norah represented the standards he had discarded, the way of life he had turned his back on. And yet. . . . And yet. . . .

The clock in the school tower chimed the quarter. Fifteen minutes to go. For Pratt the last fifteen minutes of his school career. And none of them know it, he thought sardonically. If they did, would they care? Norah might. She would be sorry. But not the others. He wasn't one of them.

Wisps of fog were drifting across the ceiling lights. Bradley coughed again.

"There stands to each person his own day. . . ."

"Oh! God!" Bradley muttered. And then aloud: "But what does that *mean*, Shearer?"

"I don't know, sir."

"'*Stat sua cuique dies.*' Can no one enlighten our friend?"

2

Pratt had found the place. "Each man has his own appointed day," he translated; "the span of life is short and cannot be retraced; but——"

"Thank you, Pratt. An adequate rendering. Continue, Shearer." But then he added, fixing his eyes on Pratt: "The sentiment is one we should do well to ponder."

Again that twinge of—what was it, remorse? He had been Bradley's favourite, once, his star pupil. But what the hell! A lot of water had flowed under the bridge since these days.

In the cloakroom, as he bent to fasten his cycle clips, someone planted a kick on his rear and sent him sprawling. He picked himself up angrily.

"You watch it——" he began, then, more quietly: "Oh, it's you." Damn! why did he have to run into Lenny to-night?

"Yeah. Just me. Couldn't resist the sitting target. . . . Say, can you lend me a fag?"

Pratt took out a twenty packet, extracted three and handed them to the other boy, who stuffed them in the pocket of his blazer. Then Pratt took one himself and put it in his mouth. He struck a match.

"For Christ's sake, Ian, have you gone stark, staring? If you're caught smoking in here. . . ."

Pratt shrugged. "O.K. Let's go." He tossed away the match and put the cigarette behind his ear.

They walked across the staff car park to the cycle shed. The fog was thickening. Their footsteps on the tarmac were muffled.

"Wouldn't say no to a draw now," said Lenny. They lit up. All round them boys were lifting bicycles from the racks, turning on the lamps, wheeling them away. Here and there other cigarettes glowed in the semi-darkness.

"See you at the Kaff to-night?" Lenny asked. His voice was soft and slow, the voice of an innocent. That's what had earned him the nickname of "Lenny"—that and his great bulk and strength. Someone had seen the film of Steinbeck's *Of Mice and Men*, and from that day Tom Ferguson was Lenny.

He wasn't innocent, though. Not in any sense. Behind the oafish exterior was a shrewd and calculating brain. Pratt was afraid of him.

"Couldn't say," Pratt answered. "Might look in later on."

Lenny grinned. "Think I don't know where you go Wednesday nights?"

Christ! surely not! Pratt's heart thumped painfully.

"Aye," the soft voice drawled on. "I followed you last Wednesday."

3

He was bluffing. He *must* be bluffing. Pratt said nothing.

"Nice bit of stuff, yon. Can't say I blame you."

He could have wept with relief. Though *why* he should be ashamed of it he couldn't analyse.

"Yes, not bad," he said lightly. "Makes a change. Don't let on to Myra, though."

"Trust me." But Lenny's eyes were on him, sizing him up. Pratt's uneasiness returned.

He took a last pull on his cigarette, dropped it beside him and ground it with his heel into the cement floor.

"Better be making tracks, I guess." Gently he eased his bicycle from its rest, running his hand lovingly over its gleaming frame.

"Nice job, that," said Lenny, watching him.

"Uh-huh."

"Set your old man back a quid or two, eh?"

Pratt was bending over the lamp. "Yes," he said, not looking up.

"Well, see you later," said Lenny.

"Later?"

"In the Kaff."

"Oh, yes. Might do. So long, Lenny."

He wheeled the bicycle away. When he had crossed the car park, he looked back. The shed was almost swallowed up in the fog. But he could see the dim glow of Lenny's cigarette. He hadn't moved.

Pratt stood on the pedal and gently free-wheeled to the gate. His encounter with Lenny had sobered him. For the first time he wondered if things might go wrong.

Funny how Lenny gave him the creeps. He ought to like him. The rest of the gang liked Lenny. Even Myra.

As he turned through the gate the last of the school buses was pulling away, fog lamps on, the driver peering through the windscreen. The street was almost deserted now. A few stragglers drifted homewards. In the car park engines were spluttering to life as members of the staff prepared to leave.

Under the lamp outside the school gate a girl stood alone, waiting. Pratt was almost past before he recognised her. It was Eileen, his sister. She hadn't seen him. He cycled on up the street.

He had gone fifty yards when he turned back. He must speak to Eileen; he couldn't walk out of her life without a word.

But he was too late. A second figure had joined her. A man. Eileen tucked her hand in his arm, smiled, and the pair of them set off briskly and disappeared into the fog.

Pratt swore. He turned his cycle once more and pedalled blindly up the road. At the corner of Drumchapel Street he had to swerve to avoid a small child who loomed in front of him.

"You bloody nit!" he shouted at the frightened child.

PART I

The Inspector

ONE

SHE WOULD be about twenty-three, Nicolson judged. Twenty-three or twenty-four. Very dark hair, cut short; good complexion; straight nose and wide generous mouth. She wore a lemon raincoat.

"Miss Pratt would like a word with you, sir," Sergeant Cubitt announced, then went out and closed the door behind him.

Nicolson offered her a chair, but she seemed not to hear. She was frankly appraising the room, taking in the bare, distempered walls, the maroon filing cabinets, the two desks with their telephones and their inkstands and their untidy litter of papers, the two coats and hats hanging on the stand in the corner.

"You share with Mr. Cameron?" she said, eyeing the brown overcoat. Her voice was low-pitched and musical, with a lilt of the Highlands.

"Yes," he said, keeping his voice expressionless.

But not expressionless enough. The quick, perceptive glance she gave him told that she had detected the nuance.

She seemed to feel an explanation was called for. "His wife's a friend of mine. . . . And of course I met him last time I was here."

"You've been here before?"

"Yes," she said, in a tone that discouraged further questions.

Now she walked over to his desk and sat down.

"I've come about my brother, Inspector," she began briskly. "He's missing."

"Since when?"

"Since he came out of school on Wednesday."

"Wednesday? But that's two days ago!"

The girl flushed. "My mother—that is, we—well, we thought we knew where he'd gone."

"And you were wrong?"

She nodded calmly. "Yes, we were wrong."

6

Nicolson stared at her. She might have been reporting the loss of a bicycle.

"All right," he said at length. "Suppose we begin at the beginning."

Her name was Eileen Pratt, and she lived in Hughenden Road. She was gymnastics mistress in Silbridge High School.

She had an older sister, married and living in England, and a brother, Ian, aged sixteen, in sixth form in the High School. On Wednesday Ian had attended school as usual and was seen wheeling his bicycle out of the school gate at ten past four. After that he had vanished.

"Wednesday was the very foggy day, wasn't it?" Nicolson interjected.

The girl nodded.

"Have you tried the hospitals?"

"I don't think there was an accident."

"Why not?"

"He came home after school and packed a suitcase and went off with it."

"But you said——"

"Nobody *saw* him. We were all out. But the case is gone, and most of his clothes."

"In other words he's run away from home?"

"Yes."

"Any idea why?"

She didn't answer.

"I mean," he went on reflectively, "a boy doesn't run away for nothing, does he?"

"Mr. Nicolson, you're new here, aren't you?"

"Yes."

"You see, Ian's——" She hesitated. "What I mean is—Mr. Cameron knows about Ian."

"Sergeant Cameron? . . . Oh! I see. He's been in trouble, has he?"

"He's on probation. . . ." Then she added angrily: "It's that crowd he hangs around with in Finghetti's Café—Gammans and Lenny Ferguson and that lot. And there's a girl, too. . . ."

"Names, please."

"What? Oh! *they* won't know where he's gone."

"Never mind. We may want to talk to them."

She gave him half a dozen names.

"And the girl?"

"Myra. I only know her first name."

Nicolson had been writing names in a pad. Now he looked up. The girl was regarding him with amused tolerance.

"Miss Pratt," he said sharply, "you do want us to find your brother, don't you?"

"Not really. I'm glad he had the guts to clear out."

"Then why come here?"

"My mother sent me. She's afraid he may have come to some harm."

"And you?"

She took a long time to answer. At length she said: "Leave me out of this. I'm only here because Mother wasn't well enough to come herself. I want no part of it."

"Where did you think he'd gone?" Nicolson asked. "At first, I mean. You said——"

"To my sister's in Liverpool. But Mother phoned this morning. They haven't seen him."

"This *morning*? The boy's been missing thirty-six hours before you even——"

She frowned. "Mother and Annette don't get along. Mother had to swallow her pride before she phoned."

A happy family, Nicolson was thinking. He sensed that relations between this girl and her mother were strained too.

"What was he wearing and what did he take with him? We'll need a complete list. . . . And a photograph, of course. Can you——"

"Mother'll tell you about the clothes. But I've brought a photograph." Pulling off her gloves, she opened her handbag and brought out an envelope. He caught the flash of diamonds from her engagement finger.

It was a passport-size snapshot of a teenage boy, as fair as his sister was dark. The face was long and narrow, with large, luminous eyes and a sensitive mouth.

Miss Pratt came round beside the inspector.

"It's like him," she said, "except——"

"Yes?"

"Well, he's a strong boy. Healthy. This makes him look like a dying duck."

"Not much family resemblance, is there?" Nicolson remarked. "I mean, you'd never guess he was your brother."

"No?" she said, regarding him stonily.

Sergeant Cubitt didn't raise his eyes as the girl crossed from the C.I.D. room and went out through the swing doors. He was typing a report, although Nicolson could see the yellow cover of a western protruding from a pile of papers beside him.

Nicolson strolled over to the desk.

"Give me the gen on the Pratt family, Sergeant," he said.

Cubitt looked up. He was a man of about fifty, florid-faced and balding. An ex-serviceman, and with the characteristics of the old sweat: a manner carefully adjusted to the rank of the person he was addressing, and a talent for avoiding work.

No one was deceived by Cubitt: his subterfuges were too transparent. Yet the station as a whole regarded him tolerantly. Even Chief Inspector Mearns, normally so demanding, allowed Cubitt liberties no one else would have dared claim.

Nicolson remained unimpressed. Servility and laziness did not appeal to him.

"The Pratts?" Cubitt was saying. Here he was on his home ground. Apart from his years in the army all his life had been lived in Silbridge: and a nose for scandal and a retentive memory had provided him with a remarkable dossier on many of its citizens. It was his one unique contribution to the work of the station. "They came to Silbridge about fifteen years ago. Live in Hughenden Road. The father's a clerk in the Labour Exchange. The mother——"

"The father's still alive, is he?" Nicolson was mildly surprised: the girl had never mentioned her father.

Cubitt grinned. "Yes, sir—in a manner of speaking, if you see what I mean. *She* wears the trousers."

"What about the family? Two girls and a boy, isn't it?"

"Yes. The oldest one's married and down in England somewhere——"

"Liverpool," Nicolson put in.

"Liverpool, is it, sir? I dare say you're right. The other girl, Eileen—that's the one you saw to-day—she's hooked too. Engaged to a teacher in the High School. Smashing legs, eh?" When Nicolson didn't respond, he hastened on: "Then, of course, there's the boy."

"It's the boy I'm interested in."

"Yes, sir. Clever lad, but weak, as you might say, sir. Easily led."

"He's got form, hasn't he?"

"Aye. Nothing much, though. A fight in a dance hall. Six months' probation. Allan Cameron was on the case. He'll——"

"The boy's missing. Run away from home."

"Fancy that, now!" Cubitt's surprise was too wide-eyed to be genuine. No doubt Eileen Pratt had unburdened herself at the duty desk first.

A telephone rang. Cubitt lifted the receiver.

"Silbridge Police Station. . . . Oh! yes, sir"—his shoulders straightened—"certainly, sir . . . about five o'clock? . . . right, sir, I'll tell him."

"That was Mr. Mearns," said Cubitt unnecessarily.

9

"Detained in Glasgow, eh?"

"Yes, sir. He said to tell you that——"

But Nicolson wasn't listening, for the swing doors had been pushed open and the burly figure of Detective-Sergeant Cameron was striding towards the C.I.D. room.

"Allan!" Cameron stopped and turned round.

"Yes, sir?" he said woodenly.

Nicolson sighed. In the six weeks he had been here he hadn't begun to penetrate the barrier of respectful hostility.

Cameron was a big man: six feet two and nearly fifteen stones, all muscle. He was in his middle thirties, about three years older than Nicolson himself; married, with two young children. A good officer, intelligent, conscientious: his record spoke for itself. Very popular in the force, both with his colleagues in C.I.D. and with the uniformed men. Only from Nicolson did he hold icily aloof.

Nicolson told him about Eileen Pratt's visit.

"I thought I'd call on the mother," he ended. "Like to come?"

Cameron glanced at the folder in his hand.

"I've been down to Records," he said, "digging out this stuff for Mr. Mearns. I'll have to make out a——"

"He's not to be back till five."

Cameron hesitated. "All right," he said. He opened the door of the C.I.D. room, tossed the folder on his desk and took his coat and hat from the peg.

Nicolson was already giving instructions to Sergeant Cubitt.

TWO

"TELL ME about Pratt," said Nicolson as he nosed his car slowly along the High Street. It was coming up to one o'clock and the men were streaming back to the shipyards.

"What that boy needs is a good hiding."

"What's he *done*, exactly?"

"It's the company he keeps. Joe Gammans and his mob. Billiards and cafés and dance halls. A High School boy, mind you, the cleverest in his year, they say."

"What was he up for?"

"Started a fight in the Empress. Damn' lucky not to get a stretch at Borstal. If his headmaster hadn't put in a word for him. . . ."

Cameron sounded bitter.

"Was he always like that?" Nicolson asked.

"Left, here. Then turn right at the halt sign. . . . No, only in the last year."

"What went wrong?"

"Oh, some boy said something to him. He couldn't take it."

"*Said* something?"

"Aye, hurt his feelings, like." It was said with an air of disgusted finality. Then he added: "A taste of the belt would do him no harm."

They had been climbing steadily. Past the hospital and the new Roman Catholic chapel; skirting the cemetery and up into the hills where within the last decade sprawling suburbia had taken over from the sheep.

Hughenden Road was on one of the highest points. It commanded a view over the trees of the cemetery to the river and the Argyllshire hills beyond. From this height the cranes of the shipyards were like Meccano models; and the yellow-funnelled steamer plying slowly upstream —that might have been a toy, too, a toy boat in a pond.

Nicolson stopped the car outside No. 18. It was semi-detached, red-roofed and white-painted. A shabby Morris stood in the short drive between the gate and the concrete garage abutting the house. The front garden was laid out in lawn as smooth and weed-free as a bowling green. "Judge a gardener by the quality of his grass," Nicolson had once read. . . .

The ringing of the bell set off a frenzied howling from a dog inside. They could hear a man's voice scolding it, then the door was opened.

He was in waistcoat and shirt sleeves. A tall man, round-shouldered, with straggly grey hair and a pale, pouchy face. His left hand gripped the collar of a large mongrel dog, which strained forward, growling.

Sergeant Cameron stretched out a hand. The dog sniffed, then gradually relaxed and gave a token wag of its tail. Released by its master, it padded back into the house.

"Gentle brute, really," said the man. "Suspicious of strangers, that's all."

Here was where Eileen Pratt had acquired the music of the West Highlands in her voice; only in her father the accent was undiluted.

"Come away in, then," he said, when Nicolson introduced himself. "My wife's expecting you."

He showed them into a lounge; a room that could have been attractive, with its big window looking out over the river, but had been ruined by all the bric-à-brac—small tables, lamps, ornaments—that had been crammed into it.

Mrs. Pratt was in an arm-chair, her legs resting on a footstool. She apologised for not getting up.

"It's my heart," she explained, with the gentle pathos of the hypochondriac. "Excitement's bad for me."

Her voice hardened when she turned to her husband. "Look at the time, Angus! Go and get on with your lunch." Pratt went out without a word. "I don't know how he can eat," she added petulantly to Nicolson. "As if nothing had happened."

Mrs. Pratt was a smaller, more fragile edition of her daughter. The same clear complexion, the same regular features. But a few strands of grey ran through her dark hair, and there was a discontented droop to her mouth.

"Eileen's told you about Ian, then?" she said.

"Yes . . . I'd like to hear the story in your own words, though."

Mrs. Pratt had been out playing bridge on Wednesday afternoon. When she came home about six there was no sign of Ian. She wasn't alarmed, because he often made himself a snack at home on her bridge day and then went out till late.

"Was nobody else at home?" Nicolson asked.

"No. Eileen was having tea with her fiancé. And Angus often drops in at the Castle on his way home on a Wednesday. He knows I'm not back till six."

When Ian still hadn't returned by midnight, his mother did become anxious. But then her husband noticed that the trapdoor to the attic was open; and, on investigation, they found a large suitcase was gone. They looked in Ian's bedroom and saw that most of his clothes had been removed from the wardrobe and chest.

"Anything besides clothes?" Nicolson asked.

"Some of his own things—his camera, one or two books, his diaries."

"He left no message?"

"No."

"Mrs. Pratt, why did you wait nearly two days before you phoned your daughter?"

"I was sure I'd hear from him. I expected a phone call, like last time. Or even a card. He wouldn't——"

"*Last* time? He's done this before?"

About a month ago, she admitted, Ian had gone off without a word one Saturday morning and had phoned the same night from Liverpool. He returned on the Monday.

"Did he pack a case with clothes then?"

"No. He only took a toothbrush and pyjamas."

"Well, it isn't just a week-end this time, is it? Didn't it cross your mind he might be leaving you for good?"

"No!" she said fiercely. "Ian wouldn't do that."

"Your daughter believes he has."

Two angry spots appeared in her cheeks. "Eileen——" she began, then checked herself. "Listen, Inspector. We've had our troubles this past year—Mr. Cameron here knows about that—" she fluttered a smile at Sergeant Cameron "—Ian's been difficult, I don't deny. But he and I are very close. He wouldn't *do* this to me."

"He wouldn't run away?"

"No." She hesitated, then added: "And if he did, he'd get word to me. He knows how I worry. Something's happened to him, Inspector. I feel it in my bones." A tear trickled down her cheek.

Nicolson instinctively disliked Mrs. Pratt. He disliked the possessive way she spoke of her son and her undisguised contempt for her husband. Yet her anxiety was genuine—he could see it in her eyes. He felt vaguely uneasy. He was also irritated with Cameron; Nicolson sensed in his silence disapproval, if not derision.

He stood up. "I must catch your husband before he leaves," he said abruptly.

Mrs. Pratt looked pained. "Angus? But he doesn't know——"

He interrupted. "Perhaps you'd describe to Sergeant Cameron exactly what your son was wearing and what he took with him." He went out.

He could hear Pratt moving about somewhere at the back of the house. Across the hall from the lounge a door stood open. Nicolson glanced in. It was a small bedroom. Or rather a study/bedroom, for it contained a cheap wooden desk as well as a bed, and shelves lined with books. School books. This must be Ian's room.

Nicolson hesitated, then walked in. The dog was stretched on a rug beside the bed. It seemed to have accepted him, for it opened one sleepy eye, feebly thumped its tail, then dozed off again.

The room was simply furnished with light oak wardrobe and chest, divan bed, desk and chair. Plywood bookshelves ran the length of one wall above the bed. The green carpet was wearing thin in placcs; the rug by the bed was probably covering a frayed patch.

Nicolson opened the wardrobe. It contained only a green High School blazer and an old and shabby raincoat; and, on the floor, a pair of football boots.

On the chest two framed photographs stood side by side. One was of Eileen, the other of a girl in tennis shorts. Nicolson thought at first this was Eileen too, but the face was thinner, the mouth smaller. It must be Annette, the older sister.

The books on the upper shelf declared the subjects Ian Pratt was taking in school: Greek and Latin texts and grammars; algebra and geometry, an introduction to the calculus; a French-English dictionary and some French novels. The lower shelf contained the boy's private library. Novels of Scott and Dickens and Trollope and Jane Austen— school prizes, probably. Nicolson took one down at random: *Pride and Prejudice*. Yes, there was the scroll on the inside cover: "Johannes Pratt in classe Litt. Graec . . ." Johannes Pratt was no sluggard, if all these were prizes. *Pride and Prejudice* was, however, unread; some of the pages were uncut.

Not so the books at the other end of the shelf. Here were the boy's real interests. Paperbacks of modern novels and plays; one or two manuals on photography and art; a book on chess; and several volumes of poetry.

Nicolson took down Palgrave's *Golden Treasury*. It was well thumbed and had been marginally annotated in many places. As he flicked through it a paper fell out and fluttered to the floor. He bent to pick it up and was startled by the voice behind him.

"Very fond of poetry, Ian. He wrote it too, you know."

Nicolson straightened up.

"I'm sorry, sir," he said. "I should have asked——"

"You've your job to do."

Pratt had his jacket on now. It didn't fit well and accentuated his round shoulders and general air of slovenliness.

" 'Wrote'," Nicolson remarked. "You used the past tense?"

"What? Oh! I see. To be sure, I think of him in the past tense. We'll not be seeing him here again."

"You don't think he'll come back?"

He looked at Nicolson in surprise. "Indeed I don't. As soon as I saw that case was gone, I *knew*."

"Why?"

"Well, it's a great muckle thing, you understand. Not what you'd take for a week-end."

"It's your case, is it, sir?"

"It is. But I haven't used it, haven't even seen it for a couple of years. I knew it was in the attic, that was all."

"Could you describe it, sir?" Nicolson took out his note-book.

"Well, it's green—imitation leather with a broken lock. It's the biggest case we have. He's taken most of his stuff with him, you understand."

"No warning at all? He didn't leave a note, did he?"

"He didn't leave a note, no. But there was plenty of *warning*. He's been threatening to leave for months. Didn't Margaret tell you?"

"No, she didn't."

Pratt peered into the mirror on the chest while he adjusted his tie.

"Ach, well, you know how it is," he said. "The rest of us could see this coming. But not Margaret. She just can't believe the boy hates her."

"*Hates* her?"

Pratt turned and faced him. "Oh! yes," he said mildly. "That's why he's gone."

"Why should he hate her?"

Pratt shrugged. "Ask your sergeant," he said. "He knows."

He walked over to the desk. He had a ponderous, stiff way of walking. As if he had lumbago. "Have you looked in here?" he asked.

Nicolson shook his head. Pratt lifted the lid of the desk.

"Ian always kept it locked. That's where his diaries were hidden away. I forced the lock last night. The diaries were gone, but——" He was rummaging among the papers in the desk. "Ah! here it is. What do you think of that?"

He had taken out a sheet of drawing-paper. In the top left-hand corner was a white crucifix; all over the rest of the sheet were black, wriggling worms. It was entitled "Despair."

"Ah! but there's a better one than that," said Pratt. He produced a sheet entirely filled in with black paint apart from the white letters in the bottom corner: "Death."

"Morbid subjects for a boy of sixteen," Nicolson remarked.

"To be sure, to be sure. He used to be happy enough, though. It's just since . . ."

"Since what, sir?"

"Ach, well, you'd best find out from Margaret . . . Or your sergeant. He knows . . . I'm not one for telling tales out of school." He shut the lid of the desk and looked at his watch. "Goodness me! It's late I'll be if——"

"Where do you think he's gone, Mr. Pratt?"

Pratt shrugged. "London, I'd say. The big city. Less easy to trace there." He sounded uninterested.

Nicolson was nettled. "It doesn't upset you that your son should run away from home?"

He smiled. "I'll miss him. I used to play chess with him. We got on much better since—well, since he fell out with his mother. But I can't honestly say I'm broken-hearted. . . . Of course,"—the exit line was flung over his shoulder as he turned to the door—"of course, it would be different if he really *were* my son."

15

He was gone; and moments later the front door slammed. Nicolson watched from the window as the Morris backed into the road and drove away.

He was angry. Bitterly, comprehensively angry. So angry that the sensation was almost pleasurable. He lit a cigarette, savouring the coolness of the tobacco in throat and lungs.

He went back to the bookshelf. Yes, there on the lower shelf, wedged between two novels of C. P. Snow, was the slim black volume, the odd man out. He had seen it before, but hadn't consciously taken it in. *Adoption and the Law.*

Cameron got into the car beside his inspector. "Would you drop me at my house, sir?" he said.

Nicolson let in the clutch without a word and drove into town in silence. He stopped the car outside the red sandstone building in Bath Row where Cameron had a flat.

But as Cameron made to get out, he stopped him.

"Not yet," he said harshly.

Cameron settled back stolidly in his seat.

"You don't like me, do you?" Nicolson went on. And, when Cameron didn't answer: "All right, but when we're on a job together, you're damn' well going to forget your likes and dislikes. D'you understand?"

"I'm sorry. I don't understand." Cameron's voice was quiet.

"Oh! yes, you do. Like this morning. The one thing I needed to know about Pratt and you didn't tell me."

"I still don't——"

"I mean that he's *adopted*. That wasn't worth mentioning, I suppose?"

"I thought you'd know." Cameron sounded genuinely surprised. "Didn't Cubitt tell you?"

"No, he didn't."

A red-haired girl in a white polo-necked sweater was at a first-floor window, gazing down at the car. Nicolson wondered if that could be Cameron's wife. Probably was; he'd heard she was a redhead. Younger than he would have expected. Nice face. . . .

Illogically his resentment was intensified.

"And another thing," he said roughly. "I asked you what sent Pratt off the rails. 'A boy said something to him'—what kind of an answer's that? *What* did the boy say?"

"He told him he was adopted. Pratt didn't know till then."

"I see. And I'm supposed to *guess* all that."

This time the charge went home. Cameron coloured.

"I'm sorry, sir," he said sullenly.

"Well, why didn't you?"

He hesitated. "It's easy to get soft-hearted over kids like Pratt. But I know him, see? And he's a bad lot. I was afraid you'd——"

"You were afraid I'd what, Sergeant?"

Cameron didn't answer.

"Well, I warn you, if that ever happens again, I'll report you. I made a ruddy fool of myself up there this morning, thanks to you."

"I'm sorry, sir," Cameron repeated woodenly.

Nicolson sighed. His anger had suddenly evaporated. Letting off steam had achieved nothing. He wondered, as so often before, why Cameron disliked him. Not jealousy, surely, though the sergeant must have had hopes of promotion himself when Inspector Green was transferred to headquarters. But Cameron must see it wasn't Nicolson's fault he had been passed over; there must be other reasons for his antagonism. . . .

"There's trouble between the boy and his mother, I gather?" Nicolson remarked.

Cameron grunted. "It's not Mrs. Pratt's fault, though. She's done all she can."

"Then what——"

"He blames her. For not letting him know he was adopted, I mean."

"It's always a mistake not to tell."

"Aye, maybe." Cameron sounded unconvinced.

Nicolson gave up. "You'd better have your lunch, Sergeant," he said wearily.

Cameron opened the car door.

"Who's the boy's probation officer?" Nicolson asked as an afterthought.

Cameron paused. "Saunders," he said. His expression was still sultry.

"I'll see him this afternoon," said Nicolson. He had met Saunders, and liked him. "And I'll look in at the school too. You take charge of the station end of it, will you? Cubitt should have the wheels moving by now."

"Yes, sir," said Cameron. As he got out of the car, the girl at the window disappeared. It must be his wife, Nicolson decided.

THREE

IT WAS the third time in a week he had lunched in Carter's Grill Room. Pie and chips, and a pot of tea. The wall clock was at 2.35 and he was the only customer.

This is what leads to ulcers at forty, he was reflecting. Hurried meals at irregular hours. Meals in pubs, in snack bars, in station buffets. He envied the married ones. He envied Cameron, with that attractive redhead to look after him and a couple of kids to give him a stake in the future.

Nicolson was missing Ruth, missing her more than he would have believed possible. Or rather, not Ruth herself. That was over. You couldn't turn the clock back. No, it was what she had symbolised.

His eye fell on the piece of paper he had pulled out of his pocket with the cigarette packet. It looked like a letter. He opened it out; it *was* a letter. No address; and the only date was "Thursday." It was written in a small, feminine hand.

My dear Ian, (it read)
How sweet of you to write me a poem. Easily my nicest present, even if I don't understand it all. (What's 'not by the shadow of a shadow'?)
Fifteen! How ancient one feels—practically middle-aged. Time's winged chariot is jet-propelled.
See you to-morrow. And Sunday, of course. We'll take a picnic if it's fine.
Love,
Norah.

He recognised it now. This was the paper that had fallen out of the *Golden Treasury*. He must have thrust it into his pocket when Pratt surprised him.

"Norah": wasn't that the name Eileen Pratt had mentioned—the girl her brother had been seeing? No, that was *Myra*. . . .

Rather a sweet letter, he thought. Naïve. And it gave a further tantalising glimpse of Ian Pratt. An interesting boy; he'd like to meet him. "A bad lot" was Sergeant Cameron's verdict. Well, he ought to know.

Nicolson stubbed out his cigarette, stood up and reached for his coat. At the scraping of his chair, the brunette behind the service counter languidly raised her eyes from the *Daily Mirror* and gave him a brittle smile. A pretty girl, but with a face as hard as flint. In his six weeks in Silbridge he hadn't seen a girl who could hold a candle to Ruth. Unless maybe that one this morning. Eileen Pratt. She had interested him. But then she was engaged. . . .

The probation officers occupied part of the warren of little rooms at the rear of the Sheriff Court.

Saunders was typing a report when Nicolson called. He was about Nicolson's age, a smallish, plump man with pink and white complexion and eyes that twinkled behind rimless spectacles.

"Paper work," he said with an expressive gesture at the typewriter. "The curse of the age. You spend ten minutes doing something useful, then an hour writing it up in triplicate.

"You look tired," he added, his eyes behind his spectacles studying Nicolson with lively concern.

"Lack of sleep, probably."

"The railway job? I read in this morning's paper——"

"Yes. We picked up three of them last night. And we know the others."

"Good."

Saunders opened a cigarette box and passed it across the desk.

"I've come about Ian Pratt," Nicolson said, as he took a cigarette.

Saunders's eyes narrowed. "Oh! yes?" His voice was non-committal. "What's he been up to?"

Nicolson told him.

When he had finished, Saunders said: "I can't honestly say I'm surprised."

"You expected him to run away?"

Saunders didn't answer directly. "Pratt's not one of my successes," he said slowly. "I can't get on to his wavelength. A pity, really," he added with a rueful smile, "for it's not often we're given material like that to work on."

"An intelligent boy, isn't he?"

"That's an understatement. Of course, I'm easily impressed, because my usual customer isn't over-endowed. But speak to Pratt's teachers —speak to Summers, or old Bradley—they'll tell you the same thing. Bradley nearly weeps at the loss to scholarship. . . ."

"What's wrong, then? Why has he turned sour?"

Saunders shrugged. "A flaw in his make-up. The fatal flaw. We all have it, they say, only in most of us, providentially, it's never exposed."

"And in Pratt's case?"

He hesitated. "To understand that, you'd need to know his background. Have you time to listen?"

Angus Pratt, Ian's father, was the son of a farm labourer from Ross-shire. He showed sufficient promise in the village school for his father, who had the inborn respect of the Scot for education, to send him at some financial sacrifice first to Inverness Academy and then to the University of Glasgow.

Angus obtained a respectable second in Economics in 1937 and entered a firm of stockbrokers in Glasgow. He was already married. In his third year at university he had met Margaret Barr, a second year medical, who had been runner-up for Charities Queen the year before. The unaccustomed unresponsiveness of the dour Highlander so intrigued her that she pursued him with single-minded determination, at first in sport and then, when she came under his spell, in unaffected earnest. His voice was her undoing; those deep, melodious tones, she used to tell her friends, set her heart a-flutter.

As for Angus, he, as always, kept his own counsel; but he was at any rate a willing partner when, in the teeth of opposition from both families, they were married at Easter, 1937. Margaret at once abandoned her studies.

Their first child, Annette, was born in March, 1938. By the time Eileen was born, two years later, her father was in the army. He served in Africa and Italy and emerged unscathed in 1945 with the rank of major.

For most of the war Margaret had done part-time nursing, leaving the children to her mother's care. What she saved was enough, when added to Angus's gratuity, to buy them a poultry farm in Galloway. A return to a desk in the city held no appeal for Angus: something in his blood, inherited no doubt from his father, drove him to seek his future on the land.

The venture was not, however, a notable success. In less than three years—in the spring of 1948—he sold out. Angus was not one to discuss his financial troubles. But it was understood that by the time he had paid his debts, he had only a few pounds to his name. And, of course, no job.

Besides which he had an ailing wife. Margaret, after a series of miscarriages, had become depressed and needed psychiatric treatment. The specialist diagnosed a craving for a son and prescribed adoption. Angus, without enthusiasm, acquiesced, and Ian was added to the family, at the age of six weeks, in May 1948.

The treatment was successful; or perhaps it was the move to Silbridge in the summer of that year. Margaret, who had never adapted herself to the isolation of the farm, blossomed again among the bright lights. Angus had found employment as a clerk in the Post Office in Silbridge; later he was transferred to the Ministry of Labour.

Angus, always taciturn, gave little outward sign of bitterness at the blows life had dealt him. He drank a little more than before, he paid less attention to his family; that was all. Imperceptibly, however, the roles of the husband and wife were being reversed. Margaret, who in the early years had left all major decisions to her husband, gradually took over the reins and became the dominant partner. Angus was reduced in status to the mere wage-earner. And even in that field he was not the sole provider; for when Margaret's father died in 1960 it was his money that paid for the house they bought in Hughenden Road.

Margaret doted on her children. She loved them all equally, she was fond of saying. And if Annette was heard to mutter occasionally that "some of us are more equal than others," well, that was the sort of precocious, wounding remark that made Annette such a *difficult* child. Naturally Ian, as the youngest, needed more attention than the other two. But their mother loved them all alike.

Nicolson interrupted.

"You're being ironical, I take it?"

Saunders grinned. "Yes. Mrs. Pratt was a rotten mother. All her affection went on the boy, and she'd none left for the other two. In fact, as they grew older she positively disliked the girls. She was jealous."

"Jealous? Of her own daughters?"

Saunders nodded. "It's not unknown. They grew up very pretty, you see."

"And the boy? How did he respond?"

Saunders looked at him quizzically. "Well, of course, I've only known Ian a few months. I have to rely on what others say about his earlier days. And when a person's changed for the worse, people tend to exaggerate how good he was before. All the same, there's not much doubt he was an unusually good-natured child. Both Annette and Eileen were very fond of him, and that's significant, considering he was his mother's favourite. Very clever at school: carried off prizes with monotonous regularity. But not just a swot. He played games passably well and by the time he was fifteen he had a healthy interest in girls. Or, at any rate, one girl."

"Norah?" Nicolson asked.

"You know about her?"

"Not really. I've seen a letter she wrote, that's all."

"I see. Well, her name's Norah Shipstone. A kid in his form. Sweet little thing. They used to go for walks on Sundays, hand in hand. All very innocent."

"Then somebody told him he was adopted?"

Saunders sighed. "Yes, someone told him he was adopted."

The Pratts had made the mistake so many adoptive parents make: they didn't tell the child. It was Mrs. Pratt's decision. She didn't want *anyone* to know that Ian was not her own son. Indeed, she hated to be reminded of it herself. There were times when she almost believed the fiction she had gradually evolved about Ian's birth. For when he reached the age of asking questions, she was not content to tell the bald lie, she had to embroider it with circumstantial detail. So Ian grew up believing he had been born on the poultry farm in Galloway on a stormy night in March and that his father, with the telephone wires down, had walked four miles to fetch the midwife.

Mrs. Pratt started with an advantage in that they had moved, while Ian was still a baby, to a town where they were not known. Even so, the truth was bound to leak out. One day, shortly before Ian's sixteenth birthday, a classmate in a fit of temper called him a bastard and made it plain he was using the word with precision. Ian was no fool: he saw by the embarrassed silence of other boys standing around that this was something to be taken seriously.

His mother's reaction was predictable: she indignantly denied the imputation. But Ian was persistent and demanded to see his birth certificate. It was then that Mrs. Pratt, terrified of losing him, made her biggest mistake. She admitted the adoption but gave vent to a scurrilous outburst against Ian's natural parents, describing his father as a crook and his mother as a drunken harlot.

Two weeks later Ian had traced his father in Edinburgh and had learned that his mother was dead.

"Who were they?" Nicolson asked.

"The parents? The father's name's Coleman. He's an insurance agent in Edinburgh, but he's had a number of other ploys in his day. A wide boy; always just this side of the law. Mrs. Pratt wasn't so far wrong when she called him a crook, though he's never actually been in trouble. Very smooth and plausible."

"You've met him?"

"Once. Your colleague Allan Cameron and I went to see him two or three months ago. An unrewarding visit."

"Cameron? Why did he go?"

22

Saunders hesitated. "He was sorry for the boy."

"He doesn't sound sympathetic now," Nicolson remarked shortly.

"When you try to help someone and get kicked in the teeth for your pains, it's apt to change your attitude."

There was an edge to Saunders's voice and his smile was frosty. Nicolson remembered that Saunders and Cameron were friends.

"What about the mother?" he asked.

The mother was from an entirely different background. The only daughter of elderly parents, she was a girl of unusual intellectual gifts. After taking a first in languages at Aberdeen, she went to the Sorbonne on a research scholarship. It was in Paris that she met Coleman, who was at that time a courier for a travel agency.

Nancy Lyall was an attractive girl, but with the naïveté of the bluestocking. Her strict upbringing and her almost total immersion in her studies had left her vulnerable to the first determined assault. Especially vulnerable to a glib and experienced charmer like Coleman. She fell at the first fence.

The affair lasted two months in the early summer of 1947. Then Coleman lost his job and returned to Scotland. Soon afterwards Nancy discovered she was pregnant. Coleman was not prepared to marry her and Nancy, her eyes now opened, didn't want him anyway. She did want the child, though, and it took the strongest pressure from her parents to make her agree to give it in adoption.

Instead of resuming her studies, she took a teaching post in a private school in England. Ten years later she died of leukaemia.

These were the facts Saunders had established from independent sources. Unfortunately the first testimony Ian Pratt had about the circumstances of his birth and adoption came from a prejudiced witness: from his father, Edward Coleman.

"I don't know what fantasy Coleman spun," said Saunders. "He's a plausible rogue and, of course, Ian would be receptive to anything his newly discovered father told him. Whatever it was, it turned him from a nice-natured boy into an embittered bolshie. . . . And it landed him in court."

"He started a rough-house, didn't he?"

Saunders took off his glasses and polished them on a handkerchief. Without them his face had the helpless look of the short-sighted. Nicolson noticed that the cuff of his shirt was frayed and that the brown suit he wore was shiny. They didn't pay these men enough. It was like the ministry: you had to have a vocation for it.

23

"Yes, he was in a fight," Saunders replied. "He was the ringleader, or so they said. Personally I doubt it. He's not a violent type."

"You're suggesting he was framed?"

"*He* suggested it. . . . And on the whole I'm inclined to believe him. It hasn't, as you can imagine, made my task any easier. To him it's one more proof of the injustice and oppressiveness of our society."

"How does he behave with you?"

"He doesn't hold it against me. But I've made hardly any headway with him. Polite sparring, that's all, and he sheers off whenever you come near the personal level. Just occasionally I've caught his interest and he's shown some animation. That's when I've had a glimpse of the quality of his mind. But most of the time we just don't communicate. I used to warn him about the company he was keeping. He'd smile and say nothing."

Saunders reached mechanically for a cigarette, then, recollecting himself, offered the box to his visitor.

"Mind you," he added thoughtfully, "for a while I did have some hope. I thought I was chipping away the barrier. But this past month. . . ." He broke off.

"Yes?" Nicolson prompted.

Saunders was lighting his cigarette. "Something's gone wrong," he said through the smoke. "He's had something on his conscience."

"Not surprising, considering the way he's behaved."

Saunders shook his head emphatically. "No, this is different. Something new . . . and another thing: he's been splashing money around. He got a new bicycle a few weeks ago. Twenty-five pounds if it cost a penny. A beautiful machine."

"His parents——"

"No. I asked Mrs. Pratt. He didn't get it from them. . . . Clothes, too. He bought an overcoat last week." Saunders laughed shortly. "I only wish I could afford one as good."

"And a trip to Liverpool."

"What? Oh! yes. And a trip to Liverpool. . . . And his *manner's* been different. You know, worried and anxious, but excited too—that's the only way I can put it. As if he were waiting for something to happen. . . ."

FOUR

SILBRIDGE HIGH SCHOOL was erected between the wars. Its four symmetrical wings formed a square, with a courtyard—quadrangle was too grand a name for it—in the middle. Architecturally it had the merits of simplicity and functional efficiency; and it had a certain solid dignity. It was, however, incapable of coherent expansion. While the post-war population bulge was rippling through the primary schools, the education authority was considering and rejecting a succession of plans for tacking on extensions to the High School. In the end the main building was left intact, and temporary huts were erected on a piece of adjacent ground acquired from British Railways.

This huddle of wooden huts was partially screened from the main school precinct by a privet hedge. On the school side of the hedge was a twenty-feet-wide strip of ground in which in summer well-drilled rows of dahlias and antirrhinums blossomed. Now, in November, the ground was bare. As Nicolson entered the main gate he could see, behind the school and to the right, a gardener at work turning over the soil.

Nicolson went under the arch and up the staircase to the first floor and entered the door on the left that bore the legend: "Music, Art and Handwork; Headmaster and Secretary." As he walked along the green-tiled corridor past the line of classrooms the thin, reedy note of a violin competed with the whirr of a lathe.

The administrative offices were grouped round the angle of the building where the corridor made a ninety degrees turn towards the gymnasium. As Nicolson approached, a boy came out of the door marked "Headmaster." A big boy, not far short of six feet, with a coarse, unhealthy face and the figure of a heavyweight wrestler. His green school blazer sat grotesquely on him. He slouched along the corridor with lowered head, and Nicolson had to step aside to let him pass.

The headmaster received Nicolson with the welcoming smile that was part of his stock-in-trade. Some people considered Dr. Huddleston a charlatan: nobody, they said, who oozed charm as he did could possibly be sincere. But perhaps charm was more important than sincerity for public relations. Whenever the school needed something out of the ordinary—an expensive piece of equipment for the physics lab or the re-surfacing of the hockey pitch—Huddleston knew the right ears to whisper into over sherry, and the money would be duly voted at the next meeting of the Education Committee. And as a pacifier of disgruntled parents no one else was in his class.

His staff on the whole rated him a tolerable, but undistinguished, headmaster. They were grateful that he rarely interfered in the teaching and gave full scope to heads of departments. But they despised him a little as a professional administrator of dubious academic credentials. His record at Glasgow University was mediocre and he had taken his doctorate at an obscure college in the States.

"Pratt?" Huddleston said when Nicolson told him why he had come. "Now, that's a coincidence. Perhaps you saw that boy who went out just now?"

"The big loutish one?"

"Loutish. H'm, yes. Yes, indeed. That describes Ferguson. Tom Ferguson, but usually known, I'm given to understand, as Lenny. A friend of Pratt's. He's the last person, so far as we know, to have seen Pratt. I've just been questioning him again."

"About Pratt, sir?"

"Yes. You see, Inspector,"—he gave a deprecatory cough—"with all due modesty, I sometimes feel I could have made a success in your profession. I can tell when a boy—when a person is lying. I have a *flair* for it."

A vain man. Vain about his looks, too, Nicolson suspected: he was almost *too* well groomed. Unquestionably handsome, but with a suggestion of effeminacy about the mouth.

"Ferguson was lying, then?" Nicolson asked.

"*Suppressio veri* rather than outright lies. When Pratt's sister spoke to me yesterday——"

"Yesterday?"

"Yes. She reported her brother hadn't returned home on Wednesday. Naturally we questioned Ferguson. He——"

"Why 'naturally'?" Nicolson interrupted.

"He's a friend of Pratt's. Almost the only one he has left. He said he'd talked to Pratt after school in the cycle shed." The headmaster turned on his dazzling smile. "That means they had a smoke. The cycle shed's the unofficial smoking room."

"You allow it, sir?"

Huddleston shrugged. "We pounce from time to time. But one can't stamp it out. . . . However, Ferguson's manner gave him away. I knew he was holding something back. So I had him here this afternoon." He paused: he was savouring this moment. "I extracted from him the information that Pratt had dinner in the Royal Hotel on Wednesday."

26

"Who with?"

"Alone."

"Expensive place for a schoolboy, isn't it?"

"You'd be surprised how much some children have nowadays. Do you know, we've a boy in upper sixth with a car. . . . However, I'm only repeating what Ferguson told me. Pratt went into the Royal at five to seven and came out an hour later."

"How does Ferguson know all this?"

"He was following him. *Tailing* him, I think, is the technical expression, isn't it?"

"But why?"

The headmaster spread his well-manicured hands. "Curiosity," he said. "It seems our young friend has made something of a mystery of his Wednesday evenings. Ferguson hoped to penetrate the mystery. But, alas, the fog defeated him."

"He lost Pratt?"

He inclined his head. "Soon after he left the Royal. . . . But why don't you speak to Ferguson yourself?"

"I will. . . . No, not yet, sir," he added, as Huddleston made to press a bell on his desk. "I'd like to hear about Pratt first."

The headmaster stood up and walked to the window. "What exactly do you want to know?" he said, his back to Nicolson.

"Anything you can tell me. What sort of person he is, and what his work's like."

A bell rang: a long, sustained note.

"That's four o'clock," said Huddleston, still looking out of the window. "If you want to see Ferguson——"

"I'll see him some other time. You were going to tell me about Pratt, sir."

There were distant muffled noises of doors being opened; and from the floors above them, scuffling of feet and banging of desks. Shrill voices floated up from outside as the first class emerged to freedom.

Huddleston turned round slowly. There was no smile on his face now.

"I spoke up for that boy," he said. "I went down to the Court and *pled* for him. One doesn't look for *thanks*, but——" He broke off.

"He didn't show his appreciation?" Nicolson suggested.

"He bit the hand that fed him. Bit the hand that fed him."

Huddleston's tone reflected the vindictiveness of the vain man who has been rebuffed.

"He's an able boy, though, isn't he?" Nicolson asked.

"Able, yes." Huddleston switched on his smile once more. "Ex-

27

tremely able, when he feels inclined. But if it's Pratt's *work* you're interested in. . . ."

He pressed the bell. The door opened and a girl came in.

"Miss Macrae, see if you can catch Mr. Bradley before he leaves. Detective-Insp——"

"Mr. Bradley's absent to-day, Dr. Huddleston."

"Indeed, yes, he's ill, isn't he? Well, ask Dr. Summers to look in. Or Mr. Troup."

It was Troup who came. A tall, slim young man with very dark hair and a pale, saturnine face, and wearing a red bow tie. He walked with a slight limp. Huddleston introduced him as the art master.

"Inspector Nicolson would like a word with you about Pratt," Huddleston explained.

Troup looked concerned. "He's still missing, is he?"

Something about Troup struck a chord in Nicolson's memory. The voice, perhaps?—a languid drawl with the suspicion of a lisp.

"I suggest, Troup, that you take Mr. Nicolson to the staff room." Huddleston turned to Nicolson. "You'll excuse me, Inspector. Letters to get off. . . ." He gestured vaguely at the desk, then stretched out his hand. "So nice to have met you. Let me know when you have any news." The smile was doing duty again.

"Culverton," said Troup as they crossed the tarmac to the school gates. He had invited Nicolson to tea in his flat.

"I beg your pardon?"

"I knew you at Culverton, though you won't remember me. You were a year or two ahead of me."

That was it. He remembered now that black hair and pale, Byronic face. Yes, and the affected voice. Troup had been a cricketer, he had made the Eleven exceptionally young. He hadn't had a limp in those days, though.

There was something else, too, that he had known about Troup, something not so creditable. He searched for it in the recesses of his memory, but it eluded him.

Troup had a furnished flat above a tobacconist's shop in Greene Road, almost opposite the school.

"I do for myself," he explained as they went in. "Can't stand landladies."

The room he showed Nicolson into was a combined studio and sitting-room. Nicolson had leisure to look round while Troup was in the kitchen making tea.

It was a big room, with a large window facing north across Greene Road to the High School. There were one or two good pieces of furniture—some easy-chairs, a studio couch of contemporary design. A walnut bookcase contained, in about equal numbers, volumes on art and paperbacks. On the wall above the fireplace were two prints by Ben Maile. The opposite wall had one large painting—a bold splash of crimson and yellow.

Dominating the room was the easel by the window and the table beside it with palette, paints and brushes.

Two or three canvases stood against the wall by the bookcase, face inwards. Idly Nicolson turned one round. It was a painting of a nude reclining on a couch. Not just any couch: it was recognisably the one in this room. And not just any nude: the face was Eileen Pratt's.

Nicolson was still studying it when Troup came in carrying a tray with tea and sandwiches.

"Ah! you recognise her?" he said. "Eileen's my fiancée, you know."

Nicolson didn't answer.

"You're not shocked, are you?" Troup asked, grinning.

"No." After all, it was none of his business.

Troup was pouring out tea. "Sugar?"

"Thanks. . . . How well do you know her brother?"

"Better than most, I should say. When trouble hit him, he turned to Art as some people turn to religion. Art with a capital 'A.' He found it a sort of catharsis, he told me once." Troup laughed. "He used to bring me drawings and paintings he'd done at home. Abstract stuff. 'Remorse,' 'Humiliation'—they all had names like that."

"I've seen a couple of them."

"Ghastly, aren't they? He'd some vague notion of what he was aiming at, but he couldn't begin to translate it into line or colour. No talent at all." He laughed again.

"You encouraged him, though?" Nicolson found his manner irritating.

"Between ourselves, old boy, only because I'm engaged to his sister. Eileen's soft on the boy and I had to pretend to be sympathetic."

"Were you surprised to hear he'd run away?"

"I wasn't *expecting* it, if that's what you mean. But—no, I'm not altogether surprised. A tiresome child. Too introspective. Running away's the sort of infantile gesture you might expect from him."

"No idea where he might have gone?"

"Well, he used to talk to me about London. He believed he could make his fortune there. Like Dick Whittington. Streets paved with gold, you know."

The doorbell rang, and Troup went out to answer it. There were low voices in the hall, then: "I think you two have met already." Troup was ushering in Eileen Pratt.

She smiled to Nicolson, then looked past him and her face turned scarlet.

"Douglas," she said angrily, "I've *told* you to hide that damned picture." The nude was lying face up on the carpet.

"Ah! well, darling," Troup's tone was amused, "our friend here's a policeman, remember. He turns pictures round and puts a microscope on them. It's his job. . . . Here, sit down and relax, for God's sake, darling. You're like one of the Furies." He lifted the canvas and put it back against the wall. "There. That better? All decent and seemly again. There's still some tea in the pot."

"I'm not staying, Douglas," she said shortly. "I only called to put off our date to-morrow. I tried to see you in school, but——"

"Why?"

"I'm going to—I'm going away on business."

Nicolson was conscious of undercurrents in the silence that followed.

"I must go," he said quickly. "Thanks for the tea."

"I'll come with you," said the girl.

Troup was sulky. "The seats are booked, and——"

Her face softened. "I'm sorry, darling, I really am. But I *have* to——"

"He won't be there, you know." Troup's voice was still petulant.

Nicolson intercepted the warning glance she flashed at her fiancé. "I must fly," she said, "or I'll miss my bus. Coming, Mr. Nicolson?"

She planted a hasty kiss on Troup's cheek, turned and went out. Nicolson followed her.

She declined his offer to drive her home, but let him take her to the bus stop in Drumchapel Street.

She didn't immediately get out. "I've five minutes," she said.

Nicolson was very conscious of her nearness, of the subtle fragrance of her perfume. The *same* perfume. He could close his eyes and imagine it was Ruth. . . .

She took the wrong inference from his silence.

"I've shocked you, Inspector, haven't I?"

"You mean the painting?"

"Please remember, Douglas is an artist—it doesn't *mean* anything, my posing for him like that."

Nicolson didn't answer.

"I wouldn't like you to draw the wrong conclusions, that's all," she continued.

"I assure you, Miss Pratt, I'm drawing no conclusions at all. It's no concern of mine."

"What I mean is, I don't *sleep* with Douglas."

She was sitting up very straight and, although it was too dark to see her face, he knew she was blushing. He liked her better than he had in the morning. She was less sophisticated, more vulnerable than she had seemed.

"Don't let it worry you," he said soothingly. Ironical, really, that she should fear his disapproval. If she knew about Ruth. . . .

"There's my bus," she said. It had appreared round the bend and was lumbering towards them.

Nicolson crossed the road with her to the bus stop.

"Who are you visiting to-morrow?" he asked abruptly.

The girl looked up, startled. Then she said rapidly, for the bus was slowing up at the stop: "Inspector, you won't tell Douglas, will you?"

He shook his head.

"Well," she lowered her voice to a whisper, "the fact is, I'm getting married to-morrow. To Dr. Huddleston."

She leapt nimbly on to the platform and waved to him as the bus moved off. Her face was lit by a smile of mischievous delight.

He wondered what a girl like that could see in Douglas Troup.

FIVE

SERGEANT McCRORIE had taken over from Cubitt at the desk. Young Gray, the new recruit, was laboriously taking down particulars of a missing dog from a man in a cloth cap.

As Nicolson came in, McCrorie gestured towards the chief inspector's room.

"He wants to see you, sir," he said.

"He's back, then?"

"Aye. Half an hour ago. Mr. Cameron's with him."

Chief Detective-Inspector Mearns was in his favourite attitude—chair tilted back, thumbs in waistcoat, pipe clenched between his teeth. Across the desk from him Cameron sat, massive and still.

"Where the hell have you been?" Mearns growled as Nicolson came in.

"A boy's disappeared from home. I've——"

"So they tell me. But what have *you* been doing?"

"Talking to people who know him."

"Well, in future keep us posted, will you? Maybe I'm peculiar that way, but I like to *know*."

"Sorry, sir."

Mearns laughed. "Forget it, Maurice," he said, at once conciliatory.

Mearns lacked confidence in handling people. He blew hot and cold. He had no close friends, because he could never relax and be natural; he was too much concerned about what people might think of him.

His failure in personal relations had undoubtedly circumscribed his career. He was now fifty and would rise no further. Yet he was among the ablest officers in the county; certainly one of the most intelligent.

He seemed taller than his five feet eleven, for he was thin to the point of gauntness. Iron-grey, bristly hair, bushy eyebrows, and the aquiline nose and sunken cheeks gave his face a forbidding, ascetic look. Only the restless eyes betrayed the weakness and vacillation.

Mearns took the pipe from his mouth and knocked out the smouldering ash.

"Get anything useful on Pratt, then?" he asked, as he brought out his tobacco pouch.

"Background material, that's all. Nothing you and Allan here don't know already, I dare say."

Mearns nodded. "You know he's been in the money recently?"

"I heard that."

"I'd like to know where he got it."

Cameron spoke then. "I still think it was the Schapiro job, sir."

Mearns shook his head decisively. "Donovan would never let a kid like that in on it."

Schapiro's, a jeweller's in the High Street, had been broken into a month ago. Although the method of operating pointed unmistakably to Larry Donovan, the police hadn't enough evidence to pull him in.

"Anyway," said Mearns, "the kid's not short of money, wherever he got it. My guess is he's over the border by now. London, like as not."

"You're assuming," said Nicolson, "that he's not still here. In Silbridge."

"I'm not assuming anything," Mearns snapped; then at once smiled apologetically. "Sorry, I'd forgotten you didn't know, Maurice. Tell him, Allan."

Inquiries had been made during the afternoon at railways, docks and bus stations in Silbridge. A booking clerk at St. Gregory's Station remembered Pratt buying a single to Glasgow on Wednesday evening.

When this news came in, Cameron went to the station himself and questioned the clerk.

"Observant chap," he said. "Could even tell me the colour of his scarf. And a green suitcase: he described that too."

"What time was this?" said Nicolson.

"About half past six. The train left at 6.40. Actually it was the 5.58, but the fog knocked the time-tables to hell that night."

"He was seen getting on the train, was he?"

Cameron hesitated. "Well, no, but——"

"You see, my information is that Pratt was still in Silbridge much later than that. IIe came out of the Royal Hotcl at eight o'clock." He recounted what the headmaster had told him.

Mearns exploded. "This isn't good enough, Cameron. You assured me Pratt left on that train."

"I did say we were looking for confirmation, sir. . . . But he bought a ticket and walked towards the platform: where else could he have been making for?"

"Damn it,"—Mearns was still angry—"he might have been going to the lavatory, he might have been going for a paper at the kiosk, he might have——"

Nicolson interrupted. "He might have been going to the Left Luggage."

Mearns glanced sharply at him. "That's a point," he said. "Have you tried there, Allan?"

Cameron was sulky. "Not yet, sir. I haven't had *time*. . . ."

The chief inspector was having his customary remorse. "Sorry, Allan, you're right: you did warn me you weren't finished. . . . Anyway, I don't see it matters much. Natural enough to dump your case and go off for a meal, then come back for a later train." He yawned. "God, I'm tired. And I've still all this to wade through." He indicated the heap of papers on his desk.

As the other two stood up, Mearns added: "Don't waste much time on this busincss. It's not our worry if a boy lcavcs Silbridge of his own free will. We've got his description out, there's nothing more we can do. . . . I'd just like proof that he's gone, though."

"So would I," said Nicolson.

Mearns looked up at him. "Have you any reason to doubt it?"

"No," said Nicolson slowly. He had no *reason* to doubt it.

"Come and have a pint, Allan."

Cameron hesitated. "I'd like to get back to St. Gregory's, sir."

Nicolson controlled his irritation. He said, mildly enough: "Have a quick one all the same. I need your advice."

They crossed the road to the Bodega. The bar was full. Business men, mostly, dropping in for a drink on their way home. Sergeant Cubitt, a whisky in his hand, was talking to a man in a checked suit. When he saw them, Cubitt beamed and raised his glass. Nicolson observed that Cameron's acknowledgment of the greeting was as frosty as his own.

Nicolson bought two lagers and took them over to where Cameron stood.

"Cheers!" he said perfunctorily, then: "You know this boy Ferguson, don't you?"

"Lenny Ferguson? I've met him."

"I thought I might talk to him to-night. At Finghetti's, if he's there."

"Oh, aye." Cameron's tone was unforthcoming.

Nicolson tried again. "I wondered—well, I know you're off duty, but I wondered if you'd come along. You know Ferguson, you know the rest of Pratt's cronies. I don't."

Why don't I *order* him to come, Nicolson was asking himself. This would be the last time; if he refused now. . . .

"All right," said Cameron. "What time?"

"Eight o'clock?"

Cameron nodded. "I'll be there."

"One other thing, Allan. Have you the list of what Pratt took with him?"

Cameron took a mimeographed sheet from his wallet and handed it to him. A print of the photograph Nicolson had seen that morning was attached.

Nicolson ran his eye down the list: Shirts, socks, ties, sweaters, underwear, three pairs of shoes, jeans, anorak, brown suit, overcoat. . . .

"Must be a big suitcase," he muttered.

. . . Camera, pocket chess set, *Under Milk Wood, The Quare Fellow*. . . .

"I wonder how many boys of sixteen would choose these for their desert island discs," Nicolson commented. Cameron didn't answer.

. . . Personal diaries, bicycle. . . .

"The bicycle's gone, has it?"

"Yes."

"Did he have it at the station?"

"The booking clerk didn't see it." Cameron was on the defensive.

"Pratt didn't buy a ticket for it, then?"

"No." Cameron swallowed the last of his drink. "But I'm not finished down there. I want——"

"All right, off you go. See you at eight."

34

Although the Royal Hotel had only twenty bedrooms, the dining-room could accommodate 120. Could, and often did. It was the fashionable place to eat in Silbridge; the *only* place, some said. It thrived on expense account lunches and west-end wedding receptions.

The dining-room was still almost empty when Nicolson went in at seven o'clock. He hadn't been in the Royal before; he couldn't afford it.

The head waiter bore down on him, smiling, and escorted him to a small table at the side. He was tall, grey-haired and dignified, with something Slavonic in the cast of his head.

"Don't go away," said Nicolson as the man pulled out a chair for him. He showed his credentials.

The smile wavered. "Yes, sir," he said, looking round uneasily. "You come into the office?" He *was* eastern European. Polish, probably, Nicolson decided.

"Hardly necessary," he said. "And anyway I want a meal."

He took out the photograph. "Recognise him?"

The man studied it, then nodded vigorously. "Yes. He come here for dinner, four, five, maybe six times."

"Alone?"

"Yes, sir—No, once with a girl, I think."

"When did you last see him?"

"This week. Tuesday, Wednesday maybe." His eyes were straying to the door; people were beginning to drift in. "Excuse me, sir. I send the waiter who serve him."

The man who came over was a little red-headed Scot with a broad Clydeside accent. He remembered Ian Pratt well.

Pratt had first had dinner here one Wednesday about four weeks ago. He had ordered a half bottle of claret, which the wine waiter refused to serve because he looked too young. He paid the bill from a wallet lined with fivers; and he was lavish with his tips.

"He was trying to impress, sir, if you see what I mean," said the waiter.

He came back each Wednesday night always alone. And on two Saturdays with a girl.

"Maybe oftener," the waiter amended. "He might have come on my night off."

"What was the girl like?"

"Cheap, sir." He shook his head disapprovingly. "Loads of eye-shadow. And blonde hair out of a bottle." He picked up the photograph and looked at it. "I was sorry for the boy."

The waiter confirmed that Pratt had been in two nights ago as usual.

"What was he wearing?" Nicolson asked. "His school uniform?"

"Oh! no, sir. He always had a brown suit on. And one of these short, fur-trimmed grey overcoats."

The brown suit and the grey overcoat were on Mrs. Pratt's list.

"Anything unusual about him on Wednesday?"

The waiter hesitated. "No . . . except he wasn't very hungry. He left half his main course. Didn't finish the ice-cream either." A thought seemed to strike him. "Has something *happened* to him, sir?"

"Not that I know of," Nicolson said, and picked up the menu.

Nicolson was studying the photograph again as he drank his coffee. Pratt's face fascinated him.

From over his shoulder a voice said: "Like Nureyev, sir. You think so? A tragic face."

Nicolson looked round, startled. The head waiter had glided up unheard.

He turned back to the photograph. Those luminous eyes stared up at him.

"Yes," he agreed. "I see what you mean."

SIX

COMING IN from the dark street Nicolson was dazzled by the fluorescent lighting and the garish reds and yellows of the decor. Cameron was seated at one of the little yellow-topped tables, a cup of coffee in front of him. The only others in the café were three teenage girls giggling round the juke box.

A young Italian girl took Nicolson's order, a raven-haired beauty with smiling eyes.

"Is that a Finghetti?" Nicolson asked when she had gone.

"Aye," said Cameron. "A daughter. It's a family concern, this. The old man serves in the fish grill next door. And that's a nephew over there." He indicated the youth in the white overall behind the counter. "They brought him in when the other sister snuffed it."

It came back to Nicolson then. A hit-and-run case four or five weeks ago, just after he came to Silbridge. A girl had been fatally injured and they had never traced the car or the driver. Nicolson hadn't himself been concerned in the case, but he remembered the girl's name had been Finghetti.

"Lucia, that was the sister's name, wasn't it?" he asked.

"Aye."

The coffee was good; better, indeed, than at the Royal.

"The gang's not here, then," Nicolson remarked.

"Not yet," said Cameron. "That's Joe Gammans's girl, though. The one in black."

As he spoke, a blast of sound issued from the juke box.

Nicolson winced. "What in hell's name's that?" he said.

Cameron grinned. " 'Gonna Miss You.' Number three in the charts. The Lumberjacks." His foot was tapping rhythmically.

One of the girls was dancing. She wore a tight black skirt and sweater, and knee-length black boots. Her hair was in a fringe low on her forehead and her eyes were two black smudges on a dead white face.

Her body and limbs pulsed to the beat of the music with rippling, sinuous, sensuous movements; her face had a faraway, dedicated expression. The other two girls looked on, also unsmiling.

Nicolson watched, at once fascinated and repelled.

"They should ban the Twist," he said. "It's sexier than a strip-tease."

"That's not the Twist," said Cameron witheringly, "that's the Shake." Nicolson laughed.

The music stopped and the girls sat down. The dark one caught Nicolson's eye, gave him an insolent stare, then said something which convulsed her companions.

The café began to fill up as the first house of the Gaumont Cinema across the road came out. But still no one had joined the three girls.

"You were right about the Left Luggage, sir," said Cameron abruptly. "Pratt left his suitcase at half past six on Wednesday."

"When did he pick it up?"

"They couldn't tell. Except it was probably after nine o'clock. There's one chap there who knows Pratt—he was the one who saw him leave the case. He thinks he'd have noticed if the boy had come back before he went off duty at nine."

"The case is gone, though?"

"Oh! yes. It's not there now. Anyway they have the counterfoil. They date-stamp it when the customer hands it back and this one's dated Wednesday. So Pratt must have picked it up that night."

"So *someone* must have picked it up that night," Nicolson amended. When Cameron didn't answer, he smiled and went on: "All right, let's not split hairs. What trains could Pratt have taken?"

Normally the service to Glasgow was about every half hour, the last train leaving at 11.12. But on Wednesday, owing to the fog and a derailment up the line, only one passenger train had left Silbridge after nine o'clock. It departed at 10.20 and crawled into Glasgow just before midnight.

"Well, that narrows things down," said Nicolson. "Have you——"

"I've given a note to the papers," said Cameron, "asking passengers to come forward. And I've been on to Glasgow. Sent them up a photograph. They're questioning the ticket collectors, taxi drivers and so on. Hotels, too, because that train got in too late for any connections."

The door of the café opened and about half a dozen youths entered. They were all in black leather jackets, drainpipe trousers and winkle-pickers. Nicolson recognised at once the massive bulk of Lenny Ferguson. But it wasn't Ferguson who dominated the group: the undisputed leader was a thickset youth with fair, curly hair, and side-levers and a scar running down his left cheek.

"Is that Gammans?" Nicolson whispered.

Cameron nodded.

Gammans and his entourage made their way to the table where the girls were sitting. The two younger ones moved over to let him sit beside the girl in black. He gave her a curt nod, then ignored her. Nicolson thought the girl looked frightened. Two of the boys went up to the counter for drinks.

"Who is Gammans?" Nicolson asked.

"Ex-approved school. Now a labourer with the Roads Department. Always spoiling for a fight. A filthy tongue and a foul temper."

"He's older than the others, isn't he?"

"Aye. He's twenty, maybe twenty-one."

"Then why——"

"He enjoys being king-pin."

An obscenity from Gammans carried over to them, followed by a chorus of coarse laughter.

"They're a scruffy lot," said Nicolson. "How could High School boys like Pratt and Ferguson get tangled with them?"

"There's your answer so far as Ferguson's concerned." Cameron gestured towards the other table.

Lenny Ferguson stood behind the others, his hand resting casually on the shoulders of a thin, fair-skinned boy.

"A homo?"

"Aye . . . And that's why he brought young Pratt into the gang."

"Pratt too?"

"No. Ferguson miscalculated there. Pratt's—" Cameron's admission was grudging, "—Pratt's normal in that way. . . . There's his girl, as a matter of fact. Myra Thexford."

Nicolson looked at the girl who had just come in. This must be the blonde that the waiter at the Royal had described. "Cheap" he had called her and he was right. Yet there was a certain animal grace about her. She crossed leisurely to where the others sat, pulled in a stool and insinuated herself between Joe Gammans and the boy on his right. The girl in black, on Gammans's other side, scowled as he turned and began to whisper to the blonde.

"Can you get Ferguson over?" Nicolson asked.

Cameron walked across and spoke to Ferguson. Although the buzz of conversation and laughter died abruptly, Nicolson was too far away to hear what was said. But he didn't miss the quick glance that Lenny Ferguson flashed at Gammans or Gammans's barely perceptible nod. Ferguson laid down his Coke and slouched across the floor, Cameron following.

"Detective-Inspector Nicolson," Cameron introduced him.

Ferguson nodded without raising his eyes, and sat down. He took a half-smoked cigarette from behind his ear, put it in his mouth and lit it. His fingers were stained with nicotine.

"We're looking for Ian Pratt," said Nicolson. "I understand you followed him on Wednesday evening. Why?"

"To see where he was going." He spoke in a slow, childish drawl. It was hard to say whether he was being deliberately insolent or not.

Cameron was in no doubt. "Don't try to be funny, Lenny," he said sharply. "It won't get you anywhere."

Ferguson shifted uncomfortably in his seat. "Well, see, we were just *curious*," he said. "Every Wednesday night he went off on his own. Even Myra didn't know where. And we wondered if—well, we were curious," he ended lamely.

"You wondered what?" Nicolson pressed him.

"Well, see, it was the *dough*. Pratt's stiff with it and he always used to be so hard up. We thought maybe he was on to some racket Wednesday nights."

"And Gammans wanted to be in on it, is that it?"

Ferguson licked his lips. "See here, I never mentioned Joe's name." He glanced furtively over his shoulder.

"All right," said Nicolson. "Tell us what happened on Wednesday. Where did you pick him up?"

"The Royal Hotel. Myra told me to try there. And Joe said—" He corrected himself. "—And I waited till he turned up."

Pratt arrived, on foot, just before seven o'clock, and went into the hotel. He emerged at five to eight and walked briskly down Main Street towards the town centre. Ferguson lost him in the fog after a couple of blocks.

"He must have slipped up a side street," he said.

"But he definitely went *down* Main Street? Away from the railway station?" Nicolson asked.

Ferguson shrugged. "That's what I told you," he said.

"When did these Wednesday evening expeditions of Pratt's begin?"

"Four—five weeks ago, I guess."

"And just about the same time he suddenly had money to burn?"

"Do you coppers never *listen?* I've told you already——"

"Lenny!" Cameron's tone was sharp.

"Yes, that's right," he muttered. "And now can I go?" He stubbed out his cigarette.

Nicolson nodded. Ferguson sauntered back and rejoined his friends.

"Just a stooge for Gammans," Nicolson remarked.

"You think so?" said Cameron.

"Well, don't you? He let it out twice there."

"Lenny Ferguson never lets things out accidentally. He's got brains, though he tries to hide it. He's in sixth form in High School, remember."

There was a scraping of chairs from the table by the juke box. Joe Gammans and his gang were preparing to depart. Gammans, with the blonde hanging on to his arm, led the way. The girl in black, with murder in her eyes, followed.

Gammans paused at Nicolson's table and called over his shoulder: "Watch your language, children. The Salvation Army's here." He smirked at the sycophantic titter that greeted his sally. The blonde at his side was doubled up with laughter.

"Miss Thexford," said Nicolson.

"Eh? Me?" She was still laughing.

"Yes, I'd like a word with you."

She clung more closely to Gammans and looked up at him in mock appeal.

He glared at Nicolson. "What about, copper?" he said.

"About Ian Pratt."

"O.K. But if you talk to Myra, you talk to me an' all."

"As you please." Nicolson indicated chairs.

Gammans turned round. "Beat it, kids," he said. "See youse all to-morrow."

The dark girl plucked at his arm. "But, Joe——" she began pleadingly.

He pushed her hand away. "Shove off, Liz," he said roughly. "Myra and me's got business to-night, eh, baby?"

The blonde giggled. "Oh! you are *awful,* Joe." The other girl stamped out.

When they had all gone, all except Gammans and the blonde, Nicolson said: "Miss Thexford, you know Ian Pratt's missing?"

She tossed her head. "I couldn't care less," she said.

"But I thought you and Pratt——"

"See what thought did?" Then she added viciously: "I learnt that smarty-pants his ABC. He was wet round the ears when I took him in hand. And if he thinks he can two-time me——"

"He's been taking another girl out, has he?"

"Too bloody true, he has," said Gammans. "Dinner in the Royal bloody Hotel and all."

"But Ferguson said he was *alone*——"

"Aye, maybe. But you don't want to believe all Pansy Ferguson tells you."

Nicolson was wondering why Gammans was so agitated. Now Sergeant Cameron suggested an answer. "Fallen out with Liz, have you, Gammans?" he remarked.

Gammans turned on him, his face suffused with rage: "What the —— is it to you, copper?"

The girl put her hand on his. "Ach, forget it, Joe," she said soothingly. "She's no' worth it. Anyway, we're no' sure it's her."

"By Christ! if I *was* sure, I'd break every bloody bone in her body, so I would."

"She's no' *worth* it," Myra repeated. "Nor him neither. I'm through wi' him, honest I am. You and me can——"

"Where did Pratt get his money?" Nicolson asked.

Gammans was still muttering angrily and Nicolson had to repeat the question.

"His money? Search me," he said dully. He didn't seem interested.

"He wasn't mean, I'll say that for him," Myra put in. "He took me to posh hotels and places. But golly! the way he went on! All them big words. You're no' like that, Joe, eh?"

Gammans grinned, his equanimity restored. "No' me." He put his arm round her and squeezed her. "I don't need words, baby." She giggled happily.

Nicolson tried one more question. "Do you know where Pratt might have gone?"

"Back to Daddy, if you ask me," said Myra.

"'Back to Daddy.' It's an idea, isn't it?" Nicolson remarked as he walked back with Cameron. "Is Coleman still in Edinburgh?"

"Who? Oh! I see, Pratt's father. Yes, so far as I know. . . . The boy won't be there, though."

"Why not?"

Cameron hesitated. "I've met Coleman, sir."

"Well?"

"Well, I just don't believe he'd want a boy hanging round."

"Not even his own son?"

"Least of all his own son."

Still, there could be no harm in finding out. . . .

SEVEN

NICOLSON TOOK the 8.17 to Glasgow, a fast, through train, popular with commuters.

He passed the journey reading the Press accounts of Ian Pratt's disappearance. *The Glasgow Herald* and *The Scotsman* had merely printed the police handout. The *Scottish Daily Express*, in a day lacking in excitement, had elevated the story to the front page, with a blown up picture of the boy flanked by smaller ones of his adoptive parents. As an appendix to the official statement, the *Express* carried an account of an emotional interview with Mrs. Pratt and some guarded remarks by the headmaster of the High School. It was competently done; yet Nicolson had the impression that the reporter's heart was not in it. It read as if he knew that Monday's edition would carry a small paragraph reporting that the boy had turned up unharmed in Aberdeen or Cardiff or Wolverhampton.

The day had started fine, but as Nicolson changed trains in Glasgow the predicted rain belt could already be seen in the clouds banking to the west. It chased and eventually engulfed them as they neared Edinburgh.

Nicolson took a taxi at Waverley Station. Grayson Street, where Coleman lived, was a short and unsalubrious street of grey tenements in the old part of the city, near the law courts, not a stone's throw from the Royal Mile.

A scraggy cat slunk along hugging the wall, partially sheltered from the driving rain; otherwise the street was empty of life.

Number 12 was on the right hand side, about half-way up. Nicolson went in through the dingy close and up two flights of stairs. A woman on her knees scrubbing the steps moved her pail aside to let him pass.

"E. Coleman" was on a door on the second floor. Nicolson pulled the bell.

A woman came to the door. After one glance at Nicolson she said firmly, "I don't need anything," and made to close the door.

But Nicolson stopped her. "I'm a police officer," he said.

The woman stared uncertainly at him. "You'd better come in, then, hadn't you?" she said.

She took him into the kitchen. A pot of soup was heating on an old-fashioned range. Over by the sink was a bowl of potatoes which the woman had been peeling when she was interrupted. The linoleum was faded and worn, much of the woodwork was worm-eaten, and there was a large crack in one of the window panes. But the room was clean. A television set stood on a trolley against the wall opposite the fireplace.

The woman took a wooden chair from beside the curtain that screened the recess bed and brought it over to the fire for Nicolson. She herself sat on a sagging arm-chair across the hearth from him.

She was a faded, colourless woman in her forties, with greying hair, a shapeless figure and hands deformed by arthritis. She wore an apron over a brown skirt and red woollen cardigan. Although she had been pretty once, as the framed snapshot on the dresser showed, now only the barest reminder of it lingered on, in the eyes and the line of the mouth.

"It'll be about the boy?" she said in a matter-of-fact tone. It was an educated voice that seemed out of place in this setting.

"Yes," said Nicolson. "You know about him?"

"Only what was in the paper this morning." She indicated the *Express* on the kitchen table.

"I wanted to see your——" Nicolson hesitated, because Cameron had said that Coleman was unmarried. He rephrased it: "I want to see Mr. Coleman."

"You just missed him. He goes out on his rounds on a Saturday morning. He'll be back at half past one."

"Has the boy been here? Since Wednesday, I mean?"

"No." The answer was given with the same weary indifference, but Nicolson had noticed a flicker of anxiety in her eyes.

"You've met him before, though?"

This time a distinct pause, then: "Only the first time, for five minutes." She laughed mirthlessly. "Eddie introduced me as his housekeeper. After that he always met him in town."

"Why?"

"He was afraid of what I might let out. I don't find it easy to lie."

"How often has the boy been here?"

"About half a dozen times that I know of. Maybe more."

"When was the last time?"

"Two weeks ago to-day. At least Eddie *said* that's who he was meeting. But you can never be sure with Eddie."

43

"Mrs. Coleman. . . ." by his pause Nicolson allowed faint emphasis to rest on the words; and the woman took her cue.

"I'm not really his wife," she said without embarrassment. "His wife left him years ago. One good thing about living here"—her eyes travelled round the shabby room—"the neighbours aren't fussy. Out in Morningside——"

"You lived in Morningside?"

She nodded. "We'd a house of our own. But the neighbours turned nasty once they found out."

"That why you moved?"

"Not really. Eddie got into debt, that's why. Drink, you know. And women." It was said without rancour, without expression even.

Answering Nicolson's unspoken question, the woman added: "After twelve years it gets to be a habit. Living with him, I mean. . . . Anyway where else could I go? I've no money, no job. He keeps me." She looked down at her hands.

"Did you know Ian Pratt's mother?" Nicolson asked.

"No. That was all over before I came on the scene. . . . But I'll show you something."

She went out of the room and came back with a yellowing photograph.

Here was where Ian Pratt had taken his looks. His mother had the same big eyes and thin, delicate face. It was her graduation photograph, and she was in gown and hood and mortar-board, a self-conscious smile on her face.

Nicolson turned it over. On the back was the photographer's name and the date of the graduation (June, 1946); below that, in a sloping hand, the words: "To Edward, with all my love, from Nancy, 16th May, 1947."

"He's kept it all these years," said the woman. "She meant more to him than any of the rest of us."

"He didn't stand by her when she had his baby, though."

"Eddie's not one to take on responsibilities. But he got very drunk, I remember, the night he heard she'd died. That was years later, of course."

"And the boy—how does Mr. Coleman feel about him?"

"You'd better ask Eddie, hadn't you?"

He was conscious again of a hesitancy, a withdrawal.

"All right," he said. "I will."

The wind had dropped and the rain was now falling in a soft drizzle. The sky was filled in all round.

Nicolson buttoned his raincoat to the neck, pulled his hat down and set off for the nearest bus stop. He had gone twenty yards when a girl crossed the street towards him. A girl in a yellow mac, her face concealed behind an umbrella. Slim legs, good ankles. As she stepped on to the pavement the umbrella momentarily raised and he saw her face. It was Eileen Pratt.

She was more surprised than he. Surprised and angry.

"You *knew* I was coming here," she said accusingly.

"I did wonder. . . ."

She continued to stare at him. Then she laughed shortly. "All right, you've stolen my thunder. Is he here?"

"Your brother? No, I don't think so."

"You don't *think* so?"

He told her what Mrs. Coleman had said.

She stood irresolute.

"Come and have lunch with me, Miss Pratt," he invited her.

She hesitated a moment longer, then smiled. "That would be lovely," she said warmly.

They lunched at the Old Waverley, at a window table overlooking Princes Street and the Scott Monument. Farther off they could just see the Castle, wreathed in mist.

"I don't like Edinburgh," said the girl, gesturing vaguely at the scene outside. "Too self-important."

"The place or the people?" Nicolson asked.

"Both. Give me Glasgow every time."

A waiter came over to take their order. Eileen studied the menu with unaffected eagerness. Extraordinarily like Ruth, this girl. The same zest for living. . . .

"What's the matter?" she said, when the waiter had gone. "Have I a smudge on my nose?"

"I'm sorry. Was I staring? It's just that you remind me of someone I used to know."

She laughed. "Never say that to a woman. We like to believe we're unique. . . . Was she nice?"

"Not bad." He was teasing her, and she laughed again.

She went off at a tangent. "What's it like to be a policeman? I mean, grubbing into people's private lives, turning over stones to see what's crawling underneath."

"You don't approve of us?"

She smiled contritely. "I'm sorry. I didn't mean to be rude. It's just

45

—well, I wish you'd let Ian alone. He's nearly seventeen and well able to look after himself."

"It was you who called in the police," Nicolson reminded her.

She shrugged. "I had to—because of Mother. Anyway, I never dreamt you'd make a national issue of it, front page of the newspapers and all that."

"Your brother's disappeared. We want to know where he is. I should have thought *you'd* want to know too."

She was silent.

"Well, don't you?" he persisted.

"I'd like to be sure he's all right," she said slowly. "But I don't want him brought back. If you find him, he'll have to go back, won't he?"

Nicolson didn't answer directly. "Why do you think he'd be better off away from home?"

"Well, he's adopted, you see, and——"

"Is that any excuse for the way he's been carrying on—getting mixed up with that gang of hooligans and so on?"

She sighed. "Perhaps not. But—well, I don't like to say this of my own mother, but she's been an utter *fool* over this business. I mean, when it came out, when Ian learned he was adopted, imagine telling him a tissue of lies about his real mother. . . . Even so, he'd have got over it but for this—this *monster* here."

"Coleman?"

"Yes. He got his hooks into Ian just at the worst moment. Brainwashed him. He was a different boy after that first meeting with his father."

"Have you met Coleman?"

She postponed her reply till the waiter had removed their soup plates.

"Yes," she said, and he was taken aback by her vehemence. "I've met him."

She had gone to see Coleman one day last summer. She was worried about Ian, who was drifting into bad company. She knew he had been seeing his father and guessed that the father was an unsettling influence.

"Did you know about Coleman before?" Nicolson interrupted. "I mean, before your brother found out?"

"Not about *Coleman*. I knew Ian was adopted, of course. After all, I was eight and Annette ten at the time. But I never knew who his real parents were."

Eileen disliked Coleman on sight.

"You either go for that type or you don't," she explained. "You know—sleek hair, dapper little moustache and knowing smirk. It makes me want to throw up. His hair's dyed, too."

However, Coleman had been sympathetic when she mentioned Ian. He said he had grown fond of the boy and would like to help.

"Was Mrs. Coleman around?" Nicolson asked. "The woman he lives with, I mean."

"At first. But she soon went out." Eileen smiled wryly. "I think it was expected of her."

After the older woman had gone, Coleman switched on all his charm.

"He was so blatant," said Eileen, "that I thought it was some eccentric form of humour. I gave him the benefit of the doubt because it's so easy to be unfair to somebody you dislike. He mistook politeness for the come hither sign; or else he'd bags of confidence in his own salesmanship. Anyway, before I knew what was happening we were in a clinch."

Eileen paused to take a mouthful of salmon: "I bit his lip," she related with satisfaction. "Hard. My teeth nearly met. That broke up the party. You should have heard his language." She shivered. "He's a *horrible* man. I saw what's underneath that revolting charm. He's got it in for society because he's a failure. A dangerous influence on Ian."

"Did you tell your brother what happened?"

"I tried to, but he wouldn't listen. He's too thoroughly indoctrinated."

"That's why you think he may be here now?"

She hesitated. "It seemed possible. But not very likely. I don't believe Coleman would want him. He'd just be a nuisance."

That corroborated Cameron's view.

"Tell me about your brother, Miss Pratt," said Nicolson. "From all I hear he's an unusual boy."

"Unusual?" She thought about it. "I suppose he is, in a way. Terrible *brainy*."

"I don't mean that. I mean—well, to *change* like that, so completely——"

"Give Ian a chance and he'll find his feet again. He's too sensitive, that's his trouble. Too gentle for this rat race."

"Not too gentle to start a fight in a dance hall, though," Nicolson reminded her.

Eileen's eyes flashed angrily. "I don't care what they say, it wasn't Ian who started it. That's just not his nature. . . . And that silly little man in court thinking he could solve everything with a stroke of the pen: half an hour with a psychiatrist, then report to your probation officer once a week. . . . It makes me sick."

The only real solution, she told Nicolson, was for her brother to get right away—away from the source of the infection, the festering love-hate relationship with his adoptive mother.

Eileen had urged him to go. "I even made him go down to see Annette last month. She gave him the same advice."

"And what about Ian himself? Did he *want* to leave Silbridge?"

"He was always threatening to Mother he'd run away, but I was never sure if he meant it. When we found on Wednesday night he'd packed a case and gone, I was *delighted*."

"Yet you're here to-day to look for him?"

"That's different," she said shortly. "This is the one place he'd be even worse off than at home. I must satisfy myself he's not here."

"You're not frightened to go back to that house after what happened last time?"

She smiled. "I don't scare easy, mister. . . . I pack a sharp tooth."

They walked back to Grayson Street. The rain was almost off and Eileen wanted exercise. She walked with the vigour and grace of an athlete.

"You're not my idea of a gym teacher," Nicolson remarked.

"How do you mean?"

"The ones I remember had deep voices and legs like tree trunks. From playing too much hockey, I suspect."

She laughed. "I never was much good at hockey. Tennis is my game. And I play golf with Douglas occasionally."

"He's a golfer, is he?"

Eileen replied defensively: "Douglas isn't just a long-haired artist, you know. He——"

"I don't despise long-haired artists. We're not all philistines in the C.I.D. If that was his painting on the wall of his studio, it's damned good. . . . So was his nude," he couldn't resist adding.

She turned and glared at him. "*Must* you bring that up?" Then she laughed. "All the same you don't like Douglas, do you?"

"I've nothing against him," he said.

But it wasn't true. Again the shadow of a memory of his school days at Culverton troubled him. Something involving Troup. And a girl. Wasn't there a girl concerned in it? But still the image didn't quite crystallise.

EIGHT

IT WAS a quarter to three when he rang the bell. He had left Eileen at the corner of Grayson Street. They agreed it was better not to arrive together.

Mrs. Coleman took him this time into the sitting-room, where a coal fire was just beginning to take the chill from the air. From the back of the house came the excited crackling of a television commentator.

"Eddie's watching the racing," said the woman. "I'll fetch him."

This room had some good stuff in it; notably a walnut bureau and an elegant, if old-fashioned, display cabinet, survivors, no doubt, from Coleman's palmier days. The carpet, however, was worn and the wall-paper faded.

The boom of the television was cut off and a moment later Edward Coleman appeared. Eileen Pratt's description had prepared Nicolson for the smooth black hair, the toothbrush moustache—yes, and the smirk. But he looked *younger* than Nicolson expected. Perhaps it was the dyed hair; only when he came close could you see the grey near the roots.

"Glad you came," he said, pumping Nicolson's hand vigorously. "I'm worried about that boy. . . . Now what'll it be—whisky? Gin?—or I've some vodka here that——"

Nicolson declined.

"Ah, well! You have your regulations, I dare say. But you don't mind if——?"

Coleman poured himself a generous whisky and added a splash of soda.

"Sit down, Inspector, sit down. . . . Yes, when Meg told me, I said to myself, 'Eddie,' I said, 'you've got to help these chaps.' Because the boy means a lot to me, Inspector, I don't mind telling you. . . . Cigarette? A whiff of the old cancer, eh?" He was on his feet again, proffering the packet, flicking his lighter.

"When did you last see your son, Mr. Coleman?" Nicolson asked.

"Did Meg not tell you? A fortnight ago. Two weeks to the very day. I thought Meg would have told you, Inspector."

"Did he say anything then about leaving home?"

"Well, he wasn't *happy*, Inspector. Of course, he wanted to come here. But I said to him 'Ian,' I said, 'it's no use building up your hopes,'

49

I said. 'The old cow'—if you'll pardon the expression, Inspector—'the old cow would have the law on us'."

"You mean his mother?"

Coleman snorted. "Some mother *she's* been . . . of course, it's my fault in a way for not being firm enough with Nancy. I wanted to marry her, see, but she was under her old man's thumb. The old skinflint said the kid was to be adopted and that was that. The bastard!"

He tossed back the last of his drink and went over for a refill. He moved with a nervous, restless energy.

"A pillar of the kirk, too." Nancy's father's offence continued to rankle after sixteen years. "Never trust them, that's what I've been teaching Ian. The respectable ones, the ones with money and power. They'll kick you in the guts as soon as look at you. You get your boot in first, that's what I tell Ian."

He was drunk; he wouldn't be talking like this unless he was drunk. He must have had a few before Nicolson arrived.

"Hot in here, isn't it?" Coleman remarked. He took off his checked sports jacket and threw it over a chair. He was wearing a maroon sleeveless pullover.

"Tell you a story, Inspector," he said, leaning forward confidentially. "A true story. You ask Meg if you don't believe me. Chap I knew, his hobby was cameras. Well, he came into some lolly, see, and he set up on his own. Photographer, see what I mean? The kind that goes round taking snaps of the kids in their own houses, you know the racket. Well, he wanted me as a partner, see, because you need a good salesman to push that line, and though I say it myself, I could sell a fridge to an Eskimo. I was all set to sign on the dotted line when—bingo, the deal was off."

"Why?" said Nicolson, because the question was expected. He was wondering what was delaying Eileen. Ten minutes, she'd said.

"I'll tell you why, Inspector. I'll tell you why. He got the thumbs down sign from some codger who knew Nancy's old man, that's why. It's all a bloody conspiracy, that's what it is." He threw the stub of his cigarette into the fire and immediately lit another. "Chaps like me don't stand a chance, Inspector. A revolution, that's what we need. A bloody revolution."

"And that's what you've been preaching to Ian, is it? Bloody revolution?"

Coleman's eyes narrowed. He wasn't as drunk as all that.

"Ah! don't pay any attention to me, Inspector." He smiled. "I'm just letting off steam. . . . Sure you won't change your mind?" He filled his own glass once more.

50

The doorbell rang, and Nicolson heard Mrs. Coleman go to answer it. A moment later Eileen burst into the room.

"Where is he?" she snapped at Coleman. She looked distraught and angry.

Coleman's lip curled. "Ah! the Virgin Mary," he sneered. "Pratt the Prude, eh?"

"Shut up. Where's Ian?" Eileen repeated.

"If you mean my son, I haven't clapped eyes on him for a fortnight."

"Then what's his bicycle doing downstairs?"

Coleman blanched. "Where?" he said.

"In the wash-house—I saw it through the window. . . . And don't try to tell me it's not Ian's."

He was rallying. "What bloody right have you to go snooping round the back——"

"Never mind that," she interrupted implacably. "Tell us about the bicycle."

Coleman took a deep breath. "It's mine," he said. "Ian gave it to me." They stared at him.

"All right, you don't believe me." He walked to the door. "Meg!" he shouted.

The woman came in.

"Tell them about the bike, Meg. Tell them how it came."

"It came by carrier yesterday," she said.

"Where from?" Nicolson asked.

"From Silbridge, I think. Johnstone's delivered it. They've a branch in Silbridge."

"All right. Thanks, Meg." Coleman dismissed her.

But Nicolson wasn't finished. "Mrs. Coleman," he said, "weren't you surprised the boy should make his father a present of a bicycle?"

"Present?" she repeated blankly. Then she caught Coleman's eye. "Oh! I see. Well, it's not the first gift he's sent."

"What else?"

"Money."

Coleman snorted in disgust. "For God's sake, Meg. . . . Here, let me tell it, before you rattle any more skeletons."

His glass was empty again. The hand that refilled it wasn't quite steady, Nicolson noticed. He was nervous. Or perhaps it was the effect of all that whisky.

"Know what Ian and I used to talk about?" he said. "Starting a business together. 'Edward Coleman and Son.' A newsagent's maybe. Or a bookshop. The boy wanted a bookshop. . . . We talked about it so much I was half believing in it myself. All my days I've slaved my guts out for other people and I've damn all to show for it. I've got brains, see, but that's no bloody use. You need capital, that's what you need, and connections—the old school tie and all that crap. The dice are loaded against the likes of me."

"Cut out the sob stuff," said Eileen. "Tell us about Ian."

He scowled at her. "Ian was dead keen," he said. "He didn't see it was just a pipe dream. Of course, he was fed to the teeth with Silbridge. The school and all that. And his family." Again he looked viciously at Eileen.

"So he sent you money?" Nicolson asked.

"Now, look, Inspector, don't get the wrong idea. It was only twice—no, three times maybe—and just a few quid altogether."

"But when?"

"All in the last month. We were supposed to be saving up, see, and this was the boy's share."

"You took money from a sixteen-year-old boy?" Eileen's tone was disgusted.

"Hell, he was rolling in it."

"Where did he get it?" Nicolson asked.

"How the bloody hell should I know?" Then, more quietly. "He said he'd won fifty quid on a premium bond."

"And the bicycle?"

"That was different. Last time I saw him—two weeks ago it was—he told me he was packing it in. 'I've had Silbridge, Dad,' he said. 'I want to come and stay with you.' 'Ian,' I said, 'it's not on,' I said. 'Not so long as you're under age. The old cow would——' "

"Yes, we've heard that," said Nicolson.

"Have you? Well, he said then he was clearing off anyway. These were his very words. 'I'm clearing off anyway, Dad,' he said. 'I'll go somewhere they'll never find me.' That's what he said. And he asked if his bike would be any use to me. 'Only if you don't need it, son,' I said. Well, as Meg told you, it arrived yesterday."

"Where did he intend to go?" Nicolson asked.

Coleman shook his head sadly. "Ah! Inspector, I wish I knew. I'm worried about the boy. I thought he'd have sent me a postcard or something."

NINE

THE REPORT lay on Nicolson's desk, with a pencilled note scribbled across it: "When you've read this, ring me—P.G.M."

It was after ten o'clock. Nicolson could hear shouting and singing as the first of the Saturday night drunks was brought in. It would be a busy night, probably. The Albion had lost at home to-day, and that usually made for trouble.

Nicolson lit a cigarette and began to read. The anonymity of the typewriter couldn't disguise the brisk, no nonsense, style of Detective-Sergeant Cameron. His reports never wasted a syllable.

A Glasgow taxi-driver had recognised the photograph of Ian Pratt. He picked him up at the taxi rank in the Central Station about mid-night on Wednesday and drove him to the Clydemuir Hotel near the Trongate.

The proprietrix of the Clydemuir, a small commercial hotel, had had a telephone call on Wednesday morning from a Mr. Thomas, booking a single room for that night. When midnight came and still no Mr. Thomas, she had written him off, but at 12.15 the taxi arrived with the boy. He signed the register as "D. Thomas" and gave his address as "London."

After breakfast on Thursday morning the boy paid his bill and phoned for a taxi. This taxi-driver too remembered the fare. He had driven him back to the Central Station where the boy said he was catching the Royal Scot. Finally a porter remembered carrying the green case from the taxi and putting it on the London train. The boy gave him a five-shilling tip.

That was the narrative, but Cameron had added notes:

Identification: First taxi-driver and porter positive the boy they saw was the boy in the photograph (i.e. Ian Pratt). Hotel-keeper thought Thomas's face was thinner and his hair not so fair, but admits she could be mistaken. Second taxi-driver doesn't remember the boy clearly.

Clothes, etc.: All agree on the grey overcoat—good quality, teen-age style, fur-trimmed. This matches Mrs. Pratt's description of her son's coat. And the green suitcase, although none of them remembers the broken lock. And brown shoes. Hotel-keeper has the impression the boy's suit was grey but concedes it might have been brown.

(Pratt is known to have been wearing a brown suit.) The others could only say the trousers were of a "light" shade.

Accent: Variously described as "funny—certainly not Scottish," "English—kind of cockney," and "Welsh." Suggests a hybrid, assumed accent.

Other characteristics: All four witnesses testify to liberality in tipping.

Conclusions: Strong probability that "Thomas" is Pratt and that Pratt is now in England. But further inquiries are suggested as follows:

1. Try to link the boy whom the taxi-driver picked up with the train from Silbridge. Time was right, but two or three other trains arrived about the same time. Taxi-driver did not notice from which platform the boy came.
2. Compare entry in hotel register with Pratt's handwriting.
3. Question staff and other guests in Clydemuir Hotel for Wednesday night.
4. Question train crew of Royal Scot and ticket collectors, porters, etc., at Euston.
5. Press publicity: ask "D. Thomas," if he exists as a separate person, to come forward.

Nicolson stubbed out his cigarette. The case for identifying Thomas with Pratt was stronger even than the report indicated, for there was one significant detail Cameron had overlooked. . . .

There was a knock on the door and Detective-Constable Bullock entered.

"About your phone call from Edinburgh, sir," he said. "Mr. Mearns asked me to——"

"Oh! yes, you've been to Johnstone's, have you? Any luck?"

"Yes, sir. Pratt left his bike with them on Wednesday about 4.20. Gave them an address in Edinburgh to deliver it to. A Mr.——"

"I know. Mr. Edward Coleman, 12 Grayson Street. That right?"

"Yes, sir."

"They're sure it was Pratt?"

"Oh! yes, sir. Chap knows him there. It was definitely him."

The time-table was becoming clearer, although there were still gaps. Pratt left school at 4.10 and handed over his bicycle to Johnstone's, the carriers, at 4.20, then walked home. He changed out of his school clothes into his brown suit, packed the green suitcase and left the house before his mother returned at six o'clock. By 6.30 he was at St. Gregory's Station (a mile and a half from his home), where he bought

54

a single to Glasgow and deposited his case in the Left Luggage. He then walked to the Royal Hotel and had dinner, coming out about eight o'clock and setting off in the opposite direction from the station.

From that point there was no trace of him until, four hours later, he engaged a taxi in Glasgow. He must have returned to the station after nine o'clock, retrieved his suitcase, and taken what proved to be the last train for Glasgow that night. He spent the night in the Clydemuir Hotel under the name of Thomas and travelled south by the Royal Scot the following morning.

Nicolson rang Chief Detective-Inspector Mearns at his house.

"Oh! you're back, are you?" Mearns's tone was peevish. "Now, see here, maybe I'm peculiar, but I like to know what's going on. This jaunt to Edinburgh, you should have *asked* me."

"I left a note for you. It was my day off, you know, sir."

"That's beside the point. And anyway what are Edinburgh going to think? We don't want to tread on toes——"

"I phoned them. They'd no objection."

Mearns sighed. "All right, Maurice, we'll say no more about it. You did find the bicycle; that's something. Did Bullock——"

"Yes, sir. Pratt left it with the carriers at 4.20 on Wednesday."

"Fine. Fine. . . . What did you think of Cameron's report, Maurice?"

The question was asked casually, but Nicolson wasn't deceived.

"I'm never happy," he said, "about identifications from photographs. So many people *want* to believe they saw the person you're looking for. Was it the Glasgow people who did the interviews or——"

"Allan Cameron was with them. He's been in Glasgow most of the day. . . . *He's* not in any doubt. Very positive person, Allan. A weakness, really."

"He did miss one thing, though," said Nicolson.

"What's that?"

"The name. The significance of 'D. Thomas'."

"I'm not with you."

"Dylan Thomas is one of Pratt's heroes."

"God, yes. That's clever, Maurice. I should have spotted that. Well, that just about clinches it, doesn't it?" And when Nicolson didn't answer: "Well, *doesn't* it?"

"I suppose so," Nicolson conceded unhappily.

When he had rung off, he tried to analyse his doubts. There were still some unresolved mysteries: Where did Ian Pratt go after he left the Royal Hotel and before he returned to the station? Where did he go these other Wednesday nights? How did he come by so much money?

But Nicolson's unease stemmed most of all from his interview with the Colemans. Edward Coleman's claim that the bicycle was a gift from his son had sounded like an improvisation. Nicolson had the strong impression that he—and his wife—had expected the boy to arrive as well as the bicycle. . . .

When he put that to Eileen Pratt she had ridiculed it. She was now satisfied that her brother wasn't with his father; and that was all that concerned her.

That night Nicolson dreamt of Ruth, for the first time in many weeks. Only her hair was darker. . . .

In the next two weeks Pratt, *alias* Thomas, was seen twenty-three times in places as far apart as Inverness and Plymouth. All these reports were investigated; all proved to be false. Pratt had vanished without trace. So had the boy, if he was a different boy, who boarded the Royal Scot on Thursday morning, 26th November. No one had seen him on the train, no one had seen him get off it.

Two hand-writing experts compared "D. Thomas, London," in the hotel register with specimens of Ian Pratt's writing. The first declared they were not by the same hand, the second was not prepared to commit himself. Appeals in the Press to Mr. D. Thomas, if he existed, to make himself known evoked no response.

After a few days the case of the missing schoolboy dropped out of the national Press; after a week even the *Silbridge Advertiser* ceased to refer to it. The police inquiries continued longer: a missing person's file is never finally closed until he is found. But long before Christmas the Pratt file was off the active list. Pratt had left Silbridge, his description had been circulated: what more could be done?

Only Nicolson had misgivings. . . .

PART II

ONE

"EILEEN!"

She gritted her teeth. "Yes, Mother?" she called.

"Bring my aspirins when you're coming, would you? My head's worse this morning."

"Yes, Mother."

Her father was spreading marmalade on his toast. "You shouldn't do it, you know," he remarked.

"What? Give her breakfast in bed?"

"You're only encouraging her. It's not as if she was really ill. . . . Ach, well, on your own head be it." He turned back to his *Glasgow Herald*.

Eileen picked up the tray and carried it upstairs.

"Good morning, dear. . . . Any letters?" Her mother's invariable greeting.

"Grocer's bill," she answered briskly, "and a letter from Annette. It's on the tray."

Mrs. Pratt sighed. "It's seven weeks to-day. . . ." Tears began to gather.

"Now, Mother, remember what the doctor said. Ian's all right. You must believe that."

God! How much longer would this go on? Every morning the same performance, almost to the word.

"Where are my aspirins, Eileen? I *told* you to bring my aspirins."

She took a deep breath. "Sorry, Mother. I'll get them."

If she speaks to me in that tone just *once* more, Eileen was thinking, I'll pack it in.

Mrs. Pratt was nibbling a piece of toast when Eileen came back with the bottle of aspirins. The letter from Annette lay unopened on the tray.

She really did look ill, propped up in bed there. Her skin was almost transparent and showed up the blue veins round her eyes. "Nothing organic," the doctor had said. But sometimes Eileen wondered. . . .

"Are you getting up to-day, Mother?" she asked.

"I'll see how I feel. . . . You might change my library books, would you?"

"Yes, Mother." Another chore; and whatever she chose would be wrong.

"Do you see much of your friend Mr. Nicolson these days?" her mother was going on.

"No." Since that day in Edinburgh Inspector Nicolson had always been "your friend." The phrase was intended to annoy; and it did.

"I want to talk to him. They must have found out *something* by this time."

"Mother, if they had, he'd have let us know."

"I don't care. I want to talk to him."

"All right, if I see him, I'll tell him. . . . I'll have to fly now."

Mrs. Pratt sighed. "You never have any time for me," she said petulantly.

"Good-bye, Mother." Eileen kissed the cheek that was listlessly turned to her and went out.

"Try to humour her," the doctor had said. But why should it all fall on Eileen? Why shouldn't her father take some of the strain?

There he was now, putting his coat on, crumpling his newspaper and stuffing it in his pocket. She had never known anyone who could get a newspaper into such a mess so quickly.

"Will you be wanting a lift?" he asked in his slow Highland drawl.

"I haven't had breakfast yet," she replied shortly.

He nodded. "I'll be off, then. . . . Oh! and—I'll be late to-night. Don't keep supper. I'll have a bite at the Castle."

That was every night this week. Easy for him to stay placid.

It worried Eileen to feel as she did about her parents. Although less openly hostile to her than to Annette, her mother had always been cold, unloving, quick to find fault. As for her father, Eileen might not exist, for all the notice he took of her. His garden and his chess—these were his only interests.

Try as she would, Eileen could summon up little affection for either of her parents. She didn't even *like* them.

Especially now, under the strain of doing two jobs at once and having it all taken for granted. These breakfast dishes, which Eileen had no time to wash now, would still be there for her when she came home in the evening. Their woman only came twice a week. And her mother had resigned from household chores to devote herself to grief and sickness.

Grief for her adopted son. Against all reason she insisted that some harm had befallen Ian. Sometimes Eileen wondered if her mother *preferred* to believe that, rather than that he'd voluntarily left her.

In spite of everything Eileen herself was glad Ian had gone. To get away from his mother was his only chance. Sensible, too, not to write: letters could be traced. She missed him, though. . . .

Coming out into the crisp, January air was like a release from prison. She took her bicycle to-day, for she had missed the 8.40 bus.

There were patches of frost on the roads, this morning. Eileen ignored them. On the long, steep stretch from Hughenden Road down to the Chapel she gave her bicycle its head, revelling in the rush of cold air on her face. Twenty yards from the halt sign at the Crane Road junction she pulled on both brakes and came to a screeching stop with the front wheel teetering on the white line. The driver of a corporation bus that was turning laboriously out of Crane Road scowled at her. She grinned back and the scowl turned to a reluctant smile. Eileen felt better.

Wednesday was a bad morning, though, starting as it did with the fourth, the one class Eileen didn't like. An awkward age, of course: girls of thirteen and fourteen are gawky and unattractive, given to tiresome giggling. This year they were a particularly unpleasing lot; and among them was one sharp-faced little vixen called Sandra Cowie, who had perfected the art of dumb insolence and of inciting to ill-advised retaliation. Eileen was proof against that kind of baiting. But it was a strain.

To-day she knew something was afoot as soon as they came into the gym dressed in their regulation black shorts and white blouses. There was an air of suppressed excitement about them which Eileen's trained eye didn't miss.

"Where's Sandra?" she said sharply.

By way of answer the changing-room door opened, and Sandra Cowie came mincing out, stark naked. Some of the girls began to giggle.

Eileen knew better than to let her anger show.

"Get your clothes on, Sandra," she said in a tone of mild impatience. "We're late already."

"Please, Miss Pratt, can I do gym like this to-day?"

"No! Don't be silly."

Sandra's scrawny little body was arched back in an odd attitude, her hands clasped behind her head. The excited titter from her classmates indicated that this was the climax of the joke. Eileen felt her cheeks go crimson as she recognised the parody of Douglas Troup's nude.

She advanced slowly on Sandra, staring hard at her till the girl straightened and dropped her eyes.

"I thought I told you to get some clothes on," she said quietly. Sandra scuttled away.

How on earth had it got out? It would be all round the school in no time. Douglas was so *careless*. But surely even he. . . .

Somehow the clock crept round to 9.45 and the class was dismissed. Still no respite, though. She had the sixth now.

She let them play netball; she felt too upset to give them exercises. The tall, graceful figure of Christine Anderson dominated the game as always, the one genuine athletic prospect the school had produced in years. Not enough ambition, though; the only thought in her head was boys. . . . And at the opposite extreme, Mary Reilly, a pathetic, tubby figure, half-blind without her spectacles, making timid, ineffectual sallies whenever the ball approached.

Eileen observed it all without consciously taking it in. She was still thinking of the humiliating scene in the previous class. But gradually her sense of proportion and her sense of humour were reasserting themselves. She would have it out with Douglas just as soon as——

She noticed the time: 10.25. Thank God!

She dismissed the girls. She would catch Douglas now—he had no class until 11.30. Nor had she.

But as she turned to the door, a girl ran up to her.

"Miss Pratt!"

Eileen turned round. It was Norah Shipstone.

"Could you—I mean, can I talk to you?" The girl was agitated.

"Well, I——" Eileen began, then changed her mind when she saw the girl's troubled face. "All right, get your things on, then come to my room."

Eileen's room was little more than a large cupboard with one tiny window. It had a desk and a couple of chairs; there was no space for more. Still, it was her own.

Norah Shipstone was the daughter of a local minister. A smallish, thin girl with brown hair in a fringe and hazel eyes; not much of a scholar and about average at games.

Eileen, usually a good judge of character, had been deceived at first by Norah's unassuming manner. It was only when Ian began to take an interest in the girl that Eileen looked closer and saw the strength of character in the eyes.

"It's about Ian," Norah began.

Eileen had guessed that. But she wasn't prepared for what came next: "I think he's dead."

It was the morning break, and the noise in the playground was rising in a crescendo. Eileen leant over and closed the window.

"Why do you say that?" she asked quietly. The chill stab of fear went through her breast.

"He hasn't written," said Norah.

Eileen sighed with relief. If *that* was all. . . . It was her mother's parrot-cry: "he hasn't written." Why should he?

"He promised he'd write," Norah added.

"Promised? When?"

"The night he disappeared."

"You saw him that night?"

The girl nodded.

"You'd better tell me about it," said Eileen.

About ten to six that night Norah had been doing her homework in the manse study when there was a knock on the window. It was the special knock Ian Pratt had once taught her.

She slipped out the back door and round to where Ian waited between the hedge and the side of the house. He was in an overcoat and had a suitcase. He had seen Norah through the lighted window, he told her.

"But I thought it was all washed up between you," Eileen interrupted.

Norah shrugged. "I think he had to talk to somebody. He was terribly worked up. He told me he was leaving home for good."

"Did he say where he was going?" Eileen asked.

"No. But. . . ."

"Yes?"

"Well, he mentioned his father—I mean, his real father. And it was then he made me promise not to tell anybody he'd talked to me. So I wondered——"

"You wondered if he'd gone to stay with his father?"

"Yes."

"He hasn't, you know. The police have checked."

Norah nodded miserably. "I still believe that's where he meant to go."

"But, Norah, what's worrying you? If he'd had an accident——"

"I wasn't thinking of an *accident*," Norah said quietly.

The bell rang for the end of break.

"Hadn't you better——?" said Eileen absently. The girl shook her head.

Eileen was on the verge of panic. Norah's matter-of-fact words had shocked her. They made far more impression than all her mother's intuitions of disaster or even Inspector Nicolson's vague misgivings. For the first time Ian's continued silence seemed sinister rather than prudent.

"You see," Norah went on, "he was mixed up in something dangerous."

Although Ian had long since discarded Norah, she was still very much aware of him and sensitive to his moods. She noticed the change in him about a month before his disappearance. Up till then he had acted like one kicking in blind rage against the injustice of society.

"He'd have come round," said Norah. "He'd too much sense to carry on like a fool for ever. He thought everybody was against him. Even me. But he'd have come round. Only . . . something happened."

She could almost put a date to it: 20th October—or perhaps a day on either side. It wasn't only that he suddenly had money. His manner was different. There was a touch of bravado in it, of desperation almost.

"Some of the things he said to the teachers, Miss Pratt, were *awful*."

Eileen nodded. She had heard tales of his impertinence.

"I don't see, though," she said, "how you make out he was in *danger*."

"I just know," Norah said stubbornly. "He was scared. I could tell. And ashamed too. . . ."

Eileen cast her mind back to Ian's last few weeks at home. The rows with his mother had been more frequent and more violent. The tension between them was so appalling that Eileen had had no thought of anything else. He did have money, though; she remembered that. He had bought the bicycle, he had bought new clothes. At the time she had assumed his mother was paying for them, perhaps trying to buy his affection.

"He said he'd send me a poem at Christmas," Norah was saying.

"A poem?"

"He said not to worry if I didn't hear before then. But he'd write me a poem for Christmas. He said not to tell anybody the post-mark."

"That was in November," Eileen pointed out. "More than a month before Christmas."

The girl flushed. "He wouldn't forget. He'd know I would worry."

"Norah, I don't want to be unkind, but Ian didn't show you much consideration before that, did he? I mean, running around with that little trollop?"

Norah looked steadily at her. "Miss Pratt, I know Ian would have sent me that poem if he could. I just *know* it."

"Have you been to the police?"

She had. They had questioned her when Ian first disappeared. In-spector Nicolson had found out she used to be Ian's girl friend and had asked her about him. Loyal to her promise, she had said nothing of the boy's visit on the Wednesday evening.

But when Christmas came and no word from Ian, Norah, on the advice of her parents, went to the police station and told the whole story.

"To Inspector Nicolson?"

"No, the other one. The big man."

"Sergeant Cameron?"

"Yes. . . . He wrote it all down and said they'd look into it. But I don't think he was interested."

He wouldn't be. It was a pretty tenuous story when you boiled it down. Not one that would impress the pragmatic Cameron.

"So now you've come to me, Norah. What am I supposed to do about it?"

Suddenly the girl looked very immature. "I don't know, Miss Pratt," she said helplessly.

TWO

"KEEP YOUR head still."

She carefully laid down her cup. "How can I drink coffee without moving my head?"

"Won't be a minute." Douglas was making quick, deft strokes with his pencil on the back of the menu, glancing at her every few seconds.

"There. How's that?" He handed her the card.

Eileen was always slightly shaken by Douglas's sketches of her. It was like hearing your own voice on tape.

"Is my mouth really as big as that?" she said doubtfully.

"Bigger." He laughed.

It was good, though. Extraordinary how he could put life and character into a face.

"One of these days," said Douglas, stirring his coffee, "I want to do another full-length of you. I thought——"

"Draped or undraped?" Eileen interrupted.

"What?—Oh! Nude, of course."

"Of course. Something else for the High School kids to snigger over."

"What do you mean?"

"Douglas, how did the Cowie child see that painting? You *promised* you'd——"

63

He smiled. "Is this why you brought me here to-day? For cross-examination?"

Normally they lunched in the school canteen. To-day Eileen had insisted on going out; they had chosen the Green Leaf.

"Partly," she replied.

"Matter of fact," he said, examining his nails, "I hung it in the art room in school. Place needed some life."

"What!" Then she saw his grin. "Darling, you shouldn't tease me like that."

"Sorry . . . Sandra Cowie can't have seen the picture. It's never been out of my flat and she's never been in it. Jenny must have described it to her."

"Oh! yes. Jenny." Eileen spoke without warmth. Jennifer Cowie, Sandra's older sister, was a typist in the Burgh Chamberlain's office, but did modelling in her spare time. Especially for Douglas Troup. Eileen was familiar with every inch of Jenny's anatomy from canvases in his studio. "I've got legs, too," she said crossly to him one day. That was when she let him paint her. . . .

She wasn't really jealous of Jenny. Or so she tried to persuade herself. It didn't *mean* anything to an artist, they said. All the same, she wished Jenny weren't quite so attractive.

"Have the children been talking?" Douglas asked.

"What do you expect? It's all round the school. Just wait till the parents get to hear. The Scarlet Woman, that's me."

Douglas yawned. "Never let the prurient-minded worry you, darling. They're always with us, like the poor."

It was typical of Douglas to be so detached and unsympathetic. He had a different scale of values from most people; it was part of his attraction for Eileen.

If only he weren't so volatile. This seemed to be one of his good days. But there were others when black depression gripped him and nothing she did or said could pull him out of it. He had been getting worse recently; or perhaps it was that her own troubles left her with fewer reserves to cope.

"You'd think," Douglas remarked, "that they'd *heat* the place. One can overlook the egg-stained table-cloth, but one prefers not to eat with one's teeth chattering. And look at——" He broke off. "You're not listening," he said accusingly.

Eileen was crumbling bread on her plate. She wondered now if she should tell him. She had brought him here to talk about Ian. But now that she was away from Norah, away from that earnest little face with its unhappy eyes, it all seemed fanciful and slightly ridiculous.

"Out with it, darling," he said. "I'm not paying fifteen bob for a meal in this icebox and having you sit silent as the Sphinx."

She told him.

Douglas wasn't impressed. "She's infatuated, that girl," he said. "Girls in that state can convince themselves of anything."

"Infatuation's not the right word. There's nothing unbalanced about her feelings for Ian. She sees his faults."

"Love, then? Is that what you call it? In a girl of sixteen?"

"I don't know." The point wasn't worth arguing. One thing she was certain of was Norah's utter devotion to Ian. Nothing would shift that. Unless perhaps his death. . . .

"Anyway," she said, "it's odd, isn't it, the way money suddenly flowed into Ian's pockets."

"Yes," Douglas conceded. "That *is* odd. . . . Any thoughts about it?"

Eileen shook her head. "Unless he stole it," she said doubtfully. "But I just can't see Ian as a thief."

"Still, it bears looking into. . . . 20th October, Norah said?"

"Yes."

"Good. You and I will investigate. . . . Now let's get out of here. Waitress!"

They went to the Public Library after school. Eileen had been umpiring a hockey match and was tired. She would have preferred to go home, but allowed Douglas to persuade her. Anyway she had her mother's books to change.

The *Silbridge Advertiser* for October had not yet been bound. Douglas took the loose copies for the week beginning 19th October into the reading-room while Eileen selected books for her mother. Mrs. Pratt had a formula for the kind of novel she would read: it had to be "romantic" and it had to be "nice"; which meant it must have no violence or unpleasantness or bear any observable resemblance to life. It took Eileen ten minutes to find two books sufficiently escapist. Already she could hear her mother's petulant "But I've *read* that one, dear."

Douglas looked smug when she joined him in the reading-room. He indicated the paper which lay open on the table in front of him. It was the *Advertiser* for Thursday, 22nd October, and he was pointing to a column headed "Local Jeweller Robbed." "During the early hours of Wednesday morning" (it ran) "thieves broke into the premises of Mr. Julius Schapiro, watchmaker, 37 High Street, and made off with a substantial haul, whose value, on a preliminary estimate, is close on £5,000. . . . Chief Detective-Inspector Mearns, Head of Silbridge

65

C.I.D., stated last night that the police are following a promising line of inquiry and an early arrest is hoped for."

Eileen remembered it now. No arrest had ever been made and the incident had led to one of those periodic flurries of indignant letters to the editor on "What are we paying our police force for?"

"What do you think of that, then?" Douglas whispered.

Eileen tried to consider it unemotionally. Ian had done so many strange things this past year that even burglary could not be confidently excluded. He certainly couldn't have done it alone. The newspaper account described it as a "professional" job; and, besides, Ian wouldn't know how to dispose of stolen jewellery. Eileen could—just—imagine him robbing someone whom he regarded as "a parasite of society" (a phrase he had picked up from Coleman). But Schapiro was a gentle little man, known to Ian, the father of one of his classmates.

"I don't believe it," she said softly to Douglas. "Was there nothing else? I thought I remembered——"

He looked sulky. "It was a lean week for crime in Silbridge. Forty-seven bars of chocolate stolen from a machine in St. Gregory's Station. A woman's handbag snatched outside the Rialto. Twenty-three and six in it, I think it said." He began to flick over the pages of the newspapers. "And then there was a charity box broken open in one of the churches. That was——"

She stopped him. "Turn back to that last page."

Yes, there it was. The photograph of a girl. That's what she had been remembering. These letters complaining of police inefficiency had been provoked by *two* unsolved crimes. The burglary at Schapiro's was one; the other was the death of this girl.

Her name was Lucia Finghetti and she worked in her father's café in Crane Road. Her body was found late on Tuesday night, 20th October, in Potter Street, not a hundred yards from her home. She had been run over, and the driver hadn't stopped. No one witnessed the accident, and the car was never traced.

Eileen had been shocked, because she had met the girl only a few days before. At a party. Or a dance. That was it. The Rugby F.P. dance. Lucia had turned up at that. A sultry Italian beauty, a little overripe, perhaps, but voluptuous.

"You know her, Douglas," she said, remembering.

"What? What are you talking about?" His tone was irritable.

"At a dance, remember?" When he still looked blank, she tapped the newspaper. "The Finghetti girl. Don't tell me you've forgotten *her*."

"I tell you, I didn't *know* the girl." He raised his voice in anger.

66

"Sh!" The elderly man reading *The Field* at the adjoining table glared at them.

They took the papers back to the counter and went out. She knew from the line of Douglas's mouth that he was sulking. She got into the car beside him in silence and he drove her back to the school where she had left her bicycle.

Eileen was almost too tired to make the effort. Not quite, though. She couldn't let him go like this.

"What's biting you, darling?" she said, as he pulled up outside the school gate.

"Biting me?" He looked at her frostily.

He was like a baby when he sulked. Even his voice seemed to change. She tried again. "What have I done, Douglas?" And, when he didn't answer: "Was it the girl? Should I not have said that about the girl?"

"Don't be silly. It's just—well, I didn't like the way you brushed aside my suggestion. About the burglary, I mean. After all the trouble I went to."

So that was it. He was offended because she hadn't enthused over his theory. Perhaps she *had* been a little cavalier.

"I'm sorry, darling," she said contritely. "I haven't brushed it aside. I can't see Ian as a burglar. But I'll mention it to the police all the same."

"To your friend Nicolson?"

It might have been her mother talking.

"Probably. Jealous?"

"Of Maurice Nicolson? Heaven forbid. We were at school together, you know."

That surprised her. "What was he like?" she asked.

"What you'd expect. Very intellectual. He won a scholarship to St. Andrews eventually."

"I wonder what made him become a policeman."

"He was always a do-gooder. Social conscience, you know. Couldn't leave people to run their own lives." Douglas *was* a little jealous, she fancied. But at least he was coming out of his sulks.

A blue Cortina crossed the tarmac from the car park and went out through the gate. Its driver waved to them as he passed.

"Your colleague's late to-night," Douglas remarked.

It was Tom King, the gymnastics master.

"He often works late. He's studying, you know."

"Studying? That muscle-man?" Douglas's tone was contemptuous.

Eileen sighed. She could foresee another crisis if she defended King. Not that she wanted to defend him. . . .

67

"It was King who took that girl to the dance," said Douglas unexpectedly.

"What girl?—Oh! Lucia Finghetti? Yes, I believe you're right."

She was the sort of girl who would appeal to King. He went for the pretty ones, on the theory that it was easier to escape from them before you became too involved. He had a new girl for each phase of the moon, more or less.

Yes, Lucia had gone to the dance as King's partner. But she had circulated a lot, Eileen remembered. It wasn't King who introduced her to Eileen: it was Douglas. And he'd introduced her as a friend, not as someone he'd just met. Yet. . . . Oh! well, what did it matter?

One other impression of that night came back—of Lucia in the powder room putting on lipstick. Something about her had made Eileen wonder if . . .

"Douglas," she said now, "would you have said that Lucia——" She broke off.

"What?" he prompted.

"Oh! nothing." It wasn't fair. The girl was dead.

"Why this interest in a girl you only met once?"

She couldn't answer. Seeing the girl's picture in the paper had brought back the shock of first reading of her death. She'd been so vital. . . .

"Come over to the flat and have a drink before you go home," Douglas invited her.

"I'd love to, darling, but——"

He sighed. "I know: breakfast dishes to wash, supper to make, ironing to do. That right?"

"Well, it's not my *fault*." She had to fight down tears. She felt so tired to-night.

But Douglas was not entirely without perception.

"Poor Eileen," he said, smiling. "You're one of life's givers, aren't you? Don't expect thanks for it, that's not the way of the world. The more you do for us, the more we batten on you. We need you, though . . . I need you."

He put his arm across and gently drew her towards him.

THREE

EILEEN'S RELATIONS with Tom King were confined to business. When she joined the High School staff three years ago he had taken her out to dinner twice in her first month. It was very respectable; he behaved impeccably; and yet Eileen was uncomfortable. When he invited her a third time, she declined. She had met Douglas Troup by then, but that wasn't her main reason. Something about Tom King repelled her.

King was tall and fair and beautifully proportioned; and he had a narcissistic pride in his appearance. After a science degree at Edinburgh he had taken a diploma in physical education at Aberdeen. Silbridge was his second post. He had served a couple of years as an assistant at Cargowan Academy.

King's choice of career was dictated by his fetish for physical fitness. Even now, in his middle thirties, he ran a mile every morning before breakfast; and he had a routine of exercises that he went through each day. He was teetotal and a non-smoker.

He smiled a lot, but without humour. He even smiled to Eileen, though it didn't disguise his dislike of her. He hadn't forgiven her for spurning his advances.

Eileen had lost count of the girl friends Tom King had had in the past three years. They came, like moths to a flame. And they went. Sometimes Eileen had the unworthy thought that King might not be as highly sexed as he liked to imply. Perhaps it was the girls who tired of him. At any rate he had not married.

He was an ambitious man, and hard-working. Competent at his job, though too strict a disciplinarian for Eileen's liking. He drilled the boys like a squad of recruits.

When Eileen joined the staff, King, although technically her superior, was full of promises of "equal partnership" and "a joint approach." It hadn't worked out like that. He did all the administration himself: ordering and issuing equipment, drawing up time-tables, arranging matches. He only consulted Eileen where it was unavoidable. For her part she was content so long as he didn't interfere in her actual teaching.

There were times, however, when she had to see him. Like this morning. She knocked on his door.

"Come in." And when she opened the door: "Ah! it's you, Eileen.

Take a pew. Be with you in a jiffy." The use of obsolescent colloquialisms made him sound at times like an elderly scoutmaster.

King's room was the antithesis of Eileen's: spacious, well-appointed, comfortable. It opened off the gymnasium and had been designed originally as an equipment store. King persuaded Dr. Huddleston it would be more useful as an office; and, despite mutterings from the rest of the staff, none of whom had a room of his own, the headmaster agreed. Much of the equipment was now stored in a shed outside.

King was working on his record cards. He was registered as a part-time research student for an Edinburgh Ph.D. He had explained once to Eileen what he was doing—something about the relationship of exercise and fatigue—but she hadn't fully understood. She found it hard to take his research seriously, because King seemed to her fundamentally a stupid man. But that was probably unfair; after all, he had an honours B.Sc. in Physiology. The pupils were his guinea pigs, and a filing cabinet was crammed with meticulous, detailed records.

"Well, now," he said, laying his cards aside. "What can we do for you?"

It was a trivial problem, yet important enough in a way. The first hockey team was due to meet Glasgow High School next Wednesday afternoon, and Christine Anderson, their star forward, had been refused permission to play. Young Harvey Pitt, who was taking the sixth for Latin during Bradley's illness, wouldn't let her off his class because her work had been so poor. While Eileen had little sympathy for her, it was a pity for the team, which was having its best season ever and was unbeaten.

"You've spoken to Pitt?" King asked.

"Yes, but it's hopeless. He doesn't know one end of a hockey stick from the other. And cares less."

King placed his fingertips together, a favourite gesture. "I think," he said judiciously, "this is a case where one might reasonably go to higher authority. Yes, I think so." He made a note on a pad.

He had his uses, Eileen had to admit. She wouldn't have dared approach the headmaster on a matter like this. King would have no hesitation. And probably gain his point too.

"I'll say this for old Bradley," King remarked, "we never had trouble like that with him. He knew that all work and no play, etc. . . . Poor old chap," he added. "He's in a bad way, I hear."

"Is he worse?" After weeks in hospital Bradley had gone through an operation just before Christmas.

"Oh! he's getting over the op., I think. But it's just a matter of time." He tapped his chest. "The usual, you know. Lung cancer."

It was what she had feared. Why did it always have to be the *nice* ones who——

"Of course," King was remarking, "if you want to go at sixty, that's the way to do it. Smoke forty a day. Personally I've no sympathy."

"Don't be so damned smug, Tom." She couldn't stop herself. "Anyway you can't measure life in years. Bradley's done more in his sixty years than——"

"Ah! well, that may be." King was smiling. "But I prefer to keep a healthy pair of lungs into my eighties."

It was one of his least agreeable traits—the satisfaction he took in the illness and death of others. It flowed from pride in his own fitness. Eileen often thought it would be salutary for him to be ill himself. But he never was. In three years he hadn't had so much as a cold.

The set smile on his face indicated that she had annoyed him. She wondered how he would retaliate. A disparaging remark about Douglas, probably, whose weediness he had commented on before now.

But no, this time he took a different line.

"Still no word from that brother of yours, Eileen?"

She shook her head.

"Not much affection between him and the family, is there? I mean, you'd think he'd put your minds at rest." If anything, the smile made the words even ruder.

Eileen had had enough. "Perhaps he's not able to send word," she said.

"I don't understand."

"The dead can't write."

For once she had shocked him into silence.

It had been a silly, melodramatic retort. All the same, as she walked back across the gymnasium that curious shiver of fear returned. Once an idea like that was planted it quickly took root.

Norah Shipstone came to see her again at break.

"Nothing yet, Norah," Eileen said at once. "I'm going to the police station to-night, but——"

"It's not that, Miss Pratt. I was wondering about Ian's diaries."

"What about them?"

Since the age of twelve Ian had kept a diary. Not the usual record of trivia; at least not after the first month or two: he quickly tired of that. He used it to record his thoughts: ideas for poems, comments on books he had read, films he had seen. He had once let Eileen read one of his diaries; it convinced her they had a prodigy in the family. Later he had become more secretive, perhaps because references to Norah were creeping in. And in the final stage, after the adoption row, he had guarded his diary like a document of state.

"Did you—did he leave them behind?" Norah asked.

"No. The police looked for them too. But all we found were the very early ones in the attic."

She looked crestfallen. "He was still keeping a diary, you know. It might have told us something. He used to write it in class. That last afternoon—the day he disappeared—Mr. Bradley caught him and took it from him. Oh! it was awful, Miss Pratt. I thought Ian was going to *hit* him."

"He got it back, though?"

"Yes, Mr. Bradley gave it back. 'Take your grubby little secrets, boy.' That's what he said."

A thought occurred to Eileen. "Lenny Ferguson was Ian's friend, wasn't he?"

"Yes."

"How well do you know him?"

"He's in my class." Norah's tone was guarded.

"He's bound to know *something* of what Ian was up to. Of course, the police have been on to him already. But it occurred to me. . . ."

"I'll use my charm on him, Miss Pratt. Though—" she hesitated, her eyes twinkling "—I'm the wrong sex. For Lenny, I mean."

"What?" Eileen thought at first she must have misheard. She gave Norah a reproving look, but couldn't keep her face straight.

Eileen went through the swing doors quietly, hoping to catch Sergeant Cubitt off his guard. It always amused her to see his lightning switch from idleness to harassed activity.

But Cubitt wasn't on duty to-day. It was the other one, the nice one, Sergeant McCrorie.

Inspector Nicolson wasn't in either; and that was a distinct disappointment. She asked to see Detective-Sergeant Cameron and was shown into the C.I.D. room.

"Hallo, Allan," she greeted him.

"Good afternoon . . . Eileen," he replied awkwardly.

Poor Allan! It embarrassed him when his private life and his work overlapped.

Eileen had met the red-headed Fiona Page in her first year at college. They were kindred spirits: both enjoyed swimming and climbing and tennis. And dancing. It was at a dance that Fiona was introduced to Allan Cameron. They were married in three months; Fiona didn't even complete her diploma. Eileen was her bridesmaid.

They had a child within a year, and their second eighteen months later. It seemed now to Eileen that much of the gaiety had gone out of her friend. And it wasn't only the cares of motherhood that weighed on her. She hadn't the easiest of husbands.

Allan Cameron had risen from nothing. Left school at fourteen. Moved from one dead-end job to another, until at eighteen he entered the police force, where he padded a beat for nearly ten years. He was dedicated and ambitious and spent his leisure in study. In 1959 his request for a transfer to C.I.D. was granted, and he was promoted a couple of years later.

He had hoped for further promotion when Detective-Inspector Green was transferred to headquarters in the summer of 1964. But Nicolson was drafted in instead. Eileen had the story from Fiona, who could see no good in Nicolson. Fiona was too uncritically in love, she fanned her husband's prejudices instead of laughing him out of them.

For prejudice was at the root of his antagonism to Nicolson. Eileen could sense it from what his wife said. Nicolson had everything Cameron most envied: education, culture, poise.

"How's Fiona?" Eileen asked.

"A wee bit tired. Donald's down with whooping cough and she's not getting her sleep. But och, we can't complain."

Belatedly he offered a chair.

"Norah Shipstone came to see you, I believe," Eileen remarked as she sat down.

"Aye."

"What do you make of her?"

"A nice wee lassie." He smiled. "But she's kidding herself. Pratt—" He corrected himself, "—Ian ditched her long ago. Why *should* he send her poems at Christmas?"

"So you're doing nothing about it?"

He made a gesture of hopelessness. "We'll not find him now, Eileen. Not unless he wants to be found. He'd money enough to see him through till he found a job. He'll be well fixed now. Trust him."

His voice declared his dislike of Ian. Yet it hadn't always been so. When Ian first got into trouble last summer, Cameron had tried to help and had been rebuffed. He had a long memory.

"Allan, that boy Thomas who was seen in Glasgow—you spoke to the witnesses, didn't you? The taxi-drivers and so on?"

He nodded.

"Are you *certain* it was Ian?"

He hesitated. "About ninety-five per cent, I'd say."

"I don't believe it was." Something about "D. Thomas"—she couldn't put a finger on it—didn't tie up with Ian.

"Oh, aye?" Cameron was unimpressed.

Eileen changed her ground. "Did you ever wonder where Ian was getting his money?"

"We did ask ourselves the question."

"Did it occur to you he might have been in on the Schapiro burglary?"

He looked keenly at her. "It did. . . . But . . . we . . . rejected it."

The hesitation didn't escape her.

"You're not so sure yourself, though, are you?" she asked.

When he didn't answer, she added: "Suppose Ian threatened to split to the police, the rest of the gang might——"

He broke in impatiently. "Eileen, we know who did the Schapiro job and, take it from me, they wouldn't hurt a fly. . . . Away home and forget it. Your brother hasn't come to any harm. And that's not only my opinion. Mr. Mearns thinks the same."

"And Mr. Nicolson?" Eileen asked innocently.

He looked at her impassively. "You'd better ask him, hadn't you?"

FOUR

"Is THAT you, dear?"

"Yes, Mother."

Eileen hung up her coat and went into the lounge. The room, as always, depressed her. Far too chintzy. And all those ghastly ornaments.

Mrs. Pratt was in an arm-chair, with a travelling rug round her legs and a book on her lap.

"You're late," she said reprovingly.

"I called at the police station. That's what kept me."

Mrs. Pratt brightened. "Is he coming?" she asked.

"Who?"

"Inspector Nicolson. I told you yesterday I wanted to see him."

Lord, yes! Eileen had forgotten. "He wasn't there, Mother," she said. "It was Allan Cameron I saw."

"Cameron would have done. Didn't you ask him?"

Eileen shook her head.

"Well, what were you *doing* there?" Her mother was becoming suspicious. "You're hiding something."

"Of course I'm not . . . tell you what, I'll ring Mr. Nicolson now and ask if he'll look in to-morrow. That do?"

It was a symptom of her mother's illness that she had developed a morbid fear of the telephone. Eileen had to do all her phoning for her.

Nicolson still wasn't in his office, but she got him at his home. He agreed to call on Mrs. Pratt to-morrow. "Any special reason?" he asked.

"She wants reassurance, that's all." Eileen hesitated, then added: "So do I."

"I beg your pardon?"

"I'd like to talk to you too."

Silence for a moment, then Nicolson said: "Well, look, suppose I come across this evening? I could see you both then."

"No, that's no good. I can't talk with Mother here. Couldn't we—couldn't we meet somewhere?"

Again a pause, then: "I'll be at home all evening. Why don't you drop in?"

Mrs. Pratt laid aside her book as Eileen came back into the room. "Well, dear, did you talk to your friend?"

"He's coming to-morrow morning."

"Did he say anything about Ian?"

"No."

"Did Cameron, then?"

Eileen looked at her compassionately. "Mother, they've no more news."

It was easier to sympathise now that she shared her mother's anxiety.

"How's the book?" Eileen asked her.

Her mother shrugged. "Not bad. . . . But that other one—I've read it before, Eileen. I'm surprised you didn't remember."

Oh, well! Fifty per cent success: above average. Eileen went into the kitchen to make supper.

Detective-Inspector Nicolson had lodgings at the east end of Crane Road, near the post office.

Eileen's ring was answered by the landlady, a tall, gaunt woman with brown hair scraped back in a bun. She looked doubtfully at Eileen before she let her in. She knocked on a door on the left and called: "A lady to see you, Mr. Nicolson." Then she retired to the back of the house.

Nicolson was in dark slacks and a cardigan.

"Nice of you to call," he said warmly.

The room was large and bleak: high ceiling, big windows, heavy, old-fashioned furniture. And on the walls portraits of frock-coated men and anæmic women.

The centre light was off, and the orange glow of a standard lamp took some of the harshness from the room. A record-player on the floor was playing a Beethoven piano sonata.

"I'll put this off," said Nicolson, bending down.

"No, leave it. I like it." Eileen took off her coat and laid it over a chair.

"There's no privacy in this room with all these worthies staring down at you," Nicolson remarked. "Don't you feel that?"

But Eileen's gaze was on the framed snapshot on the mantelpiece. Of a dark-haired girl with sad eyes. It didn't belong with Mrs. Laidlaw and her ancestors.

"Have you always lived in digs?" Eileen asked. "I mean, since you joined the police?"

There was a pause. "No, not all the time," he said. She had been gently snubbed.

He produced drinks. Eileen chose a dry sherry. Nicolson had a Scotch and soda.

Eileen watched him as he poured the drinks. Slim, almost slight in build, dark brown hair beginning to recede, good mouth and chin. Almost handsome but not quite. An intelligent, sensitive face.

She knew Nicolson was interested in her, notwithstanding the girl on the mantelpiece. It had been apparent that day in Edinburgh; it was apparent to-night.

He was the kind she might have fallen for, if she had met him in time. He'd be more considerate than Douglas. You could tell that from his eyes. Douglas had hard, selfish eyes. But the chemistry of love didn't take such things into account. . . .

With a click and a whirr the record-player changed to a new record. Bach this time.

Nicolson offered her a cigarette and lit one himself when she declined.

"Now, tell me about it," he said. "What's worrying you?"

She told him all that had happened in the past two days.

When she had finished, he asked: "What makes you so sure Thomas isn't your brother?"

She had been thinking about that. "It's the porter," she said. "The boy got a porter to carry his case from the taxi to the train. Ian wouldn't do that."

"Why not?"

"It just wouldn't occur to him. You have to be from the upper ten before you engage porters at the age of sixteen."

"The identification's pretty positive, you know. Sergeant Cameron——"

"Allan Cameron says he's ninety-five per cent convinced. That's not enough."

Nicolson was silent.

"Have you talked to Norah Shipstone?" Eileen asked.

"Not since November. She was as close as a little oyster then."

"She's opened up now. She believes Ian's dead, Inspector.

"So do you, don't you?" she added softly.

Nicolson sipped his drink. "Let's just say I'm not so confident as—as my colleagues that everything's as it seems."

"Why not?"

"Because of the bicycle, mainly. Why did he send it to Edinburgh?"

"Coleman said——"

"I know—a present to dear old Dad. But it didn't ring true. My impression was the Colemans expected Ian to turn up as well as his bicycle . . . I wonder why he didn't."

Again fear was burrowing in Eileen.

"What are you doing about it?" she asked him.

Nicolson clicked off the music. "Our investigation's *closed*, Miss Pratt," he said quietly. "So far as we're concerned, Ian's in England."

"But *you* don't believe that."

"The evidence is against me. All I have is a hunch. I'm probably wrong . . . I *hope* I'm wrong."

"But surely if fresh evidence——"

He smiled. "Ah, yes! But the promise of a poem at Christmas is hardly enough. Nor even theories about what class of boy would engage a porter."

He threw his cigarette stub in the fire and lit another.

"My hands are tied," he said. ". . . Of course, what I'd like to do *now* is question the staff of that hotel in Glasgow again. Better still if somebody who knew Ian well were to do it. . . . More sherry?"

She glanced sharply at him. Was this a hint?

"Thank you," she said. Only partly for the sherry.

As Nicolson replenished his own glass, he said suddenly: "I was at Culverton with your fiancé."

"Douglas told me."

Eileen waited. Nicolson was not one to make aimless conversation.

"I was older than Douglas, of course." He used the Christian name self-consciously. "A couple of years. Perhaps three. He was a very good cricketer, I remember."

"He still plays," Eileen remarked, "though his ankle slows him up a bit. He injured his foot, you know."

"Did he? . . . I expect he's talked to you about his schooldays?"

"Not much." "Hardly at all" would have been more accurate. Douglas was reticent about his past.

Nicolson knew something about Douglas. Something discreditable. She could read it in his face. And he was wondering whether he ought to tell her.

Eileen was annoyed. Did he seriously imagine he was going to turn her against her fiancé by some tale of misbehaviour at school?

She stood up and went over to the fire. "She's very pretty," she remarked, indicating the photograph on the mantelpiece. "Your landlady in her younger days?"

Nicolson was on his feet too. "No," he said quietly. "It's a girl I used to know."

Immediately she was contrite. Impulsively she put a hand on his arm. "I'm sorry, Maurice," she said. "I was prying."

"Never mind," he said lightly. "It's all over long ago. Ruth's married. . . . Anyway, thanks for the 'Maurice'."

"Mine's Eileen." And she added with a grin: "And my fiancé is Douglas Troup."

He smiled back. "Point taken," he said.

FIVE

DOUGLAS WOULDN'T go with her to Glasgow. He disapproved of the whole idea.

"I can't believe a police inspector would suggest such a thing," he said huffily.

"He didn't *suggest* it, darling. Anyway, what harm can it do? And Mother wants me to go. We can do a theatre in the evening."

But Douglas was adamant. It had been a mistake, she thought, to suggest they might also visit Mr. Bradley in the Glasgow Royal Infirmary. Douglas was ostrich-like in his attitude to hospitals and disease.

Eileen set off alone after breakfast on Saturday. It was a crisp, clear day. From the train she could see the snow-capped hills across the river sparkling in the sun.

In spite of herself her spirits were rising. It was good to get away, even briefly, from her mother's whining, her father's surly indifference. If only Douglas had come. . . .

She bought a couple of paperbacks for Mr. Bradley at a bookstall in Glasgow Central Station. Then after coffee at Fullers, she took a taxi to the Trongate. The January sales were in spate and the Glasgow streets were thronged with shoppers.

The Clydemuir, a small commercial hotel, was tucked away in a side street. Unpretentious but respectable, was Eileen's impression when she went in. The decor was dark, but the place looked clean.

When Eileen explained why she had come, Mrs. McLeod, the proprietrix, took her into her office and rang for tea.

"It's no bother," she said when Eileen protested. "My tongue's hanging out for a cup."

She was a stout, middle-aged woman, with hair dyed auburn and wearing too much jewellery. Her pseudo-refined Clydeside accent, together with the pencilled eyebrows and the large ear-rings, suggested to Eileen what she was: a barmaid who had married the boss.

"Your brother, was it?" she continued. "Fancy that, now! Mind you, I said to Bill at the time, 'That boy's got class,' I said."

Eileen had brought all the recent photographs of her brother she could find—about half a dozen in all. She showed them to Mrs. McLeod.

"Ach, it's no use," said the woman. "It's too long ago." She peered short-sightedly at the photographs. "No, I can't mind him clear enough. I'd be telling a lie if I said I could."

A maid brought in a tray with tea. As she turned to go, Mrs. McLeod said: "Here, have a look at these, Janet."

Janet picked up the photographs.

"Oh! it's him again, is it?" she said, flicking through them rapidly and without interest.

"You recognise him?" Eileen asked.

Janet didn't answer. She was staring at one of the snaps, a puzzled look on her face.

It had been taken on holiday in North Berwick the summer before last and showed Ian, in swimming trunks, poised on the edge of the pool.

"When was that taken?" Janet asked.

"About eighteen months ago. Why?"

"Well, he was skinnier when I saw him. His arms were like matchsticks, so they were. And you could have played the guitar on his ribs."

"And when did *you* see his ribs?" Mrs. McLeod demanded suspiciously.

When Janet took in his morning tea, the boy had been doing exercises at the window, wearing only his pyjama trousers.

"Did you tell the police how thin he was?" Eileen asked.

Janet nodded. "But that big chap, the sergeant, he says 'That's right,' he says, 'the boy that's missing, he's thin too,' he says."

But "thin" was the wrong adjective for Ian, unless in the negative sense of "not fat." He was well-developed for his age, with good chest and shoulders.

"So you think now it's not the same boy?" Eileen pressed her.

The girl stared again at the photograph. "It's his spittin' image," she said doubtfully, "except—well, like I said, he was *skinny*, see?" It was as far as she was prepared to go.

"A stupid lump," Mrs. McLeod remarked when the girl had gone out. "She never tells fibs, though. If she says the kid was skinny, then he *was* skinny."

"It wasn't Ian, then," said Eileen.

Mrs. McLeod looked sharply at her. "Ach, cheer up," she said. "You know something? Willie—that's my oldest—he's out in Australia, and not a scrape of the pen have I had since——"

But Eileen wasn't listening.

"Mrs. McLeod," she said, "that boy that was here—did he tell you *anything* about himself?"

"Not him. He hardly opened his mouth. He went about with a face as long as Leith Walk."

"Could he have been——" Eileen found it hard to express it "—could he have been *pretending* to be Ian pretending to be someone else? A sort of double bluff?"

But that was too much for Mrs. McLeod, and Eileen didn't attempt to rephrase it.

Two things more she learned from the proprietrix. When he phoned to book the room, Thomas said he was coming *down* to Glasgow. The inference was that he was speaking from somewhere farther north.

And the phone call itself: Mrs. McLeod knew the time of it within narrow limits, for she had been listening to *The Dales* on the radio. Between 11.15 and 11.30. And that again seemed to rule out Ian, who would be in class at that time. . . . But surely Cameron must have *checked* on that. . . .

"Could I see the visitors' book?" Eileen asked.

"Sure." Mrs. McLeod heaved herself to her feet. "Such a fuss the coppers made over that book. They took photos of it and dusted it for prints and——"

"Fingerprints? Did they find any?"

"Just smudges, they said. And they'd no luck in his room either. Not so much as a thumb mark. I just said to Bill, 'Say what you like about Janet,' I said, 'she doesn't skimp her work'."

Mrs. McLeod padded away, her bracelets jangling, and came back presently with the register.

"There," she said, panting slightly. "Near the bottom of the page." Yes, there it was. "D. Thomas, London." And the date. More like printing than writing.

Ian might, of course, have disguised his hand, but Eileen doubted if he could have produced anything as neat as this. She had seen this *style* of handwriting before. It conjured up a picture for her of "D. Thomas"; and a remark Mrs. McLeod had made suggested a reason for his journey.

Eileen found her way to the thoracic department at the Royal just as visiting hour began and joined the queue that was filing into men's surgical. The others made purposefully towards one bed or another, until only Eileen was left. She couldn't see Bradley and wondered if he was in the bed behind the screens.

And then she spotted him. Not in bed at all, but hunched in a chair like a little gnome, wearing a thick woollen dressing-gown over his pyjamas. He had no other visitor.

Eileen's heart contracted with pity. It was as if he had *shrunk*. His cheeks were waxen and the skin was stretched tight over the bones; already you could imagine the grinning skull beneath.

Bradley was a lonely man, respected but unloved. His sharp tongue had given offence too often.

Eileen knew him better than most. She had been to his flat with Douglas several times. Bradley tolerated Douglas because he admired his painting; art was his one consuming interest outside work.

He was far ahead in scholarship of any of his colleagues. His special field was Greek drama and his edition of Sophocles's *Antigone* had prompted more than one reviewer to wonder why a man of his academic calibre was languishing in school teaching. But Bradley had a vocation for teaching at that level and had no ambition to remove himself from it.

Eileen liked him. Once she had lost her fear of him, she discovered he could be teased. Not many others had put that to the test.

To-day he tried to hide how pleased he was to see her. In all his weeks in hospital he had had few visitors. Dr. Summers, the head of the English department, had been up several times. And Lamb, the mathematician, once. That was all.

"What about the headmaster?" Eileen asked.

Bradley smiled sourly. "I had a nice letter from him," he said.

He talked about his illness. He knew it was cancer, but believed that the operation—for the removal of a lung—had cured it. "They caught it in time," he kept saying. It was odd, Eileen reflected: he was an intelligent man, he *must* know the odds were against him. But he seemed not to encompass the possibility of death.

Even more than by his physical decline Eileen was saddened by the loss of intellectual vigour. People spoke of illness ennobling a man, giving him a new awareness, a new perspective. In her experience illness never ennobled, it always tended to degrade. Bradley's horizons had narrowed to the confines of this hospital ward. He grumbled about pains in his back, about the patient whose coughing kept him from sleeping, about the physiotherapist who handled him too roughly.

"You know what I think?" Eileen said, interrupting when he paused for breath. "I think you're just a great big baby."

He frowned and she wondered if she had misjudged. But then he put his head back and laughed weakly. "I expect you're right," he croaked.

"Here am I, all the way from Silbridge," she added, "and you haven't asked about the school. You haven't asked how the sixth are getting on since they fell into the pit. The Harvey Pitt."

He laughed again. She gave him the school gossip. She said nothing of Ian. She was here to cheer him, not to obtrude her own troubles.

But Bradley broached the subject himself.

"Any word yet from your brother?" he asked.

"No."

He shook his head sadly. "In nearly forty years I've taught no more than half-a-dozen first-class minds. Your brother was one of them."

"Was?"

"I doubt if he'll recover now. He's let his mind atrophy too long. I fear we've lost him."

"I'm afraid of worse than that," said Eileen.

But he wasn't attending. " 'Hubris'," he said. "That's what the Greeks called it. Over-weening pride. Your brother wasn't humble enough. He couldn't adjust when he learned some unpalatable facts about his parentage."

It seemed a harsh judgment.

"He needed help," said Eileen. "And sympathy. He didn't get it." It wasn't Bradley she was blaming: it was herself.

"One can't help those," Bradley was saying, "who are bent on self-immolation. That last afternoon, Miss Pratt, I confess I almost struck him."

"That was the row over the diary?"

"Yes, he was writing it in class. But it was his *insolence* that drove me to fury."

"Did you see anything in the diary?"

He ignored the question. "Of course, I was ill, I hadn't my usual resilience. It was that very night I went to the doctor. And——"

"Mr. Bradley, what was in the diary? This is important."

"Important?" Bradley looked bewildered.

"Ian's *disappeared*. We think he may be dead."

At last she had got through to him.

"Oh! you poor child," he said. "Dead! But I was told——"

She nodded. "There have been developments. We want to know what he was up to that night. . . . The diary might help."

The warning bell for the end of visiting hour rang. No one paid any attention.

"But, you know," said Bradley, "I didn't *read* it. I only glanced down the page he'd been writing on."

"Didn't you take in *anything*—a word, a phrase——"

"It's so long ago," he said fretfully. He closed his eyes and screwed up his face in concentration.

Eileen had pangs of conscience when she saw how weary he looked. "Please don't bother, Mr. Bradley," she said gently. "I shouldn't have asked."

Bradley opened his eyes. "A sum of money was mentioned," he said slowly. "£2,000, I think it was. And something about Wednesday evenings. And then there was a name that caught my eye."

The bell rang again. This time there was a scraping of chairs as visitors got up to leave.

"What name?" Eileen asked.

He frowned. "I can't remember. Except that it was an unusual name. Foreign, I think."

Bradley began to cough, gently at first, then more violently. He bent forward awkwardly, holding his chest, and his face was racked with pain. After a few moments the bout subsided and he leant back in his chair, exhausted, beads of perspiration on his brow.

Impulsively Eileen bent over him and kissed his cheek.

"Get well soon," she whispered.

As she went down the stone staircase towards the main exit, a nurse came running after her.

"Miss Pratt?" she called.

Eileen looked round.

"Mr. Bradley said—" the nurse was breathless, "—he's remembered the name. It was——" she dissolved in laughter: she had forgotten it. She went back up to the ward and returned a minute later with a scrap of paper. The name was scrawled in Bradley's spidery writing: "Lucia Finghetti."

Eileen paid one more visit in Glasgow. To the Mitchell Library. A long shot this, but she found what she was looking for. In the obituary columns of *The Times* for Thursday, 26th November last: "The death occurred at his Kensington home early yesterday morning of Rear-Admiral Sir Hector Thomas, G.C.B., R.N. (ret.). Admiral Thomas, who was 68, served in both World Wars and. . . . He is survived by his wife and two sons. The elder son holds a commission in the Welsh Guards; the younger is at Nevishaugh School in Scotland."

"The younger is at Nevishaugh School. . . ." Eileen could imagine the telephone call early on Wednesday morning, the hurried arrangements for the boy to go south. Too late to get down that day, too late to book a sleeper for the Wednesday night. So he travels part of the way on Wednesday and spends the night in Glasgow. (Why the Clydemuir? An unlikely hotel for such a boy to choose.) And he takes the Royal Scot to Euston next morning.

"Hardly opened his mouth," Mrs. McLeod had said. "A face as long as Leith Walk." An unhappy schoolboy with a suitcase travelling south in November. It had suggested to Eileen a family bereavement. It also explained why the boy had never come forward in response to police appeals in the Press. The period between a death in the family and the funeral is not one when people as a rule devour the news pages.

Eileen felt no satisfaction in having her hunch substantiated. If Thomas was now accounted for, where was Ian?

SIX

Eileen had expected hysteria when she reported to her mother. But Mrs. Pratt took it calmly: she had never believed the boy in the Clydemuir was Ian and was glad to have it proved.

"Have you told the inspector yet?" she asked.

"Mother, I'm just off the train."

"Well, phone him now, dear. That's the whole *point*. We must prod them into *doing* something."

But as Eileen turned to go, her father unexpectedly broke in: "That all you learned?"

He had been sitting by the radio, checking his coupon against the football scores. He was so self-effacing and self-absorbed that Eileen had scarcely been aware he was in the room.

"Put that wireless off, Angus," said Mrs. Pratt irritably.

He smiled, and turned down the volume very slightly. It was a small gesture of defiance, but typical. Since her illness Mrs. Pratt's tight rein on her husband had slackened.

Eileen answered his question. "No, that wasn't all." She told them what Bradley had read in Ian's diary.

Pratt switched off the radio.

"Lucia Finghetti? You're sure that was the name?"

"Quite sure."

Mrs. Pratt was fretful. "What are you talking about? What girl is this?"

Pratt smiled. "She's—she *was*—a high class tart, Margaret."

Eileen was shocked.

"You're sure of that, Father?"

He shrugged. "So they said at the time. She was killed, you know. Run over."

"I know . . . I met her once. She seemed a nice girl. Friendly."

"Aye. Just so. She could be a tart for all that." He yawned and switched on his wireless again.

But Eileen was still thinking of that night at the dance. "She knew Douglas," she said. "She came over and he introduced me. I remember she said 'you're not *like* him' when she heard who I was."

"I told you to put that wireless *off*, Angus," said Mrs. Pratt sharply.

Her husband was already on his way out. Some day her mother would go too far, Eileen reflected, observing the sultry expression on his face.

"Ian didn't know that girl," Mrs. Pratt continued dogmatically. "He never mentioned her name."

"Mother, of course he knew her. She served in her father's café. Ian must have seen her nearly every day."

"Oh it's *that* Finghetti, is it?" That seemed to satisfy her. She didn't speculate why Ian should have mentioned the girl in his diary. But Eileen did. . . .

Nicolson was not on duty when Eileen rang. She declined the offer to put her through to Sergeant Cameron but rang Nicolson's home instead. His landlady told her he was out.

"Is your friend not in?" Mrs. Pratt called from the lounge.

Eileen took a deep breath. "No, Mother."

"Well, you could try again after supper, couldn't you?" In other words: "When are you going to make the supper?"

"All right, Mother."

Her father had gone out. He was hardly ever in for his evening meal now.

"Not another *egg*, Eileen," Mrs. Pratt sniffed when the omelette was laid in front of her. "Your father boiled an egg for me at lunch."

"Don't eat it if you don't want it," Eileen snapped. But her mother was already tucking in: she loved omelettes.

"When you see your inspector friend," she said suddenly, "maybe you'd better not mention this girl."

"Why not?" Eileen was still smarting and her tone was sharp.

"Well, if she really was a bad lot, we don't want——"

"For God's sake, Mother. You tell me you think Ian's dead. And yet——"

"Don't *shout*, Eileen. It's not good for me. You know what the doctor said."

It was too much. Eileen got up from the table without a word and went upstairs.

Nicolson's flat was in darkness and there was no answer to her ring. Douglas, then. She must talk to Douglas. Another frustrating wait for a bus, then the leisurely circuitous journey through the Tarvit housing estate. She wished she had borrowed the car to-night.

"Just in time, darling," said Douglas expansively when he answered her ring. "I hoped you'd show up."

Eileen looked at him suspiciously; she had expected sulks and recriminations.

"In time for what?"

He didn't answer, but led her into the studio.

Tom King got up from a chair and greeted her awkwardly. She had no eyes for him, because facing her, on an easel, was the nude.

She swung round on Douglas. "How *dare* you!" she said angrily. Douglas shrugged. "He asked to see it. That's what he came for."

King broke in. "I had a complaint, Eileen," he said.

"A complaint?"

"From a parent. That you'd been posing for indecent pictures. I'm head of the department. It was my duty to investigate."

"There's nothing indecent——" Douglas began.

"No, no. Quite. I see that now." He was feasting his eyes on the painting.

Eileen looked at him in disgust. "No wonder the kids call you 'Peeping Tom'," she muttered. King flushed.

"Children, children!" said Douglas reprovingly. "A drink all round, that's what's needed, eh?" He went out of the room.

"Orange juice for me," King called after him. He turned to Eileen. "Sorry if I upset you, but——"

"All right, Tom." This was no time for a quarrel. "I'm glad you're here; I've something to ask you. You knew Lucia Finghetti, didn't you?"

"A little," King said, smiling. He always smiled when he was uncomfortable. "What of it?"

She told him what Bradley had seen in Ian's diary.

"Bradley?" King was momentarily diverted. "You saw the old boy, then? How is he?"

"Very ill. Dying, I think."

He nodded smugly. "Too bad . . . Lucia? I never reached first base with Lucia. Why don't you ask——" He broke off.

"Why don't I ask who?"

But Douglas had come in with the drinks.

"We were talking of Lucia Finghetti," King remarked.

"Oh! were we?" Douglas glanced at Eileen. "Gin and bitter lemon suit you, darling?"

She took the drink. "Thanks. . . . Yes, I was telling Tom that Ian mentioned the girl in his diary."

Douglas stared at her. "Did he? Well, if Ian was mixed up with her, I shouldn't broadcast the fact. Lucia was no better than she should be. He won't thank you for it."

"No, he won't," she agreed. She took a sip of her drink. "He's dead, you see."

"You *know* that?" It was King who broke the silence.

"I feel it."

Douglas grunted. "Marvellous gift this intuition. Luckily it's usually wrong."

Intuition? Eileen wasn't sure it was the right word.

"Anyway," said King, "trust the experts, that's what I always say. The police think your brother's O.K. So why worry? I was saying to Troup before you came in that you've been quite peaky lately. We can't have that."

"That's nobody's business but mine, is it?"

"Not when your work suffers. I mean, I've a responsibility to the school to——"

"Oh! shut up, Tom!" she snapped, suddenly losing patience.

He smiled. "Well, I must breeze off. I've played gooseberry long enough."

"Thank God!" said Eileen when he had gone. "What a wet!"

Douglas didn't answer.

"Darling, I warn you," she went on. "Don't be temperamental with me to-night. I couldn't stand it."

He looked at her then and his eyes softened. "Poor Eileen," he said. "You're all in, aren't you?" He sat on the arm of her chair and stroked her head. Within minutes she was asleep.

Later, much later, she opened her eyes.

"Don't move," he said sharply. He was across the room at his easel, sketching.

"What's the time?" she asked.

"Quarter past ten."

She jumped up. "Lord, it's not, is it?" She was putting on her coat.

"Where are you going, Eileen?" Douglas's voice was peevish.

"I must see Inspector Nicolson."

"Must you?" He sighed, then looked at the sheet he had been drawing on. "Ah well, it's not bad for a first sitting, I suppose."

"What is it?"

"A sketch for a painting. You can wear your clothes for this one."

"Thanks."

"Not at all. . . . You sleep prettily."

"Do I?"

"Yes. Your mouth looks smaller when——"

She laughed. "You're a wizard for left-handed compliments, darling."

"You realise, of course," said Nicolson, "that you haven't *proved* anything."

Eileen found it restful here in the soft light, she was soothed by his calm voice. He was the kind of man you told your troubles to and at once felt a weight lifted from your mind.

"We're not even sure," he continued, "that the boy in the Clydemuir *was* the boy whose father had died."

"You can check on that, surely?"

"Of course." He smiled. "Anyway, it was an inspired guess, and I'm inclined to think it's right. But it doesn't take us much farther. It doesn't prove your brother didn't leave Silbridge: it only means he wasn't *seen* leaving."

"But that's odd, isn't it? That nobody saw him at the station, or in the train, or in Glasgow Central."

"Yes," he admitted. "It's odd. Very odd."

She shivered.

"Cold?"

"No. A ghost walked over my grave."

"You look tired, Eileen. Let me take you home."

"Not yet." She was looking beyond him at a portrait on the wall. Of a soldier, in the khaki of the First World War. He was smiling, but the smile didn't match the eyes, which were hard and calculating. The effect was sinister; and it reminded her of someone. . . .

"Tell me about Lucia Finghetti," she said. "About how she died, I mean."

"She was run over by a car."

"I know. On the 20th October."

"What's special about the date?"

"It was about then that Ian suddenly had money to burn."

He glanced sharply at her. "All right," he said, "I'll tell you what I know."

At eleven o'clock that night a man was walking up Potter Street on his way home from The Boar's Head. About fifty yards short of the junction with Crane Road he stumbled over a woman's body which lay half on the pavement, but with head and shoulders in the gutter. She had terrible injuries: the wheel of the car that hit her had gone over her face. She had been dead, it was estimated later, half an hour to an hour before she was found.

No one had heard or seen the accident. Potter Street was a narrow, mean little street running from Crane Road down to Ashford Street. It was bounded on one side by warehouses and on the other by tumbledown property scheduled for demolition. Nobody lived in Potter Street any more, and not many pedestrians used it at night, for it was badly lit and the pavement was in poor repair.

"What about Lucia?" Eileen asked. "What was she doing there?"

"When Lucia was on a date, she always got the man to drop her on Ashford Street near The Boar's Head. Then she would nip up Potter Street and home. It was to stop the neighbours' tongues from wagging. Her father told us that."

"Who had she been out with that night?"

Nicolson shrugged. "We don't know. She had, as you might say, a circle of admirers. But none of them saw her that night. Or so they said."

"And the car? What was a car doing in Potter Street at that hour?"

But that was easily explained. Since Lovack Street, which ran parallel, had been limited to one way traffic, Potter Street was often used by cars as a short cut from the town centre to the upper reaches.

"He was probably driving on his sidelights," said Nicolson. "He'd never see her till he hit her. Then he must have panicked."

"Were there no clues at all? Tyre marks or anything like that?"

Nicolson hesitated. "I wasn't really in on this. It happened just after I came to Silbridge. It was Mearns's case. And Allan Cameron helped. They did find *something*, I think. . . ."

"You'll know this, though," said Eileen. "Was the girl pregnant?"

Nicolson stared at her. "Another inspired guess?"

"Not exactly. I saw her a few days before she died, and I wondered. . . ."

"You were quite right. The autopsy showed she was nearly three months pregnant. Not even her parents knew."

"Suppose it wasn't an accident," said Eileen. "And suppose Ian was there and saw it all. . . . You see what I'm getting at, Maurice?"

"Yes," he said slowly. "Murder, then blackmail, then murder again. You really have a vivid imagination."

"It's possible, though, isn't it?"

"Yes, I suppose it's possible."

"I mean, why else would Ian be mentioning her in his diary?"

"I'm afraid there's a commonplace reason," said Nicolson.

"What's that?"

"He must have met her in the café. Perhaps he knew her professionally as well."

There was a knock on the door. "Telephone for you, Mr. Nicolson," his landlady called. Nicolson went out.

He was away for some time. When he came back, his manner was more formal.

"That was Chief Inspector Mearns," he said. "They want me at the station. I'm afraid——"

She stood up. "That's all right. Time I was going anyway."

"I'll drive you home."

"No, please don't bother, Maurice. I'll take the bus."

To her surprise and disappointment he didn't protest.

It was after 11.30 and she had twenty minutes to wait for the last bus. It was unlike Nicolson to be inconsiderate. Something serious must have turned up. And then with sickening alarm came the thought it must be something to do with Ian, something he didn't want her to know.

SEVEN

SHE REACHED home ten minutes after midnight. Her father was waiting for her, in pyjamas and dressing-gown.

"Where have you been?" he asked fretfully.

"Does it matter?" He wasn't usually so concerned.

"There's been a phone call from Mr. Nicolson."

"When?"

"Quarter of an hour ago." He kept running his hand nervously through his hair.

"He said there's a body in the harbour. And they think——"

"Oh, God!" Eileen felt her head swim. She closed her eyes and bit her lip till the dizziness passed.

"He wants you to go down there."

"*Me?*" Oh, no! She couldn't face that.

Her last vestige of respect for her father was gone. He wasn't even upset by the news about Ian; only nervous in case he was made to go and identify the body.

"Where's the car key?" she said brusquely.

"Try if you like," he said, "but she wouldn't start to-day. The battery's flat."

Eileen sighed. "I'll take my bicycle," she said. "Where have I to go? The mortuary?"

"No. They still haven't got him—out yet. They want you to go to the harbour."

"Which harbour?"

"The George."

God! That was in the east end, nearly two miles away.

"What about Mother? You haven't told her, have you?"

"She heard the phone. But she must be asleep again or she'd be calling down."

"Don't waken her, then. . . . I'm off."

"I'm sorry, Eileen," he said. "I would have gone, but—well, I remember once in the war, seeing them fish a chap out who'd been in the water for weeks. I couldn't face it again. . . . Anyway it was you Mr. Nicolson asked for."

"Let me past, Father," she said contemptuously, zipping up her anorak.

The going was easy until she turned along Main Street into the east wind. The two miles took her nearly half an hour.

It was beginning to rain as she entered the west gate to the George Harbour. She had expected lights and cars and a flurry of police activity. But all was dark and still. She could just distinguish against the sky the line of warehouses and offices that served the dock; not a light in any of them.

Puzzled, she wheeled her bicycle along the dock side, between the rails that stretched the length of the harbour. The concrete was slippy underfoot and the sour-sweet smell of raw sugar was everywhere; a sugar-boat had been unloading. There was no sound but the scrunch of her footsteps and the ticking of the bicycle wheels.

It was a quarter of a mile from the west gate to the east. She had gone about half-way when she heard or imagined a step behind her. She turned sharply; but she could see nothing. She quickened her pace. A few yards farther on she heard it again, closer this time.

"Who's there?" she called, near to panic. No reply. Deliberately she turned the bicycle round so that its light shone back the way she had come. Nothing. Only the rails running away over the grey concrete into blackness. But just as her hammering pulse was beginning to quieten, the lamp's flicker picked out something else. A dark shape some ten yards to the left. She directed the beam towards it. It was a man's shoe, and a trouser leg rising from it.

Eileen dropped the bicycle and ran. Behind her there was now no attempt at concealment. Heavy footsteps thudded and she could hear the man's rasping breath. She seemed to be holding her own, until the heel of her shoe caught in a hole. She fell, and before she could recover, her pursuer was on her.

She felt a sickening blow on the side of her head, then she was being dragged, half conscious, across the concrete, her feet trailing. For a brief moment there was a delicious sense of freedom when her assailant released his hold and seemed to push her away from him. Then she hit the water.

The icy shock brought her round. She came up gasping, coughing salt water from her lungs, but clear-headed. She knew she was going to drown. She was a strong swimmer. But not dressed like this, in winter clothes and a heavy, quilted anorak; and not with this terrible feeling of lassitude. There was no strength in her arms and legs.

As she felt herself being dragged down, her hand touched something firm against the side of the quay just above the water: it felt like hard rubber. She clung to it and it supported her.

Above her Eileen heard footsteps pacing up and down. Presently a pale light shone down and began to rake the water: the lamp from her bicycle, she guessed. Backwards and forwards it went, moving systematically from west to east. As it came near, Eileen filled her lungs with air and silently thrust herself under. She stayed down as long as she could, and when she came up the light had gone.

There was a loud splash some way along from her. She guessed that the bicycle had been thrown in. The footsteps retreated. But still she waited. And after a minute or two an engine started up, and a car drove away.

She was clinging to a rubber tyre hanging over the side of the quay.

She hadn't the strength to pull herself up and climb the rope on which it was suspended. And when she shouted, her voice sounded pitifully puny.

She remembered seeing, when the lamp was shining on the water, an iron ladder perhaps fifteen feet to her left. Slowly and painfully, with frozen fingers she unzipped the anorak and tugged her arms out of it.

Then, uttering a silent prayer, she released her hold on the fender and struck blindly towards the unseen ladder. Numb from the waist down, she had to make her arms provide all the momentum. She felt she wasn't moving, and as the strength ebbed from her arms, she stretched towards the wall of the dock hoping to regain her fender. Instead her hand grasped the iron rung of a ladder. Moments later she lay panting and sobbing on the quay.

The temptation to lie there was overwhelming. But Eileen recognised that sleep was an enemy, not a friend. She forced herself to stagger towards the harbour gate. Her whole body was shuddering with cold and exhaustion and shock. Yet her mind was analysing with feverish concentration all that had happened. There had been something familiar about that man. Smell? Sound? Touch? She *must* get it: it was vital.

She was on the main road now, though she couldn't remember passing through the gate. No traffic at this hour. Wasn't there a telephone box somewhere near? Yes, she could see its pale light fifty yards along the road. Doggedly she set her sights on it.

A shoe and a trouser leg. . . . That was all she had seen. Black shoe. Dark trousers. Nothing distinctive. No, she must have smelt something. Or perhaps it had been that rasping breath. Or the feel of his hands as he dragged her to the water's edge. She had *known* him; he wasn't a stranger. But who . . . ?

She was in the kiosk now, lifting the telephone. Her eyes wouldn't focus; she couldn't see the numbers on the dial. 999, wasn't it? Well, that was easy: she could do it by touch.

It was hot in here. And why was the box moving? Like a bus. From a great distance a voice came through the telephone. But the box was now gyrating in ever-accelerating spins. The receiver slipped from her grasp. . . .

She was found unconscious on the floor of the kiosk.

PART III

The Inspector

ONE

TEN MINUTES after Eileen left him Nicolson was in Chief Detective-Inspector Mearns's room at the station.

Mearns was trying to get his pipe to go. "Where the hell's Allan Cameron?" he grumbled.

"Have you tried his home?" said Nicolson.

Mearns glared at him. "Goddammit, of course I've tried his home." His face looked more gaunt and haggard than ever.

The pipe was now drawing satisfactorily. "Here, take a look at that, Maurice," said Mearns, more calmly. He handed over the tattered remnants of a book. Some pages were missing and most of the rest were in shreds and were impregnated with maroon dye from the cover. There was a damp, mildewed feel about the paper.

"Been in the water for a while, that one," Nicolson remarked.

Mearns nodded. "See what it is, though?"

The title on the cover was obliterated but inside the type was still legible in places. A glance at a line or two told Nicolson what it was: *Under Milk Wood.* He turned back to the inside cover. An inscription had been written in indelible pencil: "I. T. Pratt, March, 1963."

"Where was it found?" he asked with a heavy heart.

A child had found it that afternoon while playing on the foreshore west of Cradock Pier. A well brought-up child: it wasn't his first expedition to the police station with useless treasure.

The book was left to dry on a radiator in the charge room. Later in the evening Sergeant Cubitt picked it up and yawned his way through a page or two.

"Say what you like about Cubitt," Mearns remarked, "it was smart of him to spot that inscription."

Nicolson grunted. "And what are we doing about it, sir?"

"I've a couple of men searching the shore now. And a diver'll go down in the morning."

"I suppose the suitcase was dumped off the end of the pier and burst open after a while."

"Aye, maybe." Mearns was unconvinced. "We've only Mrs. Pratt's word the book was in the case. The boy could have lost it on the shore months ago. And remember, Pratt was seen in *Glasgow* that night, suitcase and all. Even this bloody book"—he slapped his hand down on Dylan Thomas—"can't alter that."

"Something else can, though. It wasn't Pratt who was seen in Glasgow." Nicolson explained what Eileen had found out.

Mearns was shaken.

"Why wasn't I told?" he blustered.

"I've only just left her."

"At this hour? That's another thing. You shouldn't be interviewing witnesses in your flat. Especially young women."

"What was I supposed to do? Shut the door in her face?"

"You should have brought her to the station, that's what you should have done." Then the customary reaction set in. He smiled uncomfortably and said: "Just watch your step, Maurice, that's all. You of all people can't afford a scandal."

He knew about Ruth, then. Bound to, of course: it would be in the record. A "security risk" they had called her.

Sergeant Cubitt brought in steaming cups of tea.

"Bloody cold night, sir. Thought you might like——"

Mearns was effusive. "Don't know what we'd do without you, Cubitt. Eh, Maurice?"

Nicolson grunted sourly. He hadn't forgiven Mearns's innuendo about Ruth.

All the same it *was* a cold night. The tea was welcome.

"You haven't checked on the Thomas boy, I suppose?" Mearns remarked.

"I've hardly had time, sir."

"No, of course not." Mearns was now ingratiating. "We'll phone the Admiral's widow in the morning. Clever of Miss Pratt to spot it, anyway."

"That wasn't all Miss Pratt found out."

Mearns was apprehensive. "What else?"

Nicolson told him of the reference in Ian Pratt's diary to Lucia Finghetti.

"Just the name? That all Bradley saw?" Mearns asked.

"A sum of money was mentioned. £2,000 he thought it was. And something about Wednesday nights."

"Might mean nothing at all," said Mearns. "A few remarks in a diary, out of context."

"True. But why should he mention Miss Finghetti? . . . Unless perhaps he knew something about her death?"

"Well, if he did, it's more than we do. That's one case I'd like to have solved, Maurice."

"What happened exactly, sir? There was some kind of pointer, wasn't there?"

Mearns grunted. "There might have been, if the rain hadn't washed it out. It was a hell of a night—rain and sleet. Chap who found the body maintained he'd seen tyre marks in the slush near where the girl lay. On the pavement."

"On the *pavement*?"

"So he said. But that's not all. He told me there were footprints on *top* of the treads—superimposed, you understand? As if the driver got out and had a look, then drove on. Think of it! Ten minutes sooner and we'd have had his footprint and the tread of his tyre."

"You were too late?"

"By the time we got there, the rain was simply belting down and there wasn't a mark to be seen."

"The footprints," Nicolson pointed out, "needn't have been the driver's. . . . What size did he say they were?"

"A small man's; or a woman's."

"Or perhaps a boy's?"

Mearns looked at him thoughtfully. "I dare say they might have been a boy's," he agreed. He laid his pipe on the ash tray, put his thumbs in his waistcoat and tilted his chair back.

"All right, Maurice, let's have it. What's on your mind?"

Again Nicolson owed it to Eileen Pratt. She had planted the idea and it had crystallised while Mearns was talking.

He began with the night of Lucia Finghetti's death. Ian Pratt, he suggested, had witnessed the accident and had recognised the car or its driver. He left his footprints in the slush when he went up to where the body lay. On seeing that the girl was dead, he decided to blackmail the driver instead of reporting the accident. Significantly it was from that date that Pratt's pockets were lined with money. And at the same time his *manner* had changed: "worried and anxious, but excited too," to quote his probation officer.

He received payments to account each Wednesday for four or five weeks after Lucia's death. And the final pay-off (£2,000?) was to be on Wednesday, 25th November. Pratt intended to leave home that night and settle in Edinburgh with his natural father. But he had turned the screw too hard. . . .

On that final Wednesday Pratt dispatched his bicycle by carrier, packed a suitcase and left it at St. Gregory's station, dined in the Royal Hotel, and went off to collect his £2,000.

"And the chap was waiting with a gun?" Mearns interrupted dryly.

"Something like that. Anyway he killed him, took from his body the ticket for the suitcase and collected it at the station. Then he dropped the case off Cradock Pier."

"And Pratt's body?"

"Maybe that went over the pier too."

Mearns shook his head decisively. "I've known three suicides and a fatal accident off Cradock. Each time the body was washed ashore at Darvel Point. If the boy's dead, he didn't go that way."

"But you do think he's dead, don't you?"

Mearns got up and began to prowl about the room. "There's a hell of a lot of conjecture about it," he said. "But I'm half convinced." His eye brightened. "God, if it *is* true, the spotlight'll be on us, won't it? Might be just the break I need."

If they let you handle it, Nicolson qualified under his breath. . . .

"Yes," he agreed flatly. "It'll make the headlines." The prospect didn't thrill him.

Mearns was eyeing him quizzically. "One point you've missed," he said. "If Pratt was murdered, it's possible Lucia was murdered as well. After all, the car mounted the pavement."

Nicolson hadn't missed it: indeed Eileen had suggested it. But he wasn't yet convinced.

"What about motive?" he asked.

"The girl was pregnant."

"Did you think it might be murder at the time?"

Mearns hesitated. "As a matter of fact, it did cross our minds. We discovered she'd been putting pressure on at least one of her clients. Chap called Buller. Master joiner—you'll have heard of him?"

"Pressure?"

"Well, this was after she learned she was pregnant. She claimed he was the father. He did in fact part with some money."

"Why didn't he send her packing?" Nicolson objected. "I mean, for a prostitute to bring a paternity suit—she'd be laughed out of court."

"Lucia was no ordinary prostitute. She limited herself to two or three clients, and each of them probably imagined he was the only one. Certainly Buller did."

"I take it Buller can account for his movements the night she was run over?"

"Oh yes. He's in the clear. . . . But if she was blackmailing one, she may have tried it on others too. And perhaps one of them turned on her. It didn't seem likely at the time. But if the man has killed again. . . ."

All the same, Nicolson reflected, it was an uncommon method of murder. Difficult to get your victim in the right place at the right moment.

But the chief inspector had thought of that too. "Suppose," he said, "the killer is the man who took Lucia out that night. He drops her as usual on Ashford Street and Lucia turns up Potter Street towards home. But the car follows her. . . ." Suddenly he threw back his head and laughed. "I'm getting carried away," he said. "We should have Allan Cameron here to pour cold water. . . . Surely he's home by now." He reached for the telephone.

"It's nearly one o'clock, sir," Nicolson pointed out. "And we don't really need him to-night."

Mearns sighed. "I suppose not," he said and replaced the receiver. Mearns had faith in Cameron's judgment: he liked to have him around.

The men who had been searching the shore by torchlight came in to report. They had found nothing. The search would be resumed in the morning.

The minutes ticked past while they discussed tactics. At a quarter to two the telephone rang. Mearns yawned and picked it up. Idly Nicolson watched him. He saw the swift change of expression.

"Get your coat, Maurice," said Mearns urgently, as he hung up. "That was the hospital. Eileen Pratt's been brought in. . . ."

TWO

"No, you may not see her." Dr. Singh was polite but firm. "She is unconscious."

They were in a corridor outside the room where Eileen Pratt lay—Mearns and Nicolson and W.P.C. Elsie Richards and the young Indian doctor. Angus Pratt stood a little apart from the others.

But now Pratt sidled up to Nicolson.

"Was it him?" he said.

"What?"

"Was it Ian? The body in the dock?"

98

Nicolson stared at him. "I don't understand, sir. What body——"

He broke off as a nurse came out of the room and beckoned to Dr. Singh. After a brief, whispered conversation, the nurse went back inside and closed the door. Nicolson had the impression of controlled crisis.

"At least," said Mearns irritably, "you'll let Miss Richards sit with her?"

The doctor shrugged. "So long as she doesn't impede."

Mearns nodded to the policewoman, who knocked and went in, notebook in hand.

"And now, Doctor," said Mearns, with his eye on Angus Pratt, "where can we talk privately?"

Dr. Singh led them to a small office farther down the corridor.

"What are her chances, Dr. Singh?" Nicolson asked.

"It is early to prophesy," said the doctor. His English was correct and almost free of accent: only a certain formality in his choice of words betrayed that it was not his native tongue. "There is severe exhaustion and shock. She was in the water a long time, I think. . . ."

"She's going to be all right, though?" Nicolson persisted. He saw Mearns's eyes rest curiously on him.

Singh smiled, showing very white teeth. "She is a strong girl. . . ."

"All right if we smoke here, Doctor?" Mearns asked; and, without waiting for an answer, he took out his pipe and began to fill it. "Well, let's have it. What did she say, exactly?" His tone was brusque. He tended to be aggressive with foreigners because he didn't understand their thought processes.

"Miss Pratt was conscious for a short time while we examined her," said the doctor. "She was very frightened. 'He tried to kill me,' she kept saying. . . . Then she became delirious. There are signs of concussion and——"

"Spare us the clinical details, Dr. Singh. *Who* tried to kill her?"

Singh looked at him with cold dislike. "She did not say. I at once arranged for the police to be informed as well as her parents. I trust I acted properly?"

Belatedly Mearns saw he was antagonising his witness. "Yes, indeed, sir. Good of you to be so prompt. . . . Did Miss Pratt say nothing else at all?"

"Nothing we could understand. . . . Afterwards she began to call for someone. Has she a friend named Douglas, do you know?"

"Yes," said Nicolson shortly. "She has."

"Dr. Singh," Mearns said, "could any of the nurses have heard something you didn't?"

"No, Inspector. They heard no more than I. 'He tried to kill me'—she said that several times. Then a torrent of words: none of us could comprehend them. Then this name 'Douglas,' over and over."

"Was she implying that 'Douglas' attacked her, do you think?"

Singh shook his head. "Indeed not. She wanted to see this man. Very much she wanted to see him."

Nicolson felt unreasonably jealous.

"She phoned from a box outside the George Harbour, didn't she?" said Mearns.

"Yes."

"And you say she'd been in the water? Did you mean in the harbour?"

The doctor smiled. "It is not of medical significance which stretch of water she was immersed in. And she did not volunteer the information. It was sea water, however: that I can tell you."

"Thank you, Doctor," said Mearns, dismissing him. "—oh! and send in Mr. Pratt, if he's still here, would you?"

Dr. Singh bowed stiffly and went out.

"Difficult chap, that," Mearns remarked.

Angus Pratt came quietly into the room.

"You were wanting to see me?" he said.

"Oh yes, sir. Very sorry to trouble you at a time like this, but. . . ." Mearns was back on familiar territory. Father of the victim: treat with sympathy and respect.

There was a quality in Pratt that puzzled Nicolson. He knew his history—the history of a failure: reduced to menial employment far below his capacity; despised and downtrodden by his wife; a man without friends. Yet he didn't look *defeated*: just withdrawn into a world of his own. He must have something to cling to, something to give life meaning, to keep him from despair.

Clearly it wasn't his family. He had been indifferent to the fate of his adopted son. Now, to-night, he seemed little more affected when his daughter's life was in danger. Or perhaps he hid his feelings well. . . .

"My wife wanted to come," he was saying to Chief Inspector Mearns, "but she's ill, you understand."

"Any idea what your daughter was doing at the George Harbour at that time of night?" Mearns asked.

Pratt stared at him. "Well, it was that phone call. From you, Mr. Nicolson."

Mearns's hand, bearing a lighted match to his pipe, was arrested in mid-air. "What are you talking about?" he said sharply.

"Did Eileen not say? The doctor told me she came round for a bit."

"She never mentioned any phone call."

Pratt explained. Shortly before midnight the telephone had rung. He and his wife were in bed and Eileen was out. Pratt put on a dressing-gown and went downstairs to answer it.

The caller had announced himself as Detective-Inspector Nicolson and said that a boy's body had been found in the George Harbour and the police wanted Eileen to go down and identify it.

"He asked for your *daughter*, not you? Didn't that put you on your guard?"

"Ach, well, I knew Eileen and Mr. Nicolson were friends. . . ."

Eileen came in shortly afterwards and Pratt gave her the message. She left about 12.15 on her bicycle.

At 1.45 a.m. the telephone rang again. This time it was the hospital with news of Eileen's admission. They sent an ambulance for him as his car was out of action.

"Now, sir," said Mearns, "think carefully about that first phone call —what was the voice like? Was it like Mr. Nicolson's?"

"Ach, well, Inspector, I'm not clever at the voices. I haven't the ear, you understand. Unless they have the Gaelic, they all sound Sassenach to me."

"It was a man's voice, though—you're sure of that?"

"Oh yes!"

"Deep?"

"Kind of middling, you might say."

Mearns sighed and let him go.

"Pity there's no way of tracing that call," Nicolson remarked.

Mearns grunted. "I'm going down to the harbour, Maurice," he said, "before Baird and Mooney tramp every goddamned clue into the ground." A squad car had been sent to the George Harbour when the message from the hospital came in.

"You realise what this must mean?" Mearns added.

Nicolson nodded. "Not much doubt now Ian Pratt's dead."

"I wish to hell we could *talk* to Miss Pratt. . . . Stick around, Maurice, and chat up the nurses. Could be they heard more than that Indian joker thinks. And then get home to bed: one of us had better have a clear head to-morrow."

But the nurses had little to add. One of them—the girl Nicolson had seen earlier talking to Dr. Singh—had caught the words "I know him" repeated several times when Eileen was delirious.

"Don't take anything from it, though," said the nurse. "She was raving, poor girl."

"How is she now?" Nicolson asked.

"She'll be all right. . . . Like to see her?"

Do I make it so obvious? Nicolson wondered. He nodded.

The nurse quietly opened the door and Nicolson looked in. It was a small room with two beds, only one of them occupied. The room connected with the main ward as well as with the corridor.

W.P.C. Richards was on a chair between the beds. Her note-book had slipped to the floor and she hastily stifled a yawn when she saw who had come in. But Nicolson had eyes only for the girl on the bed.

She lay on her back, a bandage swathed round her head. Her face was as white as the bandage. She was very still.

"Are you sure——" Nicolson whispered urgently.

The nurse smiled. "She'll be all right," she repeated.

Nicolson left the hospital at half past three. Eileen was under sedation and there was no question of her waking for some hours.

He wondered if he should join Chief Inspector Mearns at the George Harbour but decided against it. Mearns had made it clear he didn't want him.

All the same he was too restless to go home. He knew now he was in love with Eileen Pratt. Hopelessly in love. He had never felt like this before, not even about Ruth. With Ruth his predominant emotion had been compassion. Not this consuming fire that engulfed him now.

"Hopelessly in love": the phrase was well chosen. Eileen was engaged to someone else, *loved* someone else. Nicolson remembered the Indian doctor's words: "Very much she wanted to see this man." . . .

He had been driving aimlessly through the dark, empty streets. Without conscious intent he turned up Greene Road towards the High School: and slowed down as he neared Douglas Troup's flat.

There was a light in one of the windows. The studio window, Nicolson was almost sure. He stopped the car. After some hesitation he got out and went up to the door. He pressed the bell.

Diagonally across the street the rectangular mass of the school stood out, one shade blacker than the sky behind it. And, farther back, the red light of a railway signal. As Nicolson waited, it turned to green. He heard the distant rumble and clanking of a goods train.

He pressed the bell again. And now a light went on above the door and footsteps approached. The door opened.

"What in God's name——" Troup was alarmed. Then, as he recognised his visitor: "Oh, it's you! What's wrong?"

"Your fiancée's had an accident," said Nicolson.

"Is she——"

"She's in hospital. But not in danger."

There was silence. Then Troup said grudgingly: "You'd better come in."

The studio was overheated and smelt of paraffin and stale cigarette smoke. A canvas on the easel was daubed with apparently arbitrary and undisciplined reds and oranges and yellows. And the untidy evidence of Troup's activity was all round—in paints and brushes and palette and in the smears on his hands and on the smock he wore over his T-shirt and brown corduroy trousers. Three bottles of beer, two of them empty, and a half-filled glass stood on a small table: and beside them a saucer crammed with cigarette stubs.

Nicolson declined the offer of beer but took a cigarette.

"What's this about Eileen, then?" said Troup, as he picked up his glass.

Nicolson told him.

"Do they want me at the hospital?" Troup asked, his eye straying to the canvas on the easel.

"Not to-night."

"Fine. . . . Well, I'm relieved she's all right." It was plain that he wanted to return to his painting.

But Nicolson wasn't ready to go yet. "I didn't say she was *all right,*" he reminded him sharply. "I said she was out of danger."

"Keep your hair on, old man."

The supercilious smile and the affected drawl were too much for Nicolson.

"How much does Eileen know about you?" he asked.

"What do you mean?"

"I was thinking of Betty Norton for a start."

It had happened in Troup's last year at Culverton. Nicolson had left school by then and although the story had percolated through, his recollection of it was vague when he met Troup again years later. But he had since refreshed his memory.

Betty Norton, the daughter of one of the housemasters at Culverton, had an illegitimate child. Douglas Troup admitted responsibility and was quietly withdrawn from the school.

Troup smiled. "My dear Nicolson, do you really imagine Eileen's going to upset herself over something that happened when I was sixteen?"

"All right, let's move on a year or two. To Alison Wright."

This time the shaft struck home. "Quite the little snooper, aren't you?" Troup said savagely. He crossed to the table and opened the last of the beer bottles.

"Sure you won't join me? No?" He filled his glass. "Don't come the puritan with me," he said. "I know all about your paramour—what's her name?—the ex-jailbird."

Nicolson controlled his anger. "The difference is that you're *engaged*. And you're still playing Lothario, aren't you?" And when there was no answer: "Well, *aren't* you? Do you want me to name them?"

Troup grinned. "Don't bother. I can see you've done your homework. . . . Actually, Eileen has only herself to blame. 'No indulgence before marriage'—that's her motto. But one can't live like a monk. I have to break out now and again. It's necessary to the creative temperament."

"But you haven't told your fiancée?"

"Why should I? . . . Once we're married, it'll be different. We're very much in love, as the saying goes."

"You don't act like it."

Troup frowned. "What is it to you?" When Nicolson didn't answer, comprehension dawned in his eyes. He threw back his head and laughed. "Good God, you've fallen for her, have you? . . . You haven't an earthly, old boy."

"Not even if I told her about——"

"You wouldn't, though, would you? I still remember a jawing you gave me in school about sneaking."

"Don't count on it," said Nicolson. But Troup was right: he had already passed up a chance to tell Eileen.

Outside a clock struck the half hour.

Troup yawned and glanced at his watch. "Four-thirty! You look as tired as I feel. How about coffee?"

"No, thanks." Nicolson stood up. "What's this you're doing?" he asked, indicating the canvas on the easel.

Troup stepped back and studied the painting. Then his shoulders sagged and he sighed.

"Hell!" he said wearily. "Another bloody fiasco."

"What's it supposed to be?" Nicolson could still see no cohesion or meaning in the picture.

"It's a recurrent dream I have. A glimpse of the eternal, you might call it, the key to the riddle of life. When I wake, I rush in here to put it on canvas before the vision fades. Like Coleridge and his *Kubla Khan*. . . ." He stared dispiritedly at the painting. "This is the result."

"Did I interrupt——"

He shook his head. "It was beyond redemption. It's always the same . . . Eileen can't understand why it depresses me. She'd rather I stuck to my hack work. Like this."

He took a sheet of paper from the table and handed it to Nicolson. A pencil drawing of Eileen Pratt asleep on a chair, done with a remarkable economy of line and sureness of touch.

This was *Eileen:* the drawing was alive.

"That's good," Nicolson said. "You've got her exactly."

"Yes, a 'good likeness'," Troup sneered. "Damn it, man, I'm an artist, not a ruddy camera." He stared again at the painting on the easel, then roughly tore it down. "It's like one of Ian Pratt's masterpieces," he muttered.

He paused, then added unexpectedly: "The boy's dead, isn't he?"

"Pratt? I think so."

"Pity Eileen had to run her head into a noose to prove it for you." A petulant note had crept into the drawling voice.

Nicolson didn't answer. He sensed that this was leading somewhere.

"It seems to me," Troup continued, "that you people don't show up too well in this affair. I mean, for instance, you *still* don't know where Pratt went on Wednesday nights, do you?"

"No. Do you?"

Troup frowned: he didn't like being rushed. "I saw him one Wednesday about eleven o'clock. A week or two before he disappeared."

"Where?"

"Across the road. Coming out of the school gate on his bicycle."

Nicolson was annoyed. "Why didn't you tell us sooner?"

"You never asked."

"You're sure it was a Wednesday?"

"Quite sure. I was on my way home from one of the Town Hall concerts, I remember." The Scottish National Orchestra gave a monthly concert in Silbridge during the winter months. Always on Wednesdays.

"Was Eileen with you?"

"No, Wednesday's the night she lets her hair down with Fiona Cameron."

"Fiona Cameron? Who's she?"

Troup looked at him in astonishment. "Don't you know? It's your colleague's wife. Eileen was their bridesmaid."

Nicolson remembered now that Eileen had once mentioned she knew Cameron's wife. He felt vaguely cheated to learn that she had been bridesmaid at their wedding. . . .

With an effort he switched his mind back to Ian Pratt.

"Any idea what Pratt would be up to in the school at that time of night?" he asked.

Troup smiled. "That's your department, old boy. We give you the facts, you draw the deductions. Right?"

THREE

A DIVER went down off Cradock Pier on Sunday morning. He soon found the green suitcase, open and with its locks burst. Enough of the contents were wedged between the supports of the pier to establish that this had been Ian Pratt's case. But there was no trace of his diaries.

At the east end of the town another diver was recovering Eileen Pratt's bicycle and her anorak from the George Harbour. An intensive search of the dockside revealed nothing: if there had been a struggle, no sign of it remained.

Meanwhile Nicolson had been on the telephone to Lady Thomas, the admiral's widow. She confirmed that her son had spent the night of 25th November in the Clydemuir Hotel in Glasgow. She was at pains to point out that it wasn't the kind of hotel David would normally patronise: he had mistaken it for the Clydesdale in looking up the telephone directory.

Nicolson then began telephoning the big Glasgow hotels to ask a question Cameron should have asked weeks ago: had anyone booked a room for the night of 25th November and failed to show up? Cameron had looked for a hotel in which Ian Pratt actually *had* spent the night. And once the Clydemuir seemed to provide the answer, he lost interest in hotels.

Nicolson guessed that Pratt probably hadn't intended to go the whole way to Edinburgh that night. He had bought a ticket for Glasgow only and had then gone off and had dinner. Even if fog hadn't disrupted the train service, he could scarcely have got to Edinburgh from Silbridge after dinner.

Knowing Pratt's predilection, in his newly-won affluence, for expensive hotels, he tried the big station hotels first. And at the second he struck oil. A single room had been booked by letter for that night by a Mr. I. T. Coleman, who gave an address in Silbridge. He didn't turn up to claim his room. The fact that it was a fictitious address merely confirmed Nicolson's suspicion that "I. T. Coleman" was Ian Pratt, using his natural father's name.

Here was proof, if any were still needed, that Pratt had never left Silbridge.

Chief Detective-Inspector Mearns arrived at his office about midday. Having listened to the reports he at once telephoned headquarters. "Ian Pratt's dead. . . ." Nicolson heard him say.

Mearns gained what he wanted: extra men were drafted into Silbridge to assist in the search for Ian Pratt's body: and Mearns was, for the present, left in charge of the investigation.

The search began in earnest that Sunday afternoon under the immediate direction of a taciturn Detective-Sergeant Cameron. Cameron had been on the carpet for his failure to trace the boy Thomas, and his face declared his resentment.

Arrangements were made to drag the canal and Stranach Loch and the smaller pools. Cameron recruited volunteers from the local mountaineering club to make the dangerous descent into the Devil's Ravine. The main body of policemen, along with volunteer civilians, began a systematic comb-out of the moors above the town.

Nicolson called on Mrs. Pratt before lunch. He brought reassuring word from the hospital about Eileen, but, as he expected, that was not her main concern. She at once asked about Ian.

All his experience had not hardened Nicolson to the task of breaking bad news. He lacked the philosophic detachment that usually becomes part of the armoury of those—doctors, nurses, policemen, undertakers— whose work takes them into daily contact with the tragedies of others. It was a weakness. Once already, over Ruth, this feeling of personal involvement had nearly ruined his career. . . .

Mrs. Pratt wanted reassurance that he couldn't give. True, there was a straw to cling to: her son's death was not yet inexorably established. But it would be false kindness now to encourage hope.

Although Nicolson had feared a scene, he was almost more disturbed by the apathetic despair with which Mrs. Pratt received his news.

She spoke wearily, but lucidly enough, about the previous night. The first phone call, she said, had come about ten minutes to twelve. Angus had just come upstairs and was starting to undress; she herself was in bed but not asleep. The second call was at 1.45. Angus was still downstairs waiting for Eileen to come back. He hadn't told his wife what the earlier message had been. But she knew something was wrong and lay in bed worrying.

"You definitely heard the phone ring that first time?" Nicolson pressed her. He had to be sure Angus Pratt hadn't invented the call.

"Yes, I heard it. I've *told* you that. And the dog barked too. He never barks except when the phone or the doorbell rings."

"Mrs. Pratt, you've believed from the start your son was dead. What did you think had happened to him? Accident, suicide, murder?"

"You wouldn't listen to me," she said fretfully. "You should have *listened* to me."

"I'm listening now, Mrs. Pratt."

"Ian was frightened, that's why he tried to run away. He was frightened."

"Frightened of what?"

Mrs. Pratt sighed. "I don't know," she said listlessly.

Finghetti's fish grill was empty when Nicolson went in with Detective-Constable Wood after lunch on Sunday; except for the proprietor himself, who was in his customary place behind the counter, scooping chips into a wire basket.

Paolo Finghetti was a small, balding man with a sallow, melancholy face. The fish grill, with the adjoining café, was open seven days a week, fifty-two weeks in the year; only on Christmas Day did it close. And Paolo in his white apron was on duty all day and every day. Once, when his father died, he had gone back to Italy for the funeral and to settle his affairs. That apart, he hadn't missed a day at business; it was his life.

His wage bill was nominal, for he employed only his wife and daughters; and now a nephew, brought over from Florence to replace Lucia. There was no outward sign of affluence. The family lived modestly in rooms over the shop and café. They had no car. But it was popularly believed that Finghetti was one of Silbridge's wealthiest citizens.

"Lucia?" he said when Nicolson explained why they had come. "But already I tell the other one, the one with the eyebrows"—Chief Inspector Mearns, Nicolson assumed—"already I tell him all I know."

"Yes, sir, but we'd like to go over it again, if you don't mind."

Finghetti spoke of his daughter without affection. "She was trash, that one. The black sheep, how you say. And lazy! God, was ever a girl so lazy? She make eyes at the customers when she should work, no? A judgment of merciful heaven was it that she is taken from us, God rest her soul!"

"Who were her friends?" Nicolson asked.

"Friends? She have no friends."

"I was thinking of *men*."

Two youths in leather jackets and crash helmets came into the shop for chips. Finghetti served them with practised speed.

"Men?" he repeated when they went out. "She have dozens of them, *hundreds* of them." He gesticulated angrily. "I tell you, if Lucia was now still here, these two boys would not out of this door have gone without she make a date with them."

"Can you give me names, sir? I mean of men she——"

"There were so many. . . ." He came out from behind the counter and crossed to where a staircase led to the flat above.

"Maria!" he called.

"My wife, perhaps she remember," he said.

As they waited for Mrs. Finghetti to come down, the raucous strains of a juke box from the café came through to them. The Sunday afternoon trade was beginning.

"Your nephew runs the café?" Nicolson asked.

Finghetti scowled. "He is lazy good-for-nothing. No better than Lucia. Anna, she do the work." His face softened. "A good girl, Anna."

Nicolson remembered the dark-haired beauty who had served him in the café last November. He turned to Detective-Constable Wood. "Nip in next door, Charlie, and get me twenty fags, would you?"

He gave him a ten shilling note and the barest nod of the head. Charlie understood. He had a way with dark-haired beauties. . . .

A woman was clumping heavily down the stairs; a stout woman, shapeless and untidy. Anna in twenty-five years, Nicolson thought wryly.

Mrs. Finghetti took a more charitable view of Lucia than her husband. "Too easy-going" was her verdict: too ready to say "yes" when the prudent answer would have been "no." Pleasure-loving, lazy—she conceded the laziness—but not vicious.

She insisted on going back upstairs for a photograph of Lucia. Again the family resemblance was unmistakable: here was a more mature, more worldly-wise Anna.

Mrs. Finghetti maintained that although Lucia had enjoyed the company of men she had not been promiscuous. Her first love had been a sailor; and she had been deeply hurt when she discovered he was already married. Since then there had been only two, or perhaps three, serious affairs.

She didn't know the names, nor could she describe the men. Lucia had never brought them to the house because of the scene her father would have created; and she wasn't one to confide much in her mother.

"These 'affairs,' Mrs. Finghetti," said Nicolson, "—you're speaking of *love* affairs?"

"But of course. What else?"

"It's been suggested"—he didn't want to hurt her but he had to put it to her—"that she had some *professional* clients."

"You mean she was prostitute? Never. Not my Lucia."

He mentioned the names Hubert Nelson and Arthur Buller, both of them known to have patronised Lucia. Mrs. Finghetti looked blank: the names meant nothing to her. There was no doubt she was genuinely shocked and indignant; and her evidence about her daughter's private life was therefore valueless.

When Finghetti, who had been serving a customer, rejoined them, Nicolson asked about Ian Pratt.

The Italian shook his head. "Names I do not remember," he said. Nicolson showed him a photograph.

"Ah yes. He come here, that boy. But since many weeks I do not see him."

"Does the gang still meet in your café? Gammans and that lot?"

"Sometimes," Finghetti admitted cautiously. "But, Inspector, they behave. This is respectable place. One little trouble and—pouf!" he snapped his fingers, "—out they go!"

"I'm not criticising. I just wondered if any of them might have been friendly with Lucia."

Finghetti nodded emphatically. "Yes. She make eyes at them and——"

But his wife broke in: "Never. Lucia have—how you say it?—larger fish to fry."

"Not even the boy Pratt?" Nicolson asked.

"Too young. She like men, not boys."

Finghetti was frowning. "Ah! Maria, you do not know your own daughter. I tell you, I *see* her. All my customers she make eyes at. Old men and little boys even. A judgment from the good God it is that she is taken from us."

Without warning Mrs. Finghetti gave way to tears and departed upstairs. Her husband gazed after her in bewilderment.

Nicolson went through to the café. The juke box was silent now. Three girls were drinking coffee at one of the little yellow tables; at another a middle-aged man was deep in the *News of the World*.

Detective-Constable Wood was having a *tête-à-tête* across the counter with Anna Finghetti. Literally a *tête-à-tête*: he was leaning so far over that their heads almost touched. As if he were telling her a risqué joke.

Perhaps he was; because as Nicolson watched, the girl showed her teeth in a delighted smile at something Wood said. They hadn't seen Nicolson, and he slipped out again. He walked to the corner of Potter Street, fifty yards along, and looked down. The street was narrow and steep; on one side was the solid wall of a warehouse, and on the other a hoarding behind which demolition was in progress. No doorway to take refuge in if someone drove a car at you. . . .

Detective-Constable Wood was waiting outside the café when Nicolson returned. He handed over the cigarettes and the change.

"Managed to tear yourself away?" said Nicolson dryly as they got into his car.

The boy blushed. "You have to work on them, sir."

"Learn anything?"

"Anna thought Lucia was terrific. But she's not all that clued in— I guess Lucia was cagey about what she told her kid sister. There was a sailor, seemingly, but that's over long ago."

"He was married."

Wood's face fell. "You know all this, sir?"

"No. Go on."

"Well, that's when she became kind of cynical, like."

"Put a price on her services?"

"Yes, sir. But Anna says she was very choosy. A small, select clientele, you might say. Never more than two or three."

"Any names?"

"There was a chap Pullar or some name like that."

"Arthur Buller?"

"Could be. Anna only heard the name once."

"And that's all she knew?"

"Well, sir, not quite. Lucia had a boy-friend as well—you know, a bloke she was *fond* of, not one of her clients. A teacher."

"*Teacher*? Is Anna sure he was a teacher?"

"Well, that's what Lucia told her. He was educated, anyway—Anna spoke to him on the phone once."

"How long had this affair been going on?"

"For about three months before Lucia snuffed it."

"And does Anna not know his name or what he looks like or any-thing?"

"No, sir. You'd understand it if you spoke to Anna. A nice kid, but you could never trust her to keep her trap shut. Lucia would be scared her old man might get to know. You'd never think it, but that wee man's a holy terror to his family. He scares the pants off Anna."

But Nicolson was not surprised.

"A teacher?" Mearns seized on the word. "Now that's damn' funny, Maurice."

Nicolson watched him as he fiddled with his pipe.

"The one with the eyebrows"—it was an apt description: heaven-sent material for a caricaturist, these eyebrows.

Mearns's face had the curious faculty of seeming to change its struc-ture according to his mood. To-day, while he was riding the crest, the features were less cadaverous, the line of the mouth less harsh. Even his eyes lacked their usual indecision.

Not that there was anything positive to justify his euphoria. Rather the reverse. The house-to-house inquiry in the George Harbour area had revealed nothing. No identifiable prints had been found either on Eileen Pratt's bicycle or on the lamp. And so far the search for Ian Pratt's body had been fruitless. Nevertheless, the thrill of taking charge of his first big murder investigation had not yet, it seemed, given place to anxiety. That would come to-morrow when headquarters began to jostle him. And the Press. . . .

Mearns was just back from the hospital, where he had been allowed a short interview with Eileen Pratt. That in its way had been disappointing too, as he now explained to Nicolson. She hadn't seen her assailant or heard him speak, and she could give no description, except that he wore black shoes.

She was, however, convinced the man was someone she knew.

"How did she arrive at that?" Nicolson asked.

Mearns shrugged. "Intuition, as far as I could gather. All the same, you must admit, Maurice, it's damn' funny now we hear the Finghetti girl was doing a line with a teacher. I mean, suppose it was a *High School* teacher—one of Miss Pratt's colleagues? See what I mean?"

It wasn't like Mearns to make bricks with so little straw.

"There's something else, is there, sir?" Nicolson asked.

Mearns grinned. "*You* told me, Maurice. About Pratt being seen leaving the school late at night, remember?"

Of course! Douglas Troup had seen him. On a Wednesday night too. Yes, it might be significant. . . .

"Like to take a bet, Maurice?" said the chief inspector. "Five bob we'll have found the body by this time to-morrow."

FOUR

MEARNS WOULD have lost his bet. By dusk on Monday, Ian Pratt's body had not been found. The canal, the loch, and the Devil's Ravine had now been eliminated; and on Tuesday the search of the moors was intensified and its area extended.

The probability that the boy was dead had been strengthened by evidence from an unexpected quarter. Mrs. Edward Coleman, having read in her newspaper on Monday morning of the renewed search for the missing boy, called at a police station in Edinburgh. She now admitted that both she and her "husband" had lied to Detective-Inspector Nicolson last November. They had been expecting Ian Pratt the week he disappeared; it had been arranged that he would come and live with them.

Coleman had been much agitated when, although the bicycle had arrived, the boy himself didn't appear. He made her promise to say nothing, if questioned by the police. But now that the Press was hinting at murder, Mrs. Coleman could keep silent no longer.

Chief Inspector Mearns went through to Edinburgh that night to question the Colemans himself.

On Tuesday morning Detective-Inspector Nicolson called at the hospital to see Eileen Pratt.

She was sitting up in bed with a newspaper. The bandage was still round her head, but she wasn't so pale.

She smiled. "How lovely to see you, Maurice. Heavens, you're soaking!" Her voice sent a warm glow through him. A *business* visit, he reminded himself.

"How are you?" he asked, laying his dripping hat and coat over the end of the other bed, which was still unoccupied.

"I'll survive. . . . No news yet?" She pointed to the picture in her newspaper of policemen combing the hills above Silbridge.

"No." He pulled up a chair and sat down. "Eileen, you've been over this already with Chief Inspector Mearns. But it's terribly important. Have you remembered any more about the man who attacked you?"

"Only what I told Allan Cameron last night."

"Cameron? He didn't tell me he'd been here."

"It wasn't a *professional* visit, Maurice."

Somehow he kept forgetting that Eileen knew the Camerons so well. And with Fiona and the children away at her mother's in Airdrie, it was natural that Allan should visit Eileen in hospital.

"All right," said Nicolson. "What did you tell Cameron?"

"It was while I was in the water, clinging to that rubber fender, that I recognized the man. . . . Of course, your senses are sharpened when you're in terror of your life. I thought I was drowning. . . ."

"You mean you *saw* him, Eileen?"

She shook her head impatiently. "You don't understand. I mean that was the moment when I knew who it was; I can't tell you *how* I knew."

"And you can't remember now?"

"Everything up to that point I remember vividly. But there my mind closes up; this feeling of horror comes back. Dr. Singh says it's delayed shock. My subconscious doesn't *want* me to remember."

"But it may come back?"

"At any time, Dr. Singh says."

Nicolson looked at her with concern. "Eileen," he said, "how many people have you told this to, apart from Cameron and me?"

"Only the doctor. And Douglas, of course."

"Well, don't repeat it to *anybody* else, do you understand?"

She smiled. "Poor Maurice. You worry about me, don't you?"

"Yes."

"Nice that somebody does. Douglas almost *blames* me—because he has to visit me here. He loathes hospitals. . . . And as for Mother, she hasn't even been to see me."

"She's not well, Eileen."

"All the same she's my *mother*. You'd think she——" She sighed. "It's always been Ian, though. She dotes on him. . . . How's she taking it now?"

"She seemed half doped on Sunday morning. Not really taking things in."

"That would be her sleeping pills. They put her out like a light every night."

"Well, she did hear the two phone calls during the night."

"Did she?" Eileen was sceptical. "She wouldn't admit she slept through them, more likely."

A nurse came in from the adjoining ward. She had a tray with tea and biscuits. Two cups.

"Don't forget your tablets, Miss Pratt."

Eileen nodded. She put two white capsules in her mouth and helped them over with a sip of tea.

"What are these for?" Nicolson asked, when the nurse had gone.

"Nerves, I think. I've been having bad dreams. . . ." She shivered, and pulled her yellow bed-jacket more tightly round her shoulders. "I keep thinking about Ian. It's—it's *horrible*. Who would want to kill Ian?"

"Blackmail's a dangerous game," said Nicolson quietly.

She sighed. "It's hard to think of Ian as a blackmailer. He was such a nice boy. You'd have liked him, Maurice, I'm sure you would."

"I'm more concerned about you, Eileen. I believe you're still in danger. You know too much."

She looked surprised. "But I've told the police everything I know."

"Have you?"

Nicolson had been thinking hard about this. Assume Eileen was attacked because of what she had found out last Saturday. That meant her assailant knew of her visit to Glasgow but didn't realise she had already, during Saturday evening, passed on her information to the police. But that was absurd: obviously the first thing she would do was go to the police.

Therefore there was some different reason for the murder attempt. The inevitable result of Eileen's discoveries in Glasgow would be to reopen the investigation of her brother's disappearance. Suppose the killer was not afraid of that in itself but of something Eileen might incidentally reveal. Something directly concerned with Ian's death. . . .

"Tell me about the night Ian disappeared," Nicolson said.

"But I told you at the time."

"Never mind. Go over it again. Every single detail, however trivial."

She went for tea with Douglas after school that day. While she waited for him in the fog outside the school she thought she saw Ian pass on his bicycle, but she could have been mistaken.

They had tea in Douglas's flat and listened to records. Douglas drove her home soon after six.

Her mother was just back from her bridge, but neither Ian nor her father was there. Her father came in around seven—his usual time—and the three of them had supper.

Eileen visited Fiona Cameron every Wednesday. The fog was so thick that night that she would have put it off if her father hadn't offered her a lift. He dropped her at the Camerons about 7.45.

Allan was just going out. He usually did on a Wednesday. He avoided Eileen when he could. As always, the evening passed quickly, and Eileen had to run to catch the last bus at 11.20. Fiona wanted her to wait till Allan returned, so that he could run her home. But she thought that would be unreasonable on such a night.

She found her mother in a panic because Ian wasn't home. Her father hadn't returned either, but eventually came in about five to twelve. And it was he who noticed the open trapdoor to the attic.

"I went up to look and I spotted that the big green suitcase was gone. I remembered it because I'd taken it on holiday last summer—in fact I broke one of the locks. Well, we looked in Ian's bedroom after that and saw all his stuff was gone."

"Go on," said Nicolson.

"But that's all. Mother assumed he'd gone to my sister's in Liverpool. I let her think that, although I doubted it myself. We went to bed."

"Next day, though. Tell me about next day."

Eileen looked tired. He hated harassing her, but this might be important.

Her chief recollection of that Thursday was of her mother hanging over the telephone in the evening, waiting for Ian to ring. Too proud to phone Annette herself; but becoming even more anxious as the hours slipped past.

Eileen herself believed Ian had cleared off for good, and she was glad. But she did report his absence to the headmaster, who surprised her by instituting an inquiry.

"Utterly futile, of course. I mean, even if Ian had come to some harm, it wasn't in the *school*. Several people had seen him leaving school the night before."

"Dr. Huddleston fancies himself as an amateur detective," Nicolson remarked.

Eileen nodded. "Yes. I was in his study giving 'evidence' for half an hour. It disorganised my day. What with that and a row I had with—with someone else. I was fizzing by lunch time."

"What was the row?"

"What? Oh! nothing to do with this business. Something quite petty."

"I'd like to hear about it all the same."

Eileen smiled wanly. "You're thorough, aren't you, Maurice? . . . Well, you know that big wooden shed just outside the gym?"

"Where you keep your sports gear, isn't it?"

"Yes. It's also a toolshed for the gardener. Tom King and I have each a key and there's a third one kept by the janitor. Old McKendrick, the gardener, is supposed to go round to the janitor's lodge when he needs the key; but as often as not he nips into the gym and borrows mine."

When McKendrick came for the key that Thursday morning, Eileen found it wasn't on her key ring and went in to borrow Tom King's. King was at his most officious and demanded to know first why McKendrick hadn't gone to the lodge for the key and secondly how Eileen came to lose hers. He marched round with them to the shed and unlocked the door, whereupon McKendrick exclaimed that somebody had been messing around in there. His spade wasn't in its proper place. . . .

"That did it," said Eileen. "We had to take an inventory of the contents to make sure nothing was missing. And at the end of it I got a lecture about leaving my keys where the children could pinch them. I nearly told King where he could put his damned keys. . . . What's the matter, Maurice?"

Nicolson was staring at her, scarcely listening. "A *spade*, did you say?"

A picture was forming in his mind of his first visit to the High School last November. Of a gardener working the ground in front of the hedge; and the dark brown of the freshly turned earth. . . .

FIVE

THE SCHOOL was closed at the end of morning classes; and digging began after lunch.

It was the sort of weather that gave Silbridge its music-hall reputation. A black, lowering sky and a downpour that had continued unabating since early morning.

Half a dozen policemen in oilskins were driving spades into the heavy clay in front of the privet hedge. Detective-Sergeant Cameron, squelching about in rubber boots, superintended the work.

Farther back, on the tarmac, a little group was huddled, watching. A pale, subdued Dr. Huddleston shared an umbrella with a fair-haired Apollo; this, Nicolson gathered, was Eileen's colleague, King. Angus Pratt was there, at Nicolson's request, and beside him stood McKendrick, the gardener, a wiry little man with red hair and glasses. The others were newspapermen.

Nicolson stood a little apart, hands in pockets, the rain cascading from his hat and streaming down his mackintosh. His eye kept straying to the gate. Mearns should have been here by now. They had phoned him in Edinburgh and he was driving straight through.

McKendrick came across to Nicolson.

"That's the wrong place they're diggin', sir," he said. "I tell't the sergeant."

That had been Nicolson's impression too. The bit they were at now hadn't been turned over when he visited the school last November; the gardener had been working ten or twenty yards farther east. But he recognised Cameron's passion for orderliness, for a systematic progression from one end of the plot to the other. He didn't interfere.

"They'll get there," he said to McKendrick.

"Aye, bloody slow about it, though." The little man spat disgustedly.

"Did you notice anything that morning?" Nicolson asked him. "I mean, had the ground been disturbed or anything?"

"I didn'y see nothin' out here. But somebody'd been larkin' about in the shed a' right."

"Because the spade wasn't in its usual place?"

"Aye, and my boots. They were stuck wi' glaur."

At the end of each day's work McKendrick always scraped the loose mud off his gardening boots and left them in the toolshed. But that Thursday morning he had found them coated with mud. Since nothing was missing and no damage had been done, it was assumed that some boy or boys had been "larkin' about."

"Did you know Ian Pratt?" Nicolson asked.

"I often gave him cuttings for his old man."

"You know Mr. Pratt, do you?"

"Aye, he's daft about his garden."

The scene of operations had now moved ten yards east. The first square was pronounced clean: they had dug down four feet, then filled it in again.

A few sharp orders from Cameron and stage two began. He had his men so deployed as to cover the area in the most economical manner. Nicolson suspected he had a mathematical formula to determine their exact positions.

Nicolson listened, mesmerised, to the squelch of spades on wet clay and the occasional sharp ring as metal encountered stone; and the thud of the earth being piled up. Behind him water gushed from a rone pipe on the roof of the shed. Outside, on Greene Road, a sizeable crowd was now spread along the railings, peering in. There was still no sign of Mearns.

Square two was completed at 3.15 and the scene shifted once more. The rain was heavier than ever. There were mutinous rumblings from the perspiring diggers, silenced when Cameron promised a break at the end of this stint.

The reporters were becoming restive. Nicolson refused to say more than he had said at the start—that there was some evidence that Pratt's body might be buried in the school grounds. They stayed on.

At 3.42 a black car swept through the school gate and pulled up beside Nicolson. Chief Detective-Inspector Mearns leapt out.

"A bloody puncture," he muttered angrily. Then: "Anything here yet?"

At that moment there was a shout from one of the policemen and the others crowded round. Nicolson and Mearns ran forward.

"All right. Stand clear," Cameron shouted and the policemen made way.

The trench here was nearly three feet deep. Looking down, Nicolson at first could see nothing but yellow clay and puddles of water. But there was a darker patch, just uncovered. Dark brown it seemed to be. As he peered closer, he saw it was cloth. And one of the patches of yellow wasn't clay: it was the rotting flesh of a human hand. . . .

PART IV

ONE

THE HOUSE was very quiet when Annette and Peter had gone. They left on Sunday, the day after the funeral. Peter had to get back to his job. Annette would have stayed on: Eileen could read sisterly concern in her eyes. But she had commitments too: her two year old twins, left with her mother-in-law in Liverpool. Besides, Eileen assured them she was all right.

Physically she was better: the headaches were less fierce now. But as soon as she was alone, depression and nagging guilt returned. Could she have saved Ian? Could she have done anything to help her mother?

Her mother's breakdown had shocked Eileen even more than Ian's death. She had been gradually conditioned to that, and the exhumation in the High School grounds was only sickening confirmation of what she knew already in her heart.

But when Eileen—against medical advice—went home last Wednesday, she was utterly unprepared for what she found. She walked from the ambulance into the house and upstairs to her mother's room. On the bed was a stranger—a woman who stared at her with blank, uncomprehending eyes.

Mrs. Pratt was in Ladgrove Mental Hospital now. Although the prognosis was said to be fair, Eileen had an intuition that her mother would never be sane again.

Angus Pratt meanwhile went on his stolid way as if these disasters were no concern of his. He had fainted, Eileen was told, when Ian's body was brought up: but that was physical squeamishness. He felt no grief that the boy was dead, and pretended to none. His honesty was, Eileen supposed, to be accounted to his credit, but it was inhuman. As was his indifference to his wife's collapse.

It brought home to Eileen how little she knew of her father, how little she understood what went on inside his mind. Even in the old days, when her mother was firmly in the saddle, when Angus Pratt was the stock figure of a henpecked husband—even then there had been something false in the picture. Looking back now, Eileen remembered the occasional half-smile that belied the submissiveness. He had listened to the nagging, then escaped to his garden, or to the pub.

At least, Eileen supposed it was to a pub. It was commonly believed —and by Mrs. Pratt it was frequently stated—that Angus Pratt spent much of his leisure hours drinking. Pratt didn't deny it, but there was no positive evidence. And he had never come home drunk.

Of late his absences had been more frequent. Almost every night he was out, and at the week-ends too. To-day, a Sunday, he had gone off after breakfast and wasn't back yet. He wasn't there to see Annette and Peter off.

Already Eileen was sorry she had let her sister go. The silence of the house oppressed and frightened her. A killer was at large: a man who had murdered her brother and attempted to murder her. *And it was someone she knew.* . . .

The doorbell rang and she went to answer it. It was Douglas Troup.

"It's the prodigal returned," he said as Eileen stared coldly at him.

He put his hands on her shoulders and made to kiss her. Eileen pushed him away.

He said pettishly. "I did *ask* you, darling."

Yes, he had asked her. Asked if he must go to the funeral. He didn't want to miss a week-end conference of art teachers at Newbattle Abbey.

Eileen sighed. "Come in," she said.

To Douglas it was a token of surrender.

"A typically *feminine* attitude, darling," he remarked as he followed her in. "To say yes and then sulk because I take you at your word."

"Don't go on about it, Douglas," she said fiercely.

He had failed her when she needed him most. She knew the conference was only an excuse: Douglas would always shuffle out of unwelcome duties.

"Actually it was a waste of time," he said. "Yap, yap, yap. I came away early. Aren't you pleased?"

She didn't answer.

Douglas smiled. "Come over here," he said. "No, on the couch. Beside me."

She sat down, and this time didn't resist when he put his arm round her. She must accept Douglas as he was, with all his imperfections. You couldn't mould a man to some ideal pattern of your own. Her mother had tried that. . . .

"No arrest yet?" Douglas asked.

She shook her head. She was out of touch. Allan Cameron had been at the funeral but had said nothing about the police inquiries. Nor had Maurice Nicolson. Her heart warmed to Maurice as she recalled his attentiveness. He had done all he could to make things easy for her.

"They're going round every house in Silbridge, did you know that?" Douglas went on.

Yes, she had read it in yesterday's newspaper. A house-to-house inquiry, they had called it.

"A bit elaborate, wouldn't you say?" he remarked. "One would think they'd concentrate on your friends, since you say it's somebody you know. . . . How does it feel to have a bodyguard, by the way?"

"A bodyguard?"

"That beefy character hanging about across the road. He's not there for his health."

"Oh, *him!* Maurice Nicolson put him there to keep the Press from bothering us."

Douglas laughed. "My dear Eileen, how naïve can you be? If you imagine our police can spare a man for *that.* . . ."

"Then what's he there for?"

"I've told you. Bodyguard. They must believe you're still in danger. . . . You haven't remembered yet who——"

"No."

"What was it, darling? His voice, or his smell, or——"

"I've told you," she said tartly. "I can't remember."

"But there must have been *something* distinctive about him. Suppose it was me, for instance. You'd have remembered my limp, wouldn't you?"

"Is this a confession?" said Eileen coldly.

"Darling, darling," he said, "that's one of the things I love about you. You've such a *literal* mind."

Douglas could be insufferably patronising. But his arm was still round her waist.

"Know the real reason I came back early from Newbattle?" he added placatingly. "I missed you. I couldn't stay away another minute."

It was probably a lie. But she was too tired to challenge it.

At six o'clock Allan Cameron called. "On business," he said. He came in and sat down.

Douglas was glad of the excuse to leave, Eileen suspected. He hadn't been at ease with her. Her bereavement put him at a disadvantage: he couldn't claim his usual monopoly of the right to feel depressed.

All the same he would have stayed if Cameron hadn't come. Eileen felt unreasonably irritated with Cameron. This was symptomatic of her ill-starred relationship with him: always they rubbed each other the wrong way. Only the common bond in Fiona preserved a semblance of civility in their dealings.

In principle Cameron was the type Eileen admired: a man who had pulled himself up by his own efforts, honest, conscientious, dedicated to his profession. If only he weren't so prickly, so quick to imagine slights. And so intolerant. He disapproved of Douglas, always had. Douglas's irresponsibility, his extravagance, his lack of respect for authority—it was predictable that these qualities would not find favour with a man of Cameron's background and training. But he disapproved equally of Maurice Nicolson; and here Eileen could find no other explanation than envy. . . .

"Your father not at home?" said Cameron.

"No."

"Aye. Well, we got his statement the other night." Cameron took a paper from his folder in the briefcase he carried. A multigraphed sheet, a questionnaire of sorts with answers added in ink. "There's just one or two points. . . ."

"You want me to break Father's alibi, is that the idea?" Eileen said dryly.

Cameron frowned. "This is routine, Eileen. It's not only your father, it's every male adult in Silbridge."

"But I gave Mr. Mearns the names of twenty, maybe thirty, people who might have stolen a key from my ring. Why not start with them? And if——"

Cameron interrupted angrily. "I wouldn't presume to teach you how to coach a hockey team."

"But I'm only asking *why*. There's ninety thousand people in Silbridge, half of them males. And why stop there? I mean, suppose the chap came down from Glasgow? That gives you another million——"

"Don't be sarcastic, Eileen. We're being thorough. This way we make sure our man won't slip through the net."

Yes, she could see that would be how Cameron liked to work. The methodical approach; the mills of God grinding slowly. Not for him the short cut, the inspired guess, nor even the reasonable assumption. Especially since the blunder in identifying the Nevishaugh boy as Ian. That had been Cameron's fault, she guessed; a rare lapse from his own meticulous standards.

"May I see your questionnaire?" Eileen asked.

Cameron took out another copy, a blank one this time, and stiffly handed it over.

It began with name, address, age, height, weight, etc. Then came the control questions. Did the subject know Lucia Finghetti? Where was he between 10 and 10.30 p.m. on 20th October? Does he own, or have the use of, a car? Where was he on the evenings of 21st and 28th October, 4th, 11th and 18th November? Does he know Eileen Pratt? Had he access to Miss Pratt's key ring on or shortly before 25th November? Where was he between 8 p.m. and 8 a.m. on 25th/26th November? Is he familiar with Silbridge High School and the gardener's shed? Where was he on Saturday, 16th January at 11.50 p.m.? And between midnight and 2 a.m. the same night? Has he a pair of black shoes? Finally there was a section headed "corroborative evidence."

"I don't understand some of these dates, Allan," Eileen said. "20th October, that's when Lucia died, wasn't it?"

"Yes."

"And of course 25th November, that was when Ian—But what's special about these other dates last October and November?"

"These are the nights your brother met the man he was blackmailing."

Blackmailing. Eileen still couldn't associate Ian with blackmail. Surely there must be another explanation. . . .

She could see the purpose of the questionnaire. Granted the basic hypotheses, then any man with an acceptable alibi for any *one* of the dates was eliminated. As the number of controls was large, only a very few names would go through the sieve. And one of these would be the murderer.

"I want you to confirm where your father was on these dates," Cameron said briskly.

"It's a long time ago," said Eileen doubtfully. "Besides—" she looked again at the dates, "—these are mostly Wednesdays, aren't they?"

"Aye. What of it?"

"Well, *you* ought to know, Allan. I'm at your house every Wednesday. Father could be running amok for all I know."

Cameron was disconcerted. "Aye, I'd forgotten that," he admitted. He consulted the sheet in which Angus Pratt's answers had been written. "But what about Wednesday, 4th November? Can you remember that one?"

"I tell you, I've no idea where he was," she began irritably. Then it came back. Her uncle, Angus Pratt's eldest brother, had died early in November. The funeral was on Guy Fawkes Day, she remembered, and her father had travelled north the previous day. The 4th November.

Cameron nodded, folded the questionnaire and put it back in his case. "Aye, well, that's that, I suppose," he said.

He asked about her neighbours. He had taken two more sheets from his case. "There's a Mr. Dunleavy—" he began.

Eileen gaped at him. "For heaven's sake, Allan, you're not suspecting *him*? He's in a wheel-chair."

"We're not suspecting anybody," Cameron amended. "Just eliminating." He ticked something on the sheet and put it aside. "And now——"

"Oh, yes!" said Eileen, "there's Clive Ferris on our other side. He's probably your man. Big, strong chap—five feet three, if he's an inch. He came in and borrowed my keys, did I tell you that? Yes, on the 24th November at 10.44 p.m. And——"

"Eileen!"

"—And of course he was doing a line with Lucia Finghetti. She——"

"Eileen!" It was almost a shout. "How can you be so frivolous when——"

But Eileen was angry too. "Well, damn it," she said, "you'll be *months* on the job at this rate. Filling up forms about people like old Mr. Dunleavy and Clive Ferris and then cross-checking with the neighbours. The thing's ridiculous. I'll bet Maurice Nicolson doesn't approve."

She had really got under his skin now. "Ah! *that's* where you've got your fancy ideas," he said. "He's no business——"

"I've never discussed it with him," Eileen said shortly. She saw that her guess had been right: there had been a battle over tactics within the C.I.D.—Cameron against Nicolson—and Nicolson had lost.

"Just the same," she couldn't resist adding, "if you'd listened to Inspector Nicolson in the first place, you wouldn't have taken two months to find Ian's body."

"Aye, he's a great man, is Inspector Nicolson. Teaches us all our business. We're just a bunch of yokels. We weren't educated at Culverton, you understand."

"Don't, Allan." The bitterness of his voice turned her anger to compassion.

"Philistines, that's us," he went on, unheeding. "Aye, well, maybe. But some of us still know right from wrong. I could tell you a thing or two about Mr. Maurice Nicolson that——"

Eileen stood up. "I don't want to hear it," she said sharply.

"Sit down!" She had never seen him angry like this before. "It's high time you realised what your smart friends are really like, Eileen. Nicolson was nearly dismissed from the force before he came here."

"I'm not *interested*."

"And do you know what for? For living with a woman of known criminal connections. Living in *sin.*"

He mouthed the word like a Free Kirk minister. And in a moment of insight Eileen recognised the primary source of Cameron's antagonism: he was a puritan.

"Aye, the old school tie did its stuff there," he continued. "If it had been me, I'd have been out on my ear. But, oh no! 'Promise you won't do it again, old boy, and we'll fix you a nice, cushy transfer'." He laughed mirthlessly. "They were going to promote me, did you know that? It was in the bag. But they had to find a place for our friend. . . ."

There was nothing Eileen could say. Allan would regret this outburst when his temper cooled. She had provoked it, and he would remember that. No hope now of a rapprochement.

What strange things you found when you probed beneath the surface! Allan Cameron was widely accepted as a placid, easy-going extrovert, a man of few words, but dependable as a rock. He *looked* the part, too, with those broad shoulders and the firm mouth and the quiet voice. Yet all the time he was eaten up inside with inhibitions and prejudices and grievances.

Poor Fiona! She had taken on more than she knew when she married Allan Cameron. Eileen was sorry for her.

She was sorry too for Maurice Nicolson. She would like to know the true story of that girl, the girl in the photograph.

TWO

EILEEN RETURNED to school on the Wednesday, again in the teeth of medical advice. She found it too depressing to be alone all day in the house.

Alone apart from Rusty. But the big mongrel was no comfort to Eileen. He had been Ian's dog; and he had moped ever since Ian went. Eileen he barely tolerated.

She was frightened. Every time someone came to the door, every time the telephone rang, her heart beat faster and she tasted the dryness of fear at the back of her throat. The memory of that night at the George Harbour was still fresh; and she knew she was still in danger.

"Knew?" Douglas would have pounced on the word. He was always teasing her about the intuitive, illogical processes of her mind. He had no faith in extra-sensory perception.

Eileen no longer argued—you couldn't win an argument with Douglas. But he didn't understand. Her "intuitive" knowledge was based on facts and logical inferences from them; only the reasoning was done by her subconscious. The conviction that a second attempt on her life was imminent must have a rational foundation, if only she could find it.

It couldn't be that the murderer knew she had recognised him and was liable at any moment to remember who he was. She had mentioned that only to the police and to Douglas; and Douglas had been warned to let it go no farther.

If she *was* still in danger, it must be because she still had some knowledge that was potentially dangerous to the murderer. But that was absurd too; she had told the police everything she knew. . . .

In the eyes of the school children Eileen had acquired a new stature. As she wheeled her bicycle through the school gate on Wednesday morning, activities in the playground were suspended while inquisitive eyes watched her respectfully. One child even came forward and asked for her autograph. Sandra Cowie—it *would* be Sandra.

Eileen wondered wryly whether she had earned her notoriety as Ian's sister or in her own right by being pushed into the dock. A bit of both, perhaps. And there had been that dreadful photograph in the *Advertiser*. They had snapped her at the funeral and blown the picture up to half page.

The staff were more sophisticated in their greeting. Vague murmurings of undefined sympathy. Murder, like cancer, was something never to be mentioned by its name.

The headmaster, however, had no such inhibitions. He called Eileen to his study for interrogation.

"Miss Pratt," he said, after a perfunctory inquiry about her health, "have you considered the possibility that your brother was murdered by a master in this school?"

"I've considered it, yes."

"So have I. So have I. . . . Tell me, you kept your key ring in your desk, didn't you?"

"*On* my desk."

Huddleston shook his head sadly. "Ah! Miss Pratt, how foolish! However. . . . When did you last use the key?"

Eileen had been over all this with Inspector Nicolson a week ago. McKendrick, the gardener, had borrowed her key on the Wednesday afternoon, the day of the fog, had locked the shed, then returned the key to her. That was about three o'clock. She put it back on her key ring and laid the ring on her desk.

"Quite so," said Huddleston. "That was my information. So the key was stolen between 3 p.m. and—when did you leave that day? 4.15?"

"It might have been taken *after* I left school," Eileen pointed out.

The headmaster frowned. "Yes, yes. But let's ignore that possibility for the moment. Now——"

"In that case," Eileen interrupted, "I can narrow the times. I had a class from 3.15 to 4. That's the only time the keys were out of my sight."

Huddleston smiled. "Ah! splendid, splendid. I hoped you'd say that . . . I've done a little exercise, Miss Pratt."

With the air of a conjuror producing a rabbit he took a paper from his desk and handed it to her. There were five names written on it: Bradley, Fry, King, Summers and Yuill.

Eileen stared blankly at the sheet.

"These, Miss Pratt," the headmaster explained, "are the *only* five members of staff who had the opportunity to remove a key from your room between 3.15 and 4 that day. All the others had a class and——"

"Mr. Bradley had a class," Eileen objected. "He had the sixth. I know because Ian——"

"Mr. Bradley was ten minutes late for his class that afternoon."

"How do you know all this, Dr. Huddleston?"

"By taking evidence. I've interviewed all the masters and—let me see —upwards of fifty pupils. You see, as headmaster one has certain advantages the police don't share. One knows how much relative *weight* to attach to conflicting testimony. And, of course,"—he smiled modestly—"one has the trained mind."

The fog on that November day, he admitted, had made his task easier. It pinpointed the day for people; they remembered it as if it were yesterday.

"What about the police?" Eileen asked. "Do they accept your findings?"

The smile was switched off. "I don't know," he said shortly. "I gave my notes to Chief Inspector Mearns at the week-end. But that young man Nicolson's been haunting the school. He's very uncommunicative."

Eileen looked at the list again. "You can cross off Mr. Bradley for a start," she said. "Unless he came out of hospital to throw me in the harbour."

"Quite so. Any others?"

"Well, there's Tom—there's Mr. King. He has a key of his own for the shed. He wouldn't need mine."

"No?" Huddleston was smiling again. She had never known anyone who could express so much by a smile.

"You surely don't suspect Tom King?" she said, astonished. King had always been a favourite of the headmaster.

But her question was too direct. "My dear Miss Pratt, I make no accusations. Not without evidence. Now if you had some *evidence* against one of these five. . . ." He left the sentence poised as a question.

Eileen shook her head.

"Ah! well, it was just a thought. Thank you for coming, Miss Pratt. Take things easily for a little, won't you?" He was ushering her out of the door, still smiling.

That smile was nauseating, Eileen thought as she walked away. A smooth, insincere man. A tailor's dummy. No, that wasn't fair: he was intelligent. But how *vain!* Always demonstrating how clever he was.

All the same the poison had done its work. She found herself going over the five names Huddleston had mentioned. Bradley was out. Summers in the role of murderer was unthinkable: he was a gentle old man, timorous and spinsterish. Fry—well, she barely knew Fry: he had only joined the staff in September. Yuill had lost a leg in the war: it certainly hadn't been Yuill who chased her along the harbour's edge. Of these four only Fry was even remotely possible.

Finally there was King. Of all her colleagues Tom King seemed to Eileen the only one with the potential for planned murder. He had the egotism of the cold-blooded killer, the conviction that his interests mattered more than anything else, even another man's life. And he had known Lucia Finghetti. . . .

"Eileen!" Think of the devil. . . . His door was open and he called to her as she passed.

"Hallo, Tom." She tried to make her voice casual.

"Come in and have a crack."

King wore a track suit. He had just come in from a run with the boys of the fifth and was glowing from the exercise. Parents had murmured about these cross-country runs in mid-winter. But the boys seemed to enjoy them.

"Take a pew, Eileen." King crossed over and closed the door behind her. A tiny prickle of fear ran up her spine. She dismissed it: nothing could happen to her here, in broad daylight.

"You look peaky," he said. "Sure you're not back too soon?"

She shrugged. "Miss Kemp's staying till the end of the week. That'll break me in gradually." Miss Kemp was Eileen's predecessor; they had brought her out of retirement to take Eileen's classes during her illness.

"Sorry about Ian," King added perfunctorily. "I was there when they dug him up."

"Why?" she asked. No good taking offence at his bluntness. The best way to deal with Tom King was to repay him in kind.

This time he took it in his stride. "H.M. asked me—needed moral support, I guess. That was a day and a half, I can tell you! He was strangled, wasn't he?"

Struck on the head, then strangled. That was the pathologist's finding. Eileen liked to believe the first blow had knocked him out.

"Terrible. Terrible." But his words were overlaid with a ghoulish satisfaction.

Or so it seemed to Eileen. Perhaps she was being hypersensitive. But she couldn't take her eyes from these big strong hands. She imagined them round Ian's throat; or thrusting her over the dock's edge.

She shivered.

"Sure you're O.K.?" He was always quick to observe signs of distress in others.

"I'm fine," Eileen assured him. "You were telling me about last Tuesday."

"Was I? Yes, that was a day and a half, all right! And we've all been on the mat since then. H.M.'s been acting Sherlock Holmes."

"H.M." was the name by which the pupils referred to their headmaster. Of the staff only King used the term: and it grated on Eileen.

"Yes," he went on, "and your friend Nicolson's been badgering us as well. I can't think why."

"Can't you? Ian was buried here. And my key was used to get a spade from the shed. The teachers are bound to come under suspicion, surely."

"I can't think why," he repeated stubbornly.

The bell rang for the end of break.

"You'll have to excuse me, Eileen," he said.

"Yes." She stood up. As she turned to go, she noticed a sheaf of typescript on the desk. Pages and pages of it.

"This your thesis, Tom?" she asked.

A fleeting expression of alarm crossed his face and was gone. "Yes," he said mildly. "Molly Macrae's been typing it. I hope to get it off this week."

Had she imagined it? To test him, she said: "Mind if I read it?"

He stared at her and said, very deliberately: "No, you may not read it."

She hadn't imagined it.

THREE

INSPECTOR NICOLSON was waiting for Eileen when she came out of the gymnasium at lunch.

"I heard you were back," he said. "I'm taking you to lunch."

"Oh no!" she said quickly. "I'm sorry. I always lunch with Douglas."

He smiled. "Your fiancé has graciously consented. A *business* lunch, of course."

"Of course." She smiled demurely as she followed him to his car.

He took her to the Royal. "Your brother used to come here," he remarked as they went in.

"So I'm told."

They had drinks in the Continental Bar. "To loosen the tongue," he said as he ordered a double gin for her. "I want you to talk."

"What about?"

"About Ian for a start. You don't mind, do you?"

No, she didn't mind. The first sharpness of her grief had dulled to a steady ache and she could think of him now; remember him. You accepted death in time, adjusted to it; you *had* to, or you went mad, like her mother. Already in Eileen's mind Ian's image was imperceptibly changing. He had lost a dimension: he had no future, only a past. He was the brother who died young, a legend in the making.

"You see," Nicolson was going on, "I can't get him in focus; I thought I understood him. A sensitive boy who went off the rails when he learned he was adopted."

"It was the *way* he found out, Maurice. And the lies Mother told him. . . . And of course getting involved with Coleman."

Nicolson was lighting a cigarette. "Yes, quite. I can understand him kicking over the traces, getting into bad company—even that fight in the dance hall. I've some sympathy for all that. But what can you say for a boy who watches a girl being killed and blackmails the killer?"

"I don't believe it, that's what I say. Not of Ian."

"You have to believe it, Eileen." His tone was impatient. "We've corroboration now. His father—his natural father, I mean—knew of it. He's admitted it. Ian told him everything except the name of the man he was blackmailing."

"And, of course, you took his word. That *dreadful* man."

"Eddie Coleman didn't exactly volunteer the information. We prised it out of him. He knew about Lucia Finghetti—and he certainly didn't get *that* from the newspapers." He sighed. "I hate destroying your illusions, Eileen. You've described Ian as a nice boy going through a difficult phase. Others have said the same—even his probation officer. But the picture's false, it *must* be false: there was a bad streak in him. . . . Take off your rose-coloured spectacles, Eileen, and tell me: *what was your brother really like?*"

"He was a nice boy going through a difficult phase."

He smiled, defeated. "Let's go in and eat," he said.

Over lunch Nicolson encouraged her to talk of her work. He was a sympathetic listener and she hardly noticed at first that he was gently pumping her. About her colleagues.

"These questions were loaded, weren't they?" she asked, when the subject had been squeezed dry.

He laughed. "I was interested," he admitted.

She asked about the house-to-house inquiry. Already the Press was becoming restive and clamouring for results.

"They'll be finished to-day," said Nicolson without inflection. "But then there's all the tabulating to do."

"Was it really necessary? I mean, that's a week gone already, and——"

But Nicolson was diplomatic. "Did you ever do jig-saws, Eileen?" he said. "I used to, when I was a kid. I was good at recognising the different *shades*. I mean, if I was working on the sky, I didn't waste time trying every single piece. I only looked at the blue ones."

"Well, naturally, but——"

"Ah! but sometimes I was caught out. I'd spend ages searching for a particular shape among my sky pieces. And all the time it was one of the ones I'd discarded as the wrong colour. Maybe there was a black cloud or something."

"Where's the moral?"

"Well, apply the analogy to this case. I'm looking for a piece of sky, and I think the High School's the right colour. But I could be wrong. And if the vital piece is outside the school, Mearns's inquiry should bring it to light."

Maurice was more loyal to his colleagues than Allan Cameron had been.

A waiter brought their coffee.

"Black?" said Eileen. "And no sugar?"

Nicolson smiled. "What's this—intuition?"

"Observation. It's not the first lunch I've had with you, remember?" He laughed.

"Have you found anything at the school?" Eileen asked, as she poured the coffee.

"A certain amount."

"The headmaster suspects Tom King," Eileen dropped it out casually.

Nicolson looked at her speculatively. "I know," he said.

"Do you suspect him?" Eileen persisted.

He made much of the business of lighting a cigarette. Then he said: "I need your help, Eileen. You're the only person who's seen the killer. You've even touched him. I know you can't positively identify him—not yet, anyway. But perhaps you could rule out some people. Assure us, I mean, that the man who attacked you definitely *wasn't*—well, say, King, for example."

"You haven't answered my question, Maurice."

"I can't answer a question like that." He spoke shortly. "Not even to you. I'm surprised you should ask."

"Oh! are you? If somebody has it in for me, I want to know who it is."

His expression softened. "I'm sorry, Eileen. Yes, you have a vested interest. All right, I can tell you this much: there is some evidence against King. And now, can you answer *my* question: could it have been King that night?"

Eileen thought about it. "I can't rule him out," she said at length. "Except——"

"Yes?"

When she was being chased along the quay that night, Eileen's impression was that she was *gaining* slightly until she tripped. Although Eileen was a good runner, she wasn't in the class of Tom King.

"Don't make too much of that," she warned Nicolson. "I didn't have my stop-watch."

He nodded. "It's a point, though. . . . Also, you spoke of a 'rasping breath,' remember? That doesn't sound like a man in prime condition, as King obviously is."

She hadn't thought of that. The panting might have been from nerves, of course.

Eileen looked at her watch. "Heavens! I'll have to get back. I don't want Miss Kemp to——"

"Nonsense. You start off with a free period this afternoon."

She laughed. "You've looked up my time-table?"

"Naturally."

"All right, give me a cigarette, Maurice, would you?" She rarely smoked, but felt the need of one now. When it was lit, she said: "Now tell me why you suspect Tom King."

"I didn't *say* I——"

She amended the question. "All right, what's the evidence against him?"

"He knew Lucia Finghetti, for a start."

"You're convinced now there's a connection between Lucia's death and what happened to Ian?"

"It seems very likely."

"Well, King certainly took her to a dance I was at."

"Yes. He claims that's the *only* time he took her out. He says one of his colleagues knew her better. . . ."

Something in the casual way this was tossed off made Eileen look at him sharply.

"If you mean Douglas," she said, "he did know her. But not well."

Nicolson smiled. "Yes. Sorry. Bad habit of mine, not saying things straight out. Comes of laying traps for people. Yes, I did mean Douglas. And Douglas admits to knowing Lucia. But, as you say, only slightly."

But he *had* been setting a trap, Eileen felt sure. He was probing whether she was aware of Douglas's acquaintance with Lucia.

Nicolson was a formidable man in this mood. There was little sign to-day that Eileen had made any personal impact on him.

"Second point against King," he continued, "is the key of the shed. It was easier for him than for any other master to remove your key. Suppose Fox, for instance, came across from the Spanish Department to the gym, somebody might see him and wonder what he was *doing* there. But nobody'd think twice about King even if they saw him go into your *room*. He'd have to steal the key, of course, to divert suspicion from himself."

Yes, that refinement had occurred to Dr. Huddleston.

"Third point," Nicolson continued, "King worked at nights in the school."

"What of it?"

"Ian was seen coming out of the High School late one Wednesday night last November. We believe that's where he went each Wednesday —to collect the levy from the blackmail victim."

"How does that implicate King in particular?"

"He works late a lot, doesn't he?"

"Once or twice a week."

"Yes, well, would any other teacher fix a rendezvous with the black-mailer at the school when there was a risk King might be there?"

"Perhaps not," she conceded. "Is that the whole of your case?"

"More or less." He hesitated. "Except he seems a bit jumpy. Nervous, you know. But perhaps he's always like that?"

Eileen stubbed out her cigarette. "No, I haven't noticed much sign of nerves. . . . Except this morning, when I asked to read his Ph.D. thesis."

She described the incident to him. "It was the way he *said* it, Maurice. 'No, you may not read it.' It sounded—well, *menacing*. And the look he gave me—it sent the shivers through me."

"What's the subject of the thesis?"

"Something to do with muscular development through exercise. He's been at it for years. He has mountains of records—the boys are his guinea pigs, you see. . . . For months now he's been writing it up. I never believed he'd actually produce something. I thought it was just a status symbol—'doing his research,' you know."

"It's hard to see what can be sinister about a Ph.D. thesis."

"I assure you——"

"I'm not doubting you, Eileen. Who's this Molly Macrae, the girl who typed it? You haven't asked her about it?"

"She's the headmaster's secretary; and Tom King's current girl friend."

Nicolson grunted. "He gets around, doesn't he? All right, I'll look into it."

It was nearly half past two. Now Eileen really must go. Not once had Nicolson by word or expression betrayed the slightest interest in her as a person. She should have been glad. She *was* glad, for his sake. Yet there was a twinge of disappointment too.

But as they went out, Nicolson said abruptly: "Why did you ask us to take our man away, Eileen?"

The sight of the "bodyguard" eternally in the street outside her house had played on her nerves. It was illogical, but she felt safer without him.

"You may still be in danger," he pointed out.

"I know."

"The man's ruthless. He's killed twice. He'll kill again if——"

"I *know*, Maurice. Don't go on about it."

He let it drop until they were in the car. "Don't take chances, Eileen, that's all," he said quietly, as he let in the clutch.

"You mean with Tom King?"

"I mean with *anybody*. Don't trust anybody. Stay in at nights and lock your door."

Eileen shivered. "You're going to get him, Maurice, aren't you?"

He took his eyes briefly from the road to glance at her. "We'll get him," he said. "It's just a question whether we'll get him soon enough."

If only her mind didn't seize up whenever she thought of that night at the harbour. . . .

"If I remembered who it was, would that be proof enough, Maurice?"

"It would help."

There was something odd about his tone.

"Do you not believe me?" she demanded. "Do you not believe I recognised him?"

"Yes," he said flatly, "I believe you. I doubt if you're going to remember, though." There was an undertone she didn't understand.

The car swung through the school gate and pulled up in the car park.

"Thanks for the lunch," Eileen said stiffly, as she got out.

Nicolson wasn't listening. He was gazing across at the school.

"Damn' funny business," he said. "I mean, coming *here* to collect his money. And why should it take so long?"

"How do you mean—'so long'?"

"Well, he was away for hours every Wednesday, apparently. And it was eleven o'clock at night when your fiancé saw him."

"Douglas? Is that where you——"

"Yes, Douglas told us he saw Ian coming out of the gate here one Wednesday."

The evidence seemed to Eileen very insubstantial. To have been seen *one* night was no proof he went there the other nights. Besides, he might just have looked in on his way home to collect his bicycle.

She put the point to Nicolson.

"I'd be happier to have it confirmed," he agreed.

"Surely *somebody* must know."

"The murderer knows. . . ."

The sound of the school bell drifted across to them.

"I've a class now," Eileen said. "Thanks again, Maurice."

He smiled to her. "Remember, Eileen, *please* look after yourself."

She could forgive a lot for the warmth of that smile.

FOUR

"STAY IN at nights and lock your door," Nicolson had said.

Yet here she was, that same night, preparing to go out. Against her better judgment, but she couldn't ignore that child's appeal.

Norah Shipstone had come to Eileen's room at four o'clock. She looked pale, with the red-rimmed eyes of sleepless nights.

"It's not true what they say about Ian, Miss Pratt, is it?" she said.

"What do they say?"

"About blackmail."

Eileen wondered who was spreading that around. There had been no mention of blackmail in the papers.

"It's not like Ian, is it?" she answered diplomatically.

"It's a filthy lie," the girl answered hotly. "Ian wouldn't do such a thing."

Eileen warmed to her; loyalty was a quality she appreciated. But Norah was too young—she oughtn't to be brooding like this.

"Try and forget him, Norah," she said gently. "You've all your life ahead of you. There'll be other boys."

The girl seemed not to hear. "That crowd know something," she said.

"What crowd?"

"The gang Ian used to knock about with. Joe Gammans and that lot."

"Know something about what?"

"About Ian. About what happened to him."

There was a knock on the door and Tom King looked in.

"Time you weren't here, Eileen," he began briskly, then caught sight of Norah. "Oh! sorry," he muttered.

Norah stood up.

"Don't go," said Eileen quickly. She didn't want to be left alone with King, not after what Nicolson had said.

"Well, I'm off," he said. "Early night for once. All work and no play, you know. . . ." He was wearing his good overcoat, Eileen noticed. Molly Macrae would be waiting, no doubt.

Still he lingered in the doorway. "I shouldn't stay much longer, Miss Pratt," he said. "First day back, remember. You look peaky."

"I'm going soon," said Eileen, stifling her irritation. Even when you were frightened of him, his clichés could still exasperate.

He went out. His footsteps receded across the gymnasium. There was the click of a key turning in a lock. Then the creak of the swing doors to the corridor, and he was gone.

"Well, I did what you suggested, Miss Pratt," Norah was saying, "I've been seeing Lenny Ferguson and——"

But Eileen wasn't listening. King had locked his door. He had never done that before, not in all the time she had been here.

"—so I'm meeting him to-night. And I'm *scared*, Miss Pratt, and I wondered if you'd come with me."

"Meeting Lenny Ferguson?"

She knew by the hurt look on the girl's face that she had made a gaffe.

"I'm sorry, Norah. My mind was on something else. You'd better tell me again."

Norah had been cultivating Lenny Ferguson, prising out of him every last thing he knew about his former friend, Ian Pratt. It couldn't have been easy, for Lenny was not given to confidences, nor was he susceptible to female charm.

But Eileen guessed that charm wouldn't be Norah's weapon. She was single-minded, and her persistence would wear him down.

Not that he had, in the end, a great deal to offer. He himself knew no more than he had admitted to the police; of that Norah was satisfied. But he did let it out at last that Myra Thexford knew something.

"Who's Myra Thexford?" Eileen interrupted.

"Ian's—Ian's ex girl-friend. She's living with Gammans now."

Norah had gone to see her. But Myra was too much for her.

"Oh! it was *awful*, Miss Pratt, simply awful. The things she said to me!"

All the same Myra did admit—or, rather, she boasted—that she knew something Inspector Mearns would give his eye teeth for.

"So I'm seeing Joe Gammans to-night," Norah concluded.

"Gammans? Why?"

"Myra doesn't keep anything from him. Lenny told me that."

Lenny had arranged for her to meet Gammans to-night in Finghetti's Café. The whole gang would be there, all except Myra, who was ill.

And Norah was frightened. She had tremendous spirit, she would go —alone, if necessary—but she was frightened. Layabouts like Gammans were beyond her experience.

"Will you come with me, Miss Pratt?" she asked.

"You won't come to any *harm*, Norah." Eileen didn't want to go. She was very tired. And she too was frightened: and with more cause than Norah.

But she couldn't reject the appeal of those hazel eyes.

"I'm taking the car to-night, Father."

Angus Pratt looked up from his newspaper, peering over his spectacles.

"I'm sorry, dear," he said, "but I'm going out."

"Maybe. But not in the car."

He laid the newspaper down then. "I'm afraid I need it, Eileen." His voice was still gentle, but firm.

"Can't you stay at home for once? Where do you *go* every night?"

He didn't answer. He had turned back to the *Advertiser*.

Eileen snatched the paper from him and threw it down. "I asked you a question, Father," she said.

Her rage was the accumulation of years of pent-up resentment. She had quarrelled with her mother often enough; but you couldn't get close enough to Angus Pratt even to quarrel with him. He was adept at sliding away, at giving under pressure. You never came against anything solid; sometimes you wondered if he *existed* at all.

Even now he avoided the issue. "Very well," he said. "I'll not be arguing. Take the car." He bent down and retrieved his newspaper.

He wasn't even angry. That was the greatest insult of all: the indifference. Somewhere along the line he had lost interest in his family. The death of his adopted son, his wife's insanity—they seemed to mean *nothing* to him.

Eileen had won her point. But she was too upset to stop there.

"I wonder you bother to come home at all," she said. "Wouldn't it be simpler if you just slept there as well?"

She had caught his attention now.

"Slept where?" he asked.

"Wherever it is you go every night."

The flicker of interest in his eyes died. He yawned and scratched his nose.

Eileen turned away. She was disgusted by that flabby, pouchy face with its bulbous nose and big ears and untidy hair. She hated the way he slouched in his chair, the slovenly way he dressed—that old jacket he was wearing was a *disgrace*.

Once you had lost respect for a person, all his little idiosyncrasies, even his physical oddities, became major irritations. For Eileen the worst part was the feeling of guilt. "Honour thy father and thy mother": she honoured neither of them. For her mother she felt only the pity she would have given to anyone mentally sick; there was no love in it. And her father didn't even evoke pity.

Eileen backed the Morris into the road. The street lamp showed up scrape marks on the fresh green paint of one of the gate posts. Even her father's driving was slovenly.

She was to call for Norah at 7.30. With time to spare, she was content to coast along, letting her anger simmer down. It was an ominous sign, losing her temper like that, a sign that her nerves were beginning to crack. She had been living from moment to moment, from one disaster to the next, never letting herself dwell on the enormity of what was happening. A reflex protective measure. But the protection was wearing thin.

Deliberately she drove past the manse and slowly circled the block again. The hands of her watch were edging 7.30: two minutes more would do no harm. She didn't *want* to start the next chapter. It was safer here in the car, insulated from the dangers that threatened from outside.

Once as a small girl Eileen had spent a week of misery in the house of a relative of her father somewhere up north. She couldn't remember now the occasion of the visit: her mother must have been ill, she supposed. Eileen had been terrified of the woman and used to lie in bed in the mornings watching the clock inexorably creep round to the hour when she had to get up. At eight o'clock there would be a thunderous knock on the bedroom door and that harsh, cracked voice would call: "Are you up, child?" And Eileen would steal two minutes more. . . .

It was a weakness, this procrastination, the reluctance to face harsh reality. She knew too that it accounted for the film that glazed over her recollection of that night at the George Harbour. Deep down she didn't *want* to remember.

"You look fab, Miss Pratt," said Norah.

That probably meant she had too much make-up on. Eileen had been deliberately lavish with the mascara and the eye-shadow, for she felt this was one occasion when over-emphasis might be an asset. She had seen Joe Gammans and was aware of his reputation; and she had an instinct for how this scene ought to be played.

Norah, by contrast, looked absurdly young and ingenue. There was an eagerness in her face that she was trying, not entirely successfully, to subdue. This was an adventure, pleasurable now that the responsibility was taken from her shoulders. When you were sixteen, you couldn't grieve *all* the time.

They were too early. The only other customers in Finghetti's were a couple holding hands at a table in the corner; they looked as if the confetti had just been combed out of their hair.

Eileen ordered coffee for herself and hot chocolate for Norah. The girl who served them was beyond question a Finghetti. The likeness to Lucia was very marked: the same black hair and olive complexion and long, straight nose. This girl was younger, though, and not quite so striking.

Shortly before eight o'clock a group of teenagers came in and took noisy possession of the café. From their proprietorial air Eileen deduced that these were the residents—the Gammans mob. But Gammans himself wasn't among them, nor Lenny Ferguson.

Eileen's head was throbbing.

"Do you find it hot in here?" she asked.

"What?" Norah's eyes had been feasting on the group laughing and chattering round the juke box, on their stylised clothes, the leather jackets and narrow trousers of the boys, the loose sweaters and short skirts of the girls. "No, I'm not specially hot," she replied inattentively.

Eileen must have a temperature, then. Her forehead was damp with perspiration and she was getting waves of heat. But she didn't take off her coat or even loosen it. That could wait. . . .

Lenny Ferguson came in, accompanied by a young, slim, very fair boy. He looked quickly round till he spotted Norah. The knowing smile on his face froze when he saw who was with her. He stared unbelievingly at Eileen for a moment, then sidled slowly across to join his friends.

The voices were muted now, like an orchestra tuning up. Indeed the whole scene reminded Eileen of the prelude to a concert. First the players coming on to the platform and taking their places, then the leader; and then the expectant pause before the conductor appeared.

He came soon afterwards, making an entrance that was no less effective for its quietness. He ignored the sycophantic greetings that were shouted to him and stood just inside the door. Lenny hastened over and began to whisper to him, nodding furtively at the table where Eileen and Norah sat. Gammans swivelled round and looked at them with amusement. Then he walked slowly across.

"You're Norah, eh?" He addressed himself only to the young girl.

"Yes," she whispered, glancing nervously at Eileen.

"Lenny says you want to talk to me?"

Norah nodded dumbly.

"O.K., chicken. Up off your behind and over here."

He indicated the two tables that had been pushed together over by the juke box. There was a scraping of chairs as the gang ranged themselves round, pleasurable anticipation on their faces. Two seats had been left vacant at one end.

Eileen was glad now she had come to-night. It was clear that Norah had been brought here to be made a fool of: she was to be the evening's entertainment.

"Why don't you sit down here, Mr. Gammans?" Eileen said. "There's more room. And more privacy."

He glanced briefly at her. "Keep your nose out of this, lady."

Eileen didn't answer. But slowly, indolently, she unbuttoned her coat, withdrew her arms from it, and let it slide off her shoulders on to the chair behind her.

There was a gasp from Norah, and from across the floor, wolf whistles.

She wore a thin white sweater, moulded to her figure; and it was obvious she wore nothing underneath.

"Get me another coffee, would you?" she said casually to Gammans.

He hesitated. From behind him his supporters shouted profane encouragement and advice. Eileen represented a challenge, a threat to his reputation that he daren't shirk.

"O.K., sister," he said. "One coffee coming up." He went over to the counter.

Norah was staring at Eileen open-mouthed. Eileen without change of expression gave her a broad wink; but the girl continued to look shocked.

Eileen hoped she had read Joe Gammans's character correctly; and hoped, too, he had something worthwhile to disclose. It would be a pity if her sophisticated strip-tease had been for nothing.

She watched him as he brought over the coffee. He was powerfully built, with the strength that comes from years of sustained physical labour, and with a rugged handsomeness that the scar running down his left cheek did nothing to diminish.

A man to be reckoned with. A natural leader—you could see it in his carriage, in the confident, almost contemptuous set of the mouth. A man, who, in a different environment, might have risen high. And yet . . . no misfortune of parentage or background could explain why, at the age of twenty, he was leading a pathetic gang of callow teen-agers.

There must be something lacking in him. Eileen suspected it was intelligence. It was said nowadays that there was no relation between depth of brow and capacity of brain; but Eileen clung to the old superstition. By her standards Gammans must have an abnormally low I.Q.

He put down the coffee in front of Eileen. He himself was drinking Coca-Cola.

"Thanks, Mr. Gammans," said Eileen.

"Name's Joe."

She smiled. "Thanks, Joe."

He produced a crumpled packet of cigarettes.

"Fag?"

Eileen took one. He lit it, and his own, then as an afterthought offered the packet to Norah, who shook her head.

Eileen's cigarette tasted foul. Turkish, perhaps, or could it be—but no, this crowd weren't *vicious* enough for that.

"You're Ian Pratt's sister?" Gammans asked.

"Yes."

"You're no' much like him."

"Ian was adopted."

"Oh aye, so he was."

Gammans was sparring for position. Eileen could read his mind, or thought she could. His eyes kept shifting downwards from her face: he was puzzled as well as intrigued.

"You know, Joe," she said confidentially, "Ian thought you were tops."

"No kiddin'?" He preened himself. He *must* be stupid if he fell for that line.

"Aye, if he'd stuck wi' us," he added, "he'd 'a been a' right. If he'd just tell't us what he was up to, but I didn'y find out till too late. We thought it was a bird he was chasin'."

Here was her chance: he had brought up the subject himself. But she judged it was to soon. He must know she was here to pump him; she couldn't expect him to surrender so quickly and for so little reward. She hoped Norah wouldn't chip in here; but no, Norah was transfixed, struck dumb.

"Yes," said Eileen, "I dare say you're right. He'd got very secretive. He never told any of us at home either."

Gammans grinned. "Aye, well, can you blame him? Wi' a mum and dad like he had, eh?"

Gammans bent his head closer and dropped his voice. "Know something? It was me that straightened him out about his old man."

"What do you mean—'straightened him out'?"

"He used to mump about his Ma all the time. He didn'y know his old man was ten times worse." Then, seeing Eileen's puzzlement, he laughed. "For Christ sake, are you in the dark an' all? What sort of a bloody family are youse, anyway? Are youse all stone blind?"

Angus Pratt, he told her, had for years been carrying on an affair with Miss Macdonald, who owned The Shepherd's Bush, a pub in Edencraigs, the small town five miles inland from Silbridge.

Eileen wasn't shocked, nor even much surprised. It explained a lot.

Gammans had been edging his chair round, closing the gap between himself and Eileen. Now his hand was on the table moving towards hers. She didn't draw away: and she steeled herself not to flinch when his hand finally closed over hers.

Across the room a transistor radio roared into life. Gammans swung round angrily. "Shut that ——— noise off," he shouted.

Suddenly Eileen lost her fear of him. In turning round he had jerked her arm up so that it was obvious they were holding hands. He was playing to the gallery. He was as ill-at-ease as she; but he had his reputation to preserve.

The time was ripe now. "Joe," she said coaxingly.

"Uh-huh?"

"Ian thought such a lot of you, Joe. You'd like to help him wouldn't you?"

He grinned. "You cann'y do much for a stiff, can you?"

"Well, help *me*, then. To find out who killed him."

"The polis've been at me a'ready," he said warily. "Yon ———— Cameron, and Nicolson and that lot."

"What did you tell them?"

He snorted. "I tell't them ———— all, that's what I tell't them."

"But you'll tell me, Joe, won't you? *Please*, Joe." She squeezed his hand and smiled.

It was an elaborate charade they were acting. Joe Gammans might be stupid, but not to the extent of believing a girl like Eileen Pratt would throw herself at him within ten minutes of meeting him. He was attracted: she knew lust when she saw it. But he was nervous of her; Eileen was out of his class, beyond his experience. He was content to *appear* to be making a conquest.

Eileen recognised that if she had misread him, the consequences could be serious, and she would have herself to blame. It was a risk she was prepared to take.

Without too much prompting Gammans told her what he knew. Ian's unexplained absences on Wednesday evenings had roused jealousy and suspicion in Myra Thexford, who believed he was two-timing her. Eventually Gammans, at her request, set Lenny Ferguson on to following him. But Lenny lost him in the fog; and Ian was never seen again.

Ian himself, under pressure, had once told Myra he visited a teacher in the High School on Wednesdays. She hadn't believed him: he was given to teasing her, often in language she couldn't fully comprehend. However, weeks later—long after Ian had disappeared—a girl who lived near the school mentioned to Myra that she used to see him going into the school at night.

"Ian didn't say which teacher, did he?" Eileen asked.

Gammans snorted. "Christ, you want jam on it! No, he didn'y."

"Or *why* he went to see him?"

"No. . . . But it wasn'y what you're thinkin'. Ian wasn'y queer. No' like his pal, Lenny."

Eileen asked the name of the girl who had seen Ian go into the school at night. But Gammans jibbed at that. She didn't press the question, the police would trace the girl easily enough.

"Well, thanks a *million*, Joe."

"That's O.K." His right arm was now encircling her. Well, that was the price, still not too high. But when his hand threatened to become more adventurous, she gently disengaged herself.

"I have to go, Joe," she said regretfully. She glanced at Norah. "Time Norah was home."

He understood. And he bore no ill will. "Yeah, sure, baby. Sure." He raised his voice a fraction. "Well, I'll gie you a buzz, eh?"

Eileen took her cue. "Yes, do that, Joe. Silbridge 2298."

She had her coat on now and he was shepherding her to the door, his arm resting casually on her shoulder. Norah followed in a trance. The eyes of all the room were on them.

"S'long, then . . . Eileen"—he almost choked over the name—"See you."

FIVE

HAD IT been worth it? She had learned nothing new. Only what Inspector Nicolson already believed—that Ian had gone to the school on Wednesday evenings. To see a teacher. "Only"? Nicolson would be glad to have it confirmed. It was evidence he could probably never have elicited himself.

So much for the credit side. It had been won at a cost. Here was Norah, pressed as far along the seat of the car, away from Eileen, as she could, silent and disapproving.

"Do you think he'd have told *you* all that?" Eileen asked.

Norah didn't answer.

Eileen was tired now, and her headache was worse. She wanted to drop Norah and go home to bed. But she couldn't let her go like this; she must make the effort to explain. She stopped the car.

"I know what you're thinking, Norah," she said. "You think that was cheap and degrading. Perhaps it was. I'd do worse than that, though, to find out who killed Ian. . . . It was the only way. He'd never have talked otherwise. He had to shine in front of his gang."

Still Norah was silent.

Eileen couldn't keep exasperation from her voice. "Don't you understand at all, Norah?"

"He was such a—a *loathsome* man," Norah burst out.

"I've known worse," said Eileen shortly.

"And these others, with their long hair and their filthy language. Horrible, horrible."

"Ian didn't think so."

Norah sprang to his defence. "That was just a—a phase. You know what drove him to it. He didn't belong there, with these—these *scum*."

The self-righteous tone was an echo of her father, the Reverend George Shipstone, the exponent of muscular Christianity, the man who believed society wasn't nearly tough enough with its young hooligans. And constantly said so.

"They're human beings," Eileen said gently. "They need understanding and help."

It was no use, though. You couldn't change with one sentence a person's whole outlook and scale of values. You shouldn't even try.

Eileen sighed. "I'll take you home," she said, switching on the ignition. They drove back in silence.

As she got out of the car, Norah said awkwardly: "I'm sorry, Miss Pratt."

"What for?"

"For being rude. I'm sure you did what you thought best." She had obviously been practising the speech in the car.

Eileen didn't cavil at the ambiguous apology. "All right, Norah," she said. "Good night."

"Good night, Miss Pratt." And Norah scuttled through her gate as if the devil were at her heels.

Eileen was deflated. Her joust with Gammans had briefly recaptured for her the thrill of the footlights, her adolescent dream of a career on the stage. But the excitement of it had gone sour. She couldn't forget the hurt disillusionment on Norah's face.

It had been an impulse, an intuitive understanding of how she might get through to Joe Gammans. Eileen envied people who could resist such impulses, who could coolly evaluate the consequences and come down on the side of caution. She wasn't calculating enough.

Her instinct had been right: she had found probably the only means of persuading Gammans to talk. But long after that was forgotten, her brazenness would be a byword. Lenny Ferguson had been a spectator; and the tale would lose nothing in his telling of it. Nor was it agreeable to be despised by Norah Shipstone.

The urge to go home to bed had left her. She wanted to talk to Douglas.

He had been avoiding her. Two phone calls, and a brief word to-day in the staff room—these had been her only contacts with him since Sunday. And even then he hadn't stayed long.

Eileen knew the reason: the aura of death still clung to her; her brother's funeral was too fresh in the memory. A spineless creature, Douglas. Still, you couldn't write your own formula for the man you fell in love with; and Douglas had remarkable gifts of his own. And he loved her; all else paled before that.

It was 9.15 when Eileen drew up outside his door. He usually went out on a Wednesday, to a cinema or the theatre, sometimes to a pub. It was Eileen's night for visiting Fiona Cameron.

To-night, however, there was a light in his studio window. She rang the bell.

There was some delay before Douglas came to the door.

"Anything wrong?" he asked. He didn't sound overjoyed to see her.

"Not really. . . . Aren't you going to let me in?"

He hesitated, then stood aside to let her pass. "You should have let me know," he muttered peevishly. "I'm *working*."

Scattered on the studio floor were half-a-dozen crumpled, discarded sketches. On the easel was the finished drawing. Of a nude seated combing her hair. As with all Douglas's work the face was instantly recognisable: this was Jennifer Cowie, his favourite model.

From the kitchen came the clink of crockery. A girl's voice called: "I can't find the sugar, darling." A moment later she came into the studio.

Eileen hadn't met Jennifer Cowie before except on canvas. But she felt she had known her a long time—known and disliked her. She had the same little *gamine* face as her younger sister, Sandra. Not a beautiful face, not even pretty. And her figure—if Douglas presented it faithfully—was too thin, her legs too long. Yet the total effect, Eileen had to confess, was good.

Jennifer wore a dressing-gown, loosely tied at the front, and a pair of Douglas's slippers. She was carrying a tray with two cups of steaming Nescafé and a plate of biscuits. She stopped short when she saw Eileen. "I'd better make another cup, hadn't I?"

"Yes, Jenny," said Douglas, "you do that."

He turned to Eileen. "Let me take your coat, darling."

She shook her head. She wasn't going to compete with *that*.

"Well, sit down, anyway. . . . If you'd only *told* me, Eileen." Suddenly he grinned. "There are compensations in being an artist after all. This would be a tricky situation to explain otherwise."

Jennifer came back with Eileen's coffee.

"Sugar, Miss Pratt?" Her smile was cruel like Sandra's.

"No, thanks. . . . And call me Eileen." She smiled sweetly back.

Douglas sensed the undercurrents. "Girls, girls!" he said pacifically. "Put the claws back in. . . . We were just finished, weren't we, Jenny?"

146

Jennifer cocked her head quizzically at him. "Were we?" Then, glancing at the drawing on the easel: "Oh, that! . . . Yes."

She turned to Eileen. "We didn't expect you, Eileen. I thought you went to Fiona Cameron's on a Wednesday?"

The damned insolence! She was practically boasting that the modelling was a blind. Just as well Eileen could trust Douglas.

"I've been at Finghetti's," she said. "Talking to Joe Gammans."

"Who's Joe——" Douglas began, then corrected himself. "Oh, *him*. You've been slumming, have you?"

"Eileen's in the auxiliary C.I.D., didn't you know?" said Jennifer. "Personal assistant to Detective-Inspector Nicolson." She infused an insult into the word "personal."

"It was about Ian, was it?" Douglas asked.

"Yes." Eileen accepted a cigarette, her third to-day.

"I hoped you'd learned your lesson, darling. Once bitten, you know. . . . Why do you do it? From what one reads, every policeman in Scotland's been drafted into Silbridge. Do you think they need your services? That's intellectual arrogance, my girl."

It was to protect Norah that she'd gone to Finghetti's to-night. Or was it? So hard to be honest about your motives. This restless activity helped to silence her conscience. It gave her an excuse not to wrestle with her recollections of the night at the George Harbour. Her mind still shied from that.

Eileen wanted to talk to Douglas alone. But Jennifer, sprawled comfortably on the couch, her feet tucked under her, showed no inclination to go.

Eileen stubbed out her cigarette, not half smoked. This one tasted odd too; she must be ill.

"And did Mr. Gammans come up to expectations?" Douglas asked. Jennifer sniggered.

"He told me one or two things, yes."

"Such as?"

Eileen didn't answer, but stared meaningfully at the other girl.

"Don't mind me, Eileen. Douglas and I have no secrets from each other, have we, dear?" Her playful laugh took none of the sting out of the remark.

"Now, now, Jenny!" Douglas reproved her, but inattentively. He turned back to Eileen. "What did he tell you?"

Well, why not? "The man Ian saw on Wednesday nights was a teacher, and they met at the school."

"That would be Tom King, then," Jennifer said at once. "He's the only one who's ever there at nights. Unless you count old H.M."

Dr. Huddleston's house was in the school grounds, adjoining the tennis courts.

"Anyway," Jennifer was going on, "you're in the clear, Douglas. I'll give you an alibi for a Wednesday night any time you need it."

"Don't be a bloody little fool," said Douglas.

She wagged a finger at him. "Temper, temper! . . . Be a dear, Eileen, and give me my bag. . . . On the floor beside your chair. . . . Thanks."

It was an ornate plastic handbag, vulgar and pretentious. Eileen smiled grimly as she passed it over: Douglas, she knew, would share her opinion of it. Anyone who carried an object like that around must be devoid of taste. Perhaps that was why Douglas always painted her with her clothes *off*.

Jennifer took a tissue from her bag and dabbed her lips. "That was good," she said, putting her cup and saucer back on the tray.

Perhaps she would go and get dressed now, and take herself off. But no. "How about another fag, Rembrandt?" she said. Douglas tossed her the packet.

As he lit her cigarette, she said between puffs: "Don't be so snooty about the alibi. *You're* a teacher in the High School, remember." She returned to Eileen. "Don't worry, Eileen. I can vouch for him. I was *modelling* for him, you understand." She trilled with laughter.

Eileen stood up. "I've enjoyed our little chat, darling," she said dryly to Douglas.

"Don't rush off," he said. "Jenny's a bitch but she's harmless. Anyway, she's just going. *Aren't* you, precious?" He took hold of Jennifer's arm and tried to coax her to her feet.

She shook him off roughly. "I'll go when I'm good and ready," she said, scowling.

Eileen was already on her way out. "Good night, Jenny," she called over her shoulder. The girl didn't answer.

Douglas hurried after her. "I'm terribly sorry about this, Eileen, but——"

"I know. You weren't expecting me."

"Well, don't go all huffy, darling. I knew you two wouldn't mix. That's why I've always kept you apart."

"The mistress and the fiancée, you mean?"

From the studio Jennifer's voice called: "Douglas!"

"Shut up!" he shouted angrily. He turned back to Eileen. "You can't mean that, darling! You can't believe I'd get embroiled with a cheap little skate like that?"

"Why not? She has a body, hasn't she? That's all a mistress needs, I'm

148

told." Eileen's head was splitting. She felt the world was using her harshly, and she had to lash out at someone.

"Darling, *please*. You must believe me."

She pulled herself together, digging her nails into the palm of her hand. "I'm sorry, Douglas," she said wearily. "Yes, of course, I believe you."

"Thank God for that," he said: and kissed her.

"Douglas!" Jennifer's voice was petulant. "How long are you going to be out there?"

Eileen broke away. She laughed, half hysterically.

"Go in and paint her, Douglas," she said.

She did believe him. Douglas wouldn't deceive her: she trusted him absolutely.

All the same he should have sent that girl packing. He must have seen Eileen was desperate to talk to him alone. But, no, he let Jennifer stay and taunt her. Openly taunt her; and he didn't intervene. Protection was something Eileen wouldn't find in her marriage: she would have to fight her own battles.

The lounge window was lit when Eileen got back to Hughenden Road. Her father hadn't gone out, then. He would be at one of his chess problems, no doubt.

She stopped the car outside the gate. She couldn't face going in yet. She knew how her father would greet her. "You're back, then," he would say, without raising his eyes from the chess board. She would make him a cup of tea and he would say "Thank you, dear," and move his bishop. And, if he remembered, he would bid her good night when she went to bed.

Eileen was restless and miserable; she desperately needed company, a friendly voice. Douglas had let her down to-night. She thought of Fiona, but the hour was too late; and Allan would be there. She even considered calling on Maurice Nicolson—until she remembered how little she was wearing under her coat, and blushed. . . .

As she sat there in the car, her father's shadow passed across the window blind. Seeing him set Eileen thinking of The Shepherd's Bush and the woman he visited there. At once she was consumed with curiosity. She must go and see the place. It would be something to do, something to anaesthetise for a short time this aching depression . . . and for once she had the car.

SIX

TEN-THIRTY STRUCK as Eileen joined the hill road out of Silbridge and changed down to third for the long zig-zagging climb to Edencraigs. Certainly too late to call on Miss Macdonald. The pub would be closed half an hour ago, if the licensing hours in Edencraigs were the same as in Silbridge.

Not many things *were* the same in Edencraigs. It was a non-industrial community, a dormitory for the more affluent commuters to Glasgow and to Silbridge and a place for the elderly rich to retire to. One of the prettiest small towns in Scotland and very exclusive, although its future was threatened by the tentacles of suburbia stretching out from Silbridge on the one side and from Garnock on the other.

The Shepherd's Bush was on the main street next the post office. A long, low building in mock Tudor style. The walls had recently been painted and were gleaming white. The big oak door was shut.

Eileen parked the Morris on the other side of the street. A man and woman were talking outside the pub; farther down an elderly man was exercising his dog. Otherwise the street was deserted. Not like Silbridge at this hour; but there were very few *young* people in Edencraigs.

The couple outside The Shepherd's Bush said good night and the man walked briskly away. The woman hesitated, then crossed the street to the car. After peering at the number-plate, she came round to the driver's window. Eileen wound down the window.

"I thought it was his car," the woman said. Her voice was from the Highlands.

"You must be Miss Macdonald?" said Eileen.

"Just so. And you'll be Eileen, I'm thinking?"

They were sizing each other up. Not easy, in the dark.

"If you'd like to come in——"

They crossed the street and the woman opened the big door. The entrance to the bar was on the left; Miss Macdonald led Eileen through a door on the right.

She switched on the light. Eileen was vaguely conscious of a pleasant sitting-room.

But her eyes were on Miss Macdonald. She could hardly have been more surprised. Her face was lined and her hair almost white. She was thin, too—not slim, but *thin*, with the angular, sexless thinness of the elderly.

"I'll take your coat, Miss Pratt."

"No." Eileen felt her cheeks go hot. "No, thanks. . . . I'm a little shivery." It was true, though it wasn't why she kept her coat on.

Miss Macdonald looked at her. "You shouldn't be out," she said severely. "I'll make you a hot toddy. Sit you down."

"Please don't bother, Miss Macdonald."

But the woman had already gone out.

Eileen had time to take stock of her surroundings. There was a refreshing simplicity about this room. Chairs that were comfortingly inviting, subdued lighting, and an absence of ornamentation—the whole effect was restful. So different from the sitting-room at Hughenden Road.

On a small table stood a framed photograph of a young man in a kilt. A handsome youth—well, perhaps not *handsome*, the nose was too big —but a strong face and good figure.

There was something familiar about his features. Eileen crossed over to have a closer look. It was her father.

"He was eighteen when that was taken." Miss Macdonald had come in silently. "Just before he went to the university."

"You knew him then?"

"I've known him all my life. We grew up together. I was even—well, we were engaged, sort of."

Eileen looked at her again. Her father was—what?—forty-eight, forty-nine perhaps. Surely this woman was *older*.

"I'll be forty-nine in April," said Miss Macdonald dryly, reading her thoughts. "Your father has worn better, that's all. . . . Here, drink this while it's hot."

It was lemon and sugar, powerfully laced with whisky. The first mouthful felt like molten tar; but it stopped the shivers.

"You're pretty," said Miss Macdonald. "Prettier than your mother."

"You know my mother?"

"We've met."

Eileen sipped her drink. "You were telling me about your engagement," she remarked encouragingly.

The woman smiled. "I wasn't," she said.

Eileen believed you could read a person's character from his smile, by relating the mouth to the eyes. A smile could reveal the insincerity of Dr. Huddleston, the cruelty of Jennifer Cowie and her sister, the smugness of Tom King. Or it could reflect genuine kindliness and goodness. As did Miss Macdonald's.

"I wish you *would* tell me," said Eileen.

Miss Macdonald looked keenly at her. "It's not a pretty story," she said.

"Never mind. I've a right to hear it."

"Why?"

"He's my father."

The woman was still staring at her, puzzled. "He never told me what you were like," she said slowly. "He ought to have told me." She sighed. "All right. But remember, I'm prejudiced. You'd best be dividing by two everything I say. . . ."

Janet Macdonald attended the same village school as Angus Pratt. They played together as small children and even after Angus went to Inverness Academy, she continued to see him in the holidays. Their relationship ripened with the years and it was generally assumed in the village that they were "bespoke."

It was certainly so assumed by Janet. But when Angus came home from the University one Christmas vacation, it was with news of his engagement to Margaret Barr, a medical student.

There had been no warning; his letters to Janet had never mentioned the girl. He was secretive by nature and it was characteristic of him to say nothing until his mind was made up.

Janet was deeply hurt and humiliated. She left the village, where she had been helping her mother in the post office and general store, and took a post in Aberdeen. When war broke out she joined the W.A.A.F.

She ran into Angus in Cairo in 1944. She let him take her for dinner. Seven years had passed since he jilted her: it was too long to harbour a grudge, especially in the emotional climate of a war.

Angus drank more than was good for him that night. He confessed that his marriage had been a mistake. He had been carried away by Margaret's vivaciousness and sophistication: he hadn't seen how little lay behind it. He was almost dreading the end of the war, when they would be reunited.

Angus wanted to go to bed with Janet that night. She refused. The invitation was too casual, the outcome of sentiment and intoxication. Besides, it would have been unfair to Margaret. Janet didn't know Margaret at that time. . . .

Although their paths didn't cross again for three years, Janet no longer thought of Angus with hatred, only with regret. They corresponded in a desultory way. Angus invited her more than once to stay at the poultry farm—"Margaret would love to have you," he always said.

Janet refused these invitations. She recognised the potential danger of the situation, for she was still in love with Angus. She preferred not to put her self-control to the test.

After the war Janet had taken a post as a counter assistant in a big Glasgow store. It was there that she met Margaret Barr.

Margaret knew about "the girl from home," and was jealous of her. She made Angus tell her where Janet worked, and went to Glasgow to see her.

She was all sweetness and warmth. She insisted that Janet, as an old friend of her husband, must come and stay with them in Galloway. Janet was not deceived: she guessed the invitation was loaded; but the temptation was too great. She arranged to spend her fortnight's holiday that year at the farm. The autumn of 1947.

"I remember that," Eileen broke in.

"But you were just a child."

"I was seven. I remember you. You slept in the bedroom in the attic and you used to make clothes for my doll." It was coming back now. She had liked "Aunt Janet," who always had time to play with her. Then there had been the night with all the shouting, and her mother in hysterics, and next morning Aunt Janet was gone. Annette and Eileen had written it off as one more instance of the inexplicable behaviour of grown-ups.

"There was a row, wasn't there?" Eileen said now.

Janet looked at her compassionately. "It was a terrible thing we did, your father and I, but she—she *engineered* it all. She wanted it to happen. She wasn't sane, even then."

Janet found relations between Angus and his wife at breaking point. Margaret nagged him constantly, in front of her, even in front of the children. She desperately wanted a son, and she took it out on her husband because she couldn't have one.

Every night she would retire early to bed, setting the stage for a seduction scene. The release of tension on her departure made the temptation almost irresistible. One night—about the middle of Janet's second week at the farm—they succumbed. And Margaret caught them *in flagrante delicto*. Her trap had been sprung.

Janet, of course, had to go. But from Margaret's point of view she was only a pawn in the game. Margaret now had what she needed: a bargaining counter. Her terms were simple: Angus must sell the farm and move back to civilisation; and he must agree to their adopting a son. Until then he had firmly refused to do either.

"Why did he agree?" Eileen asked. "Why didn't he just leave her? It wasn't because of his family. He never took any interest in Annette or me."

"Just so. You and your sister were tarred with your mother's brush. He's a powerful hater, is Angus. . . . He didn't leave her because—

well, because it didn't suit him to lose his respectability. Your father's never for doing anything that doesn't suit him." Janet was smiling, but there was a trace of bitterness in her voice.

Angus had extracted one concession from his wife. He could continue to see Janet Macdonald, so long as he was discreet and there was no scandal. Margaret agreed to this in the belief that it would consolidate her hold over him; in the event, it was his salvation.

In one other respect Angus turned the bargain to his advantage, this time without his wife's knowledge. Margaret, who had no head for business, believed him when he said he had sold the poultry farm at a heavy loss.

"In fact," said Janet, "it was the money he made from the sale that bought this pub."

Eileen was shocked. "He set you up in business here?"

"It's all been paid back. I made him treat it as a loan. . . . He wanted me near him. Not in the same town, but near him."

It was perhaps a speculative stroke, because Janet had no experience of running a pub. But they engaged a good barman and Janet's native shrewdness did the rest.

For more than fifteen years Angus, with his wife's connivance, had visited Janet at least once a week. Occasionally Janet's conscience troubled her, but not often. Angus's marriage was a failure and nothing could have saved it; all she was doing was to make life tolerable. For her own part the arrangement was an acceptable compromise. If she couldn't have Angus to herself, this at least was preferable to grinding out an unrewarding spinsterhood in Glasgow. Running her own business absorbed her; and she schooled herself to be indifferent to the occasional sniggers and half-heard remarks about her in the bar.

To begin with it was an affair in the accepted sense. But as the years went by, it was companionship Angus looked for rather than passion.

"You get past that sort of thing," Janet remarked. "Women especially. Angus still has his fling elsewhere from time to time, but that doesn't bother me. This is like home to him—his real home. We sit and relax, just chatting, you know, or listening to the wireless."

"What about the bar? Don't you have to——"

"Dermott attends to that—the man you saw me talking to to-night. And his wife helps out. I just look in occasionally to let them see that I'm there. . . . No, I can sit here with Angus all evening if I want. It's very peaceful."

Eileen guessed that she was idealising the relationship. Janet looked older than her years, and unsure of herself. For all her protestations she probably had many a turbulent session with her conscience: her upbringing in a tight little Highland community would see to that. Moreover, Angus Pratt couldn't have been the easiest of companions; he was basically a selfish man, and even the favourable climate of The Shepherd's Bush wouldn't change him.

Eileen ought, perhaps, to have suspected something of this sort years ago. But her father's habit of going out one or two nights a week "to meet his friends," as he put it, or "on the booze," as her mother used to mutter darkly, had grown up with Eileen and it never occurred to her to question it. Not until these last few weeks. And all the time her mother had known. . . .

"Tell me, Eileen," said Janet hesitantly. "Suppose your father were to—well, to move in here, how would you feel about it?"

"He's practically moved in already, hasn't he? I never see him." She hadn't meant to sound so aggressive.

"Do you *want* to see him? Does he mean anything to you?"

"He's my father." Eileen knew she was being unreasonable. This was the sort of thing Douglas constantly pulled her up for: woman's logic, as he called it. There was no bond between her and her father; they disliked and despised each other. Living in the same house could only be irksome to them both. Yet still she felt aggrieved that he should go.

Janet sighed. "Just so. . . . Anyway, he's not very willing himself. He's a terribly *respectable* man, your father."

Well, that was one word for it.

"Do the police know about this?" Eileen asked.

"Oh yes. A Mr. Cameron came out last week to talk to me. Angus had told him about—about us."

So the only person who didn't know was his daughter.

Eileen took out a handkerchief and mopped her brow.

"Are you all right, Eileen?" Janet's voice was anxious.

"Yes, I'm all right." Only hot and tired and depressed, with throbbing head and aching back. . . . Perfectly all right.

"When's the wedding?" Janet asked. "Angus told me you were engaged."

"Date's not fixed yet. Early summer, we hope."

"He's a teacher, isn't he?"

"Art master in the High School."

Silence. Then, articulating carefully, Janet said: "Not Douglas Troup?"

"Yes. Do you know him?"

"I've heard of him." Her tone was flat.

Eileen waited, then said, with slight impatience: "Well, Miss Macdonald?"

"I'm sorry, Eileen. I shouldn't have spoken. It's none of my business."

"You can't leave it there now." Eileen was angry.

Janet bent down to poke the fire. "All right. . . . Has he ever spoken of Alison Wright?"

"No. Who's Alison Wright?"

"The daughter of a friend of mine. *She* knew Douglas Troup. She has his child."

"I don't believe it!"

Janet shrugged. "As you please. . . . There's an affiliation order against him."

Eileen stood up. A moment of dizziness made her grip the back of her chair.

Janet came quickly across. "Are you sure you're——"

"I'm perfectly well, thank you," Eileen snapped. Then she relented. It wasn't Janet's fault: she was only the bearer of the news, not its author. "I'm sorry, Miss Macdonald," she said contritely. "I'm not myself tonight. How long ago was it?"

"The child's three and a half."

Self-pity was a luxury Eileen didn't allow herself. She had seen it so often, and despised it, in her mother.

But to-night, as she drove home from Edencraigs, she was wallowing in it. She couldn't help herself. What she had just heard about Douglas had been the last straw.

The story might, of course, be false; but Janet Macdonald didn't seem the kind of woman to spread unconfirmed tittle-tattle.

Only four years ago—that was what stuck in Eileen's throat. Douglas had once confessed that he had sown a wild oat or two when he was still at school. Since then, he assured her, he had never strayed from the straight and narrow.

If he deceived her over that, could she trust him in anything? She thought of Jennifer Cowie, padding about in his slippers, making his coffee, calling him "darling." True, she had been trying to impress Eileen, but all the same . . . there had been something *possessive* about her that hinted at more than a professional relationship between artist and model.

Eileen had put the Morris away in the garage when the significance of the car standing on the road outside, with its sidelights on, struck her. She went back to have a closer look.

It was a black police car. A uniformed policeman was nodding gently over the wheel.

SEVEN

THEY WERE in the sitting-room, Inspector Nicolson, Sergeant Cameron and her father.

Eileen saw the look of concern on Maurice Nicolson's face.

"Are you all right, Miss Pratt?" he said.

Eileen looked at herself in the mirror above the fireplace. Lord, no wonder they all kept asking. Her face was the colour of chalk.

"I'd like a drink," she said. She sat down.

"Where have you been, Eileen?" her father asked.

She looked at him coldly. "At The Shepherd's Bush in Edencraigs."

"Oh aye?" Apparently unconcerned, he ambled to the door. "I'll be getting your drink. Whisky, eh? And a spot of the craitur for you, gentlemen?"

They declined. Pratt went out.

"You ought to be in bed, Miss Pratt," said Nicolson.

Eileen shrugged. "You've been waiting for me?"

"Yes. It won't take long. If you're sure you feel up to it?"

She nodded. She was past caring now.

Nicolson took a folded sheet from his pocket and handed it to her. "Don't look at it yet," he said quickly. The results of the house-to-house inquiry had now been analysed. He described the machinery—Eileen heard, through a fog, the words "controls" and "punched cards" and "Powers-Samas." She grasped the essential fact that on the slip of paper she now held were the names of the only seven men in Silbridge who might have murdered her brother.

Her father came back carrying two glasses. He handed one to Eileen and took the other over to his chair beside the table with the chess board.

As he made to sit down, Nicolson said quickly: "Do you mind, sir? We'd rather like to talk to your daughter alone."

Pratt seemed about to protest but thought better of it. "Well, it's past my bed-time anyway . . . 'Night, Eileen." And he drifted out, still carrying his drink.

"You mean," said Eileen, "that these are the only seven with no alibi for the night Ian was killed?"

She sipped her drink and grimaced. The whisky must be almost *neat*.

"Rather more than that," said Nicolson. "We assume it's the same man who killed Lucia Finghetti and your brother and who tried to murder you. And that it's the same man your brother visited on each of the five Wednesdays before his death."

A prickle of doubt entered Eileen's mind. "Go *slower*," she wanted to say. "Give me it step by step."

But Nicolson was continuing: "On that hypothesis, there are only seven men in Silbridge who could possibly——"

"Only four, really," Cameron interrupted.

Nicolson nodded. "Yes, as Allan says, three of them can almost certainly be crossed off, though it's not watertight. That leaves four."

He spoke formally, as if he were giving a Police College lecture. Eileen guessed that he was trying to lighten her ordeal by taking any personal element out of it. Or perhaps it was his *own* feelings he had to keep under control.

"You said, Miss Pratt," Nicolson continued, "that your assailant was someone you know. The shock of seeing his name may jog your memory. . . . That's why we're here to-night."

Eileen slowly unfolded the paper. She fumbled a little—the effect of the whisky, probably. Or perhaps excitement.

"The top four names are the probables," Nicolson was saying.

Eileen read the other three names first, screwing up her eyes to bring the page into focus. "Wilfred Anderson, Frederick McLaren, Joseph Smith." The names meant nothing to her, unless perhaps Frederick McLaren was Freddie, the teller in the Royal Bank. But his surname was McLaggan, wasn't it?

She took a gulp of her whisky, then forced herself to look at the upper group of four names, her heart thumping wildly. "Edward Huddleston, John Laird, Thomas King, Thomas Richardson."

Eileen was conscious of anti-climax, of a feeling of—what was it?—disappointment? relief? A name her subconscious had expected was not there.

The others were watching her expectantly.

"I only know Tom King and Dr. Huddleston," she said flatly. "Are you sure it has to be one of these two?"

"One of these *four*," Cameron corrected her.

"I don't *know* the other two," Eileen said impatiently. "Besides, they're not teachers in the High School."

Cameron grunted. "Aye, well, we've only your impression it's somebody you know."

Nicolson ignored him. "I take it, then, Miss Pratt," he said, "the experiment has failed? We haven't unlocked the door for you?"

Eileen shook her head.

"We'll not keep you, then. And please——"

"It was a teacher, though," she interrupted. "It was a teacher Ian went to see on Wednesday nights." She recounted what Joe Gammans had told her.

She had the curious sensation of being detached from her body, of standing aside and watching and listening to herself speak. This must be the extreme of tiredness; or else she was drunk.

She was watching Nicolson too, watching the look of concern under the polite, official mask. She was grateful for it.

But all he said was: "Well, thank you, Miss Pratt, that's been most helpful." His voice seemed to come from a great distance. "Please don't get up. We'll see ourselves out."

She listened to the front door close; moments later a car started up and drove off.

She lay back in her chair and closed her eyes. In a minute, in five minutes, she would force herself to go upstairs to bed. . . .

"Not even got your coat off yet?" Her father's voice wakened her. She sat up, startled. "What time is it?"

"After two o'clock. I never heard you come upstairs and I wondered. . . ."

He was in his pyjamas and that shabby, grey dressing-gown. Did he have a more glamorous one at The Shepherd's Bush, Eileen wondered hysterically.

"Should you not be in bed?" he asked. Then without waiting for an answer: "Did you see Janet to-night?"

She winced as the pain shot through her head.

"Janet?"

"At The Shepherd's Bush."

"Yes, I saw her."

"How did you find out?"

"For God's sake, Father, not to-night! I've had enough."

"I wouldn't be wanting you to get the wrong impression, Eileen. You see, your mother——"

"Yes, yes, I got the whole romance from Miss Macdonald. And now——"

"Ian liked her."

He had said about the only thing that could have caught her attention.

"Ian? Did *he* know?" But of course he did. Somebody had told her that already to-night. Gammans, probably.

"Aye, just so. He was a wee bit upset at first. But when he met Janet, he soon came round."

How Ian must have changed! Time was when he had doted on his mother. It was unthinkable that he should countenance his father's mistress. But afterwards—after he learned about his adoption. . . . Yes, looking back now, Eileen recalled that there had developed latterly between Ian and his adoptive father a bond of—well, not affection, for Angus was incapable of it—but mutual tolerance. Reaction against the mother. Recognition, perhaps, that both in their different ways had been her victims.

Eileen looked at her father with renewed interest. It was so easy to dismiss him as a self-centred introvert—as indeed he was. But he was intelligent; and even an introvert had eyes to see what was going on around him.

"Father," she said, "have you any theory about all this?"

"All what?"

"About who murdered Ian?"

He took a long time to answer. "Aye," he said. "I've my own ideas about that."

"Yes?" she prompted him.

There was a strange expression on his face. If she hadn't known him, she would have said it was compassion. "I'd rather not be saying," he replied. "Like as not it's wrong."

She didn't press him. She was afraid to press him.

"I was wondering, Eileen," he said, "now you know about Janet, how would it do if I was to be moving in with her? Go and stay there, I mean. Would you mind very much?"

This was what he had come down to ask. Nothing—neither Eileen's tiredness nor speculation about Ian's murder—must be allowed to divert him from it.

Eileen's brief moment of sympathy was gone.

"I'd be delighted, Father," she said.

EIGHT

IT WAS almost noon when Eileen woke. Her head ached when she sat up in bed. But she felt cool and refreshed: last night's fever was gone.

Downstairs the telephone was ringing; probably it had wakened her. She pulled on a dressing-gown and ran down to answer it.

"Where in God's name have you been, darling?" Douglas's voice was anxious. "I've been ringing and ringing."

"I was tired. I overslept."

"Are you feeling better? You looked ghastly last night."

"Much better, thank you." She was trying to keep her voice neutral, but the resentment must have shown through.

"You're not still sulking, are you? Honestly, darling, you're the most *unreasonable*—Here, what about lunch? We'll straighten it out over lunch."

"No, thank you, Douglas," she said formally.

She heard him swear under his breath. She expected him to hang up: Douglas was not one to persist when his olive branch had been rejected.

But no. He continued: "You missed all the drama down here this morning."

She caught her breath. "How do you mean?"

"They've been giving your colleague, King, the third degree. All the top brass. Mearns, Nicolson, the lot. Even an old codger with whiskers that I think must be the chief constable."

"Are they still there?"

"No, they marched him off half an hour ago."

"They've arrested him?"

"Well, he wasn't actually in *handcuffs*, darling."

Why did the news depress her? Depress her even more than the festering suspicion of Douglas's unfaithfulness?

"Hallo! Are you still there?" he said anxiously.

"Yes."

"When shall I see you? Are you coming in this afternoon?"

"I might," she said, and rang off.

She had doubts, that's what was wrong. Doubts of King's guilt. He fitted all the facts known about the killer: he was a teacher in the High School; he had known Lucia Finghetti; and he had no alibi for any of the relevant times. Moreover, psychologically he was a credible murderer. Yet Eileen was almost certain King was not the man who had chased her along the dock's edge and thrown her into the water. If now the police were going to arrest him, she would have to do something about it. . . .

Breakfast or lunch? She compromised by heating soup and following it with a bacon sandwich and coffee.

She took her coffee over to the dining-room window. It was a cold, bright day. Although the sun had been shining for hours, there was still frost on the roof-tops. The air was so clear and still that she could see smoke rising straight up from chimneys on the houses across the river.

The one o'clock hooter from Bryant's yard sounded; usually you couldn't hear it at this distance. There was the steady drone of cars in

161

low gear climbing the hill past the hospital. The white-collar workers coming home for lunch.

Eileen was irresolute. Her instinct was to stay home, to let events take their course. Douglas had described her interference as intellectual arrogance. Perhaps he was right.

Last night was like a bad dream: she had no wish to resurrect it. It was so much easier to stay on the wings. And safer. She still had a presentiment of danger.

She had also, however, a restless conscience.

It was 1.20 when she put her bicycle in the cycle shed. The playground was almost empty. But one or two boys, who must have gobbled their lunch, were already sliding down the icy track that had been formed on the frosted tarmac near the headmaster's house.

Eileen entered the school by the side door and climbed the stair to the gymnasium. A smell of stale tobacco hung about. From Chief Inspector Mearns's pipe, probably.

She knocked on Tom King's door and tried the handle. It was locked. She muttered a frustrated imprecation.

There was a master key to all the rooms. The janitor had one; so had the headmaster. . . .

Eileen went through the swing doors and along the deserted corridor towards the administrative offices, her heels clip-clopping on the tiled floor. Nervously she knocked on the outer door, went through Miss Macrae's room, knocked again on the door of the inner sanctum.

A voice called: "Come in."

Eileen almost panicked. He *couldn't* be here at this time. He always crossed to his house at one o'clock and came back at two. You could set your watch by him.

Fighting down her consternation, Eileen went in. Easy enough to invent some excuse for calling.

"A melancholy occasion," said Dr. Huddleston, vaguely indicating a chair. "I thought I'd call the school together after lunch and say just a few words. I've been roughing out some notes." He pointed to a manuscript on his desk.

"I don't understand," said Eileen.

He looked at her as if only now realising who she was. "I beg your pardon, Miss Pratt. The news came through just on one o'clock. Poor old Bradley passed away this morning."

"Oh no!" A picture of the pathetic little hunched figure in the hospital came back to Eileen.

"A merciful release, I'm given to understand." He shook his head sadly. "It's a reminder of our mortality, Miss Pratt. We all have our own appointed day, as it were." He paused for a respectful moment or two, then said briskly: "And now, what can we do for you?"

"It doesn't matter," Eileen muttered. "Some other time."

"Not at all, not at all. I've finished this." He indicated his manuscript obituary. "Short and simple, that's what Bradley would have wanted."

Eileen could almost hear Bradley's sardonic snort.

"Yes, Miss Pratt," Huddleston continued, "in my position one acquires the faculty of switching one's mind instantly to a new subject. Already to-day I've dealt with two crises—first the business of the unfortunate King and now this." He smiled. "I'm sure your problem can be solved too."

"As a matter of fact," said Eileen abruptly, "it concerns Tom King."

The smile never wavered. "Oh yes?"

"I understand the police have——"

He nodded vigorously. "Yes, indeed. They've taken him to the police station for further questioning. That's the formula, isn't it? . . . I don't mind telling you, I've had my suspicions of King."

"You did tell me, Dr. Huddleston. Yesterday."

"Did I?" He was pleased. "Bless my soul, so I did. . . . But I'm digressing. You were saying, Miss Pratt?"

Boldly she told him the truth. "I came to borrow your master key. I wanted to go into Tom King's room."

Her words had at last obliterated the headmaster's smile. "Did you indeed?" he said frostily, picking an invisible thread from the lapel of his immaculate grey suit. "And if I wasn't here, you were going to *take* the key?"

"I'm sorry, Dr. Huddleston. But, you see,"—she had to engage his interest—"I had to get in while he wasn't there."

"May one ask why?"

"To examine his thesis. To find out why he doesn't want me to read it."

"Authors are apt to be coy," he suggested.

"This wasn't coyness: this was fear."

The challenge was too tempting for the headmaster. He took a key from the drawer of his desk. "Come, Miss Pratt," he said.

He rationalised as they traversed the corridor together. "A Ph.D. thesis," he remarked, "should be a contribution to the general store of knowledge. The *general* store. It's wrong to lock it away where others may not benefit." Huddleston would have found justification for robbing a bank.

The thesis lay on the desk where Eileen had last seen it. King had clearly been at work on it, proof correcting. He was about half-way through.

The thesis itself was short: not much more than a hundred pages. But there were voluminous appendices.

"I'll start at the beginning," said Huddleston, settling himself in King's chair. "You can look at these charts and things." He thrust the appendices across the desk.

Silence while they read. Within two minutes Eileen knew her task was hopeless. There were masses of statistics on these sheets: tables of measurements, times, distances: graphs with intersecting red, green and black curves. On one page her eye caught the fatal words "differential calculus." Her mind reeled as it always did in the presence of even the most elementary mathematics.

Besides, she wasn't comfortable here. It was one thing to read a man's private papers in the hope of finding evidence in his favour; the headmaster, she knew, was looking for evidence *against* him, for clues the police had missed.

He was reading quickly, laying each page tidily on the desk as he finished it. It was impossible to tell what he thought of it: his face had settled into its customary expression of benign smugness.

The school bell interrupted him. He started, looked at his watch. "Dear me," he said mildly.

He gathered the sheets together, tapped them on the desk to make them even, and stood up.

"We'd better lock the door again," he said, waiting for Eileen to precede him.

She didn't move. "May I read it?" she said, indicating the thesis, which he had put back on the desk.

Huddleston hesitated. "Why not?" he said at length. "I don't think our colleague will be back to disturb you. Give the key to Miss Macrae when you're finished." At the door he paused, and added: "With all due respect, Miss Pratt, I fear the point may elude you. It's rather subtle in its way." He went out.

Eileen began to read. The first chapter defined the scope of the inquiry, summarised previous work on the subject, and outlined the methods King had used to obtain his results. Eileen had finished the chapter before the most significant feature of it struck her: the perfection of style. It was written with an economy and precision of words that pleased and astonished her. So unlike the pompous, cliché-ridden language in which Tom King couched his departmental correspondence.

She read on, and soon the conviction grew that King was not the author. The narrative flowed smoothly and easily, each sentence leading logically and inevitably to the next.

If King didn't write it, who did? The answer wasn't difficult. She remembered a remark on her brother's last report card: ". . . a remarkable feeling for language." This was how Ian wrote—even to the use of the semi-colon. It had been his one idiosyncrasy: he tended to overwork the semi-colon. Tom King, on the other hand, had never found the need for a semi-colon in his life.

This must have been what Ian was doing these Wednesday nights in school. Writing King's thesis for him. But *why?*

"Enjoying it?"

Eileen jumped, scattering the type-written sheets. Tom King stood in the doorway, staring at her.

"I'm sorry, Tom," she said. "I'm only trying to help."

"To help! You've been spying on me, the lot of you. I'll not forget." He laughed angrily. "Gave you a shock, though, didn't I? You thought I'd be behind bars, eh?"

"I'm glad——"

"Don't give me that. You all think I did it, don't you? You all think——"

"Tom, I *know* you didn't."

That stopped him.

"What are you up to, then?" he asked suspiciously.

She didn't answer directly. "Ian wrote this, didn't he?" she said, indicating the thesis.

"What do you mean? That's my thesis. *I* wrote it."

"Don't be a fool, Tom. You didn't write this. And I'd bet my last dollar Ian did."

King pursed his lips mulishly and said nothing.

"Oh, for God's sake!" she said impatiently. "Why do I bother?" She stood up and stalked to the door.

"All right," he said, defeated. "But all your brother did was improve the grammar. I mean, I'm not asking for the degree for my *grammar*, am I? The real work's all *mine.*"

King's story was not very coherent, mainly because he was at pains to play down Ian's contribution. Eileen had constantly to interpret and adjust from her knowledge of King's character, and of Ian's.

So far as she understood it, the thesis was concerned with the physiological effect of exercise in the development of muscles. Ian had been one of the numerous guinea pigs for the experimental work. Unlike the other recruits, Ian was not content to be passive research material and even, Eileen gathered, made some useful suggestions. His interest dropped, however, as in most other things, after the row with his mother over his adoption.

King was ready to begin writing the thesis last September. But he found, as others have found before him, that this was not the easy part of research. Indeed the task was beyond him: after six weeks he had made no progress. Eileen suspected that grammar and syntax were not, as he claimed, the main stumbling-blocks. He had too *much* material, it was too intractable. He lacked the orderly brain to marshal his evidence in logical sequence.

In despair he called on Ian Pratt for help. Ian was the one person who understood what he was trying to do and who had the intellectual and linguistic gifts that were needed. King offered him ten guineas if he would collaborate in the writing without revealing his part in it.

Ian agreed. Why? Eileen wondered. Not for the money. At that time—last October and November—Ian was liberally supplied with funds from some other source. No, the project must have caught his imagination.

So he started spending Wednesday evenings with King in the school. He kept his promise to tell no one what he was doing. He wouldn't want to anyway. Gammans and his friends would have derided him.

"Did he finish the thesis?" Eileen asked.

King frowned. "I told you, Eileen, Ian didn't *write* it, we did it together."

"All right, did you finish it together?"

"No. He—we were on the final chapter. He was supposed to come that foggy night, the night he——"

Eileen stared at him. "You were expecting him here that night?"

"Yes. But he never turned up. I had to finish it off myself later on." He sounded as if he still bore a grudge.

"What time did you expect him?"

"He usually came at the back of eight and stayed till after eleven. But he'd told me he couldn't stay late that night. There wasn't much left to do anyway."

"How long did you wait for him?"

"Till about nine o'clock."

"You didn't hear anything, did you?"

"Not a sound."

King had been shaken by his ordeal at the police station. That was evident not only from his unaccustomed pallor but from the way he was allowing Eileen to dominate the conversation. He hadn't yet reminded her he was head of the department. . . .

"Tom, what was Ian like when he was here with you?" In the last four or five weeks of his life Ian was supposed to be blackmailing a murderer. Strange time to write somebody's thesis for him.

"Very efficient," King admitted grudgingly. "A quick worker."

"I don't mean that. Did he seem worried?"

He considered it. "Tense, I'd have said. Wound up. Sometimes I thought he was just doing the job to keep his mind off something else."

That sounded plausible.

"How much of all this have you told the police?" Eileen asked.

For the first time he smiled. "Nothing. That's what the lawyers always advise."

"Suppose they charge you. What then?"

"We'll cross that bridge when we come to it."

The swing doors creaked and there was the chatter of boys' voices and the tramp of feet across the gymnasium to the changing room.

King looked out. "That's my class," he said, glancing at his watch. "I'll have to——"

He broke off in astonishment. "It's half past two!" he exclaimed. "Where have they *been* all this time?"

"The headmaster was addressing them in hall," said Eileen. "About Mr. Bradley. He died this morning."

"Did he really? Poor old chap! His number was up, of course, but I didn't expect it so soon."

Eileen saw the gleam in his eye, the straightening of the shoulders. This was the kind of news to restore his confidence.

"Just shows you!" he said sententiously. "You can't play old Harry with your lungs and get away with it. Well, Eileen, if you don't mind." The noise outside his door was getting louder.

"Yes." She stood up. "I think you ought to know, Tom," she said carefully, "that I'm going straight to the police station."

"Listen to me, Eileen." He moved swiftly to the door and barred her way. "I've sweated my guts out for four years for this degree and I'm not having it snatched away now. If you say one word to *anybody* about——"

"Get out of my way, Tom."

"Not till you promise——"

"Oh, shut up!" she said impatiently. "I don't care whether you get a Ph.D. or a knighthood. I want to find out who murdered Ian, that's all I want."

She pushed past him, and he didn't resist. But as she opened the door, he muttered: "Well, by God, I hope you do, Eileen, I hope you do!"

Eileen was crossing to the bicycle shed when she was hailed from the car park. It was Dr. Summers, at the wheel of his Anglia. She went over to him.

"May I offer you a lift, Miss Pratt?" he said, raising a metaphorical hat. "I'm going into town."

"Thank you," she said. It was, although she didn't know it, a fateful decision.

She liked Summers. A gentle, donnish man. One of the few who had refused to take offence at Bradley's acid tongue. A faithful visitor at the hospital, he was genuinely upset by his colleague's death. He was on his way to the post office, he explained, to send a telegram to Mrs. Bradley.

"But they've been separated for *years*," Eileen exclaimed.

"I think she ought to be told all the same."

"Surely the hospital——"

He shook his head. "Arthur told them he was a widower. I'm the only one who's kept in touch. My wife and I used to know them both. A great pity it was, a great pity. . . ."

Eileen asked to be dropped at the police station.

"Any news yet?" he said as he pulled up.

"No."

"A tragic business, that. Tragic. You know, Miss Pratt, Arthur Bradley and I scarcely agreed about anything; sometimes he wasn't *tolerant* enough, I felt. But on the subject of your brother we were of the same mind. One of the most gifted boys we've ever taught. And basically an extremely nice one."

"The police say he was a blackmailer," Eileen blurted out.

Summers was shocked. "Oh no, Miss Pratt, not that! You musn't believe that."

"I'm afraid not, miss," said Sergeant Cubitt, leaning on the desk. Leaning *over* the desk, almost. Eileen guessed that he approved of her legs.

"They're in Conference," he added, his voice giving the word a capital. "With the chief constable."

"Mr. Cameron, then?" Eileen almost hoped the answer would be no.

But Allan Cameron was available. She was taken along a corridor to a bare rectangular room, with a table and some wooden chairs.

As always her hackles rose a little when she saw Cameron coming in. No reason for it: a natural antipathy. And the feeling was mutual. It was worse now since his outburst that night against Maurice Nicolson. The memory of that indiscretion would always lie uneasily between them.

"I've been talking to Tom King," Eileen said without preamble.

"Have you, now?"

"He told me something you ought to know."

Cameron frowned. "I wish you'd keep out of this, Eileen."

"I can't help myself, Allan. I feel—well, *responsible*. I ought to have recognised the man that night."

He shrugged. "All right, then, what did King say?"

She told him. The gleam in his eye declared his interest.

"He admitted Ian went to see him every Wednesday?"

"Yes."

"And that he'd an appointment with him for the night of the murder?"

"Yes. Ian never turned up."

"Aye, well, maybe." Cameron was sceptical. "Anyway, thanks, Eileen. That's useful. He wasn't so frank with us." He was shepherding her to the door.

Eileen was irritated. Cameron plainly regarded her evidence as corroboration of the case against Tom King.

"I'd like to talk to Inspector Nicolson," she said firmly. "Can't you interrupt him, just for two minutes?"

Cameron flushed and said stonily: "I'm afraid not. But I'll give him your message. If you can trust me to do that."

She did see Nicolson, though. As she crossed the duty room towards the exit, Inspector Mearns's door opened and Nicolson came hurrying out, pulling on his coat. He almost collided with Eileen.

"I beg your pardon," he said: then smiled when he recognised her. "How are you? You look better to-day."

"Maurice——" she began.

"Sorry. Must dash. Talk to Allan Cameron." Then, as an afterthought. "And listen, Eileen. No more of last night's nonsense. Stay home to-night. Don't be tempted out for *anything*." And he was gone.

It was 3.40. Hardly worth going back to school except that she had left her bicycle there. She decided that if a 3A bus came first, she would take it and pick up her bicycle; but if it was a 6, she would go straight home. It was a 6. The workings of fate are seldom obvious at the time. . . .

NINE

Four-fifteen. Two hours at least till her father would be home. Eileen knew the time had come to face the issue she had shirked so long. She must retrace that night at the harbour, every second of it.

Even now she procrastinated. She would get her cigarettes first from the kitchen. She glanced into Ian's room as she passed. There was Rusty asleep on the floor beside the bed—where he had always slept when Ian was alive.

The sight of the dog stiffened Eileen's resolution. She settled in an arm-chair in the lounge with a cup of tea and a cigarette, shut everything else from her mind, and turned back the clock. . . .

At once the pain and horror of it came surging back. The shock of her father's message, the back-breaking pedalling into the wind and rain, the eerie blackness and silence of the harbour, the ticking wheels and the flickering lamp as she followed the rails along the dock side. And then that other sound that warned her she wasn't alone. The trouser leg and black shoe. The chase. The rasping breath. The blow on the head, and those powerful hands gripping her.

All this Eileen could remember clearly and contemplate without panic. Up to there, she felt sure, there had been nothing to indicate the man was someone she knew.

And afterwards? The struggle for survival in the icy water, the desperate clinging to the rubber tyre. And the man walking up and down above her. The thought of that sent a shiver through Eileen. A shiver of horror. Because that was when she had recognised him. . . .

The *footsteps* had been familiar, that's what it was! She tried desperately now to hear those footsteps again but her subconscious resisted.

Never struggle with an elusive memory, they say: you'll only drive it deeper. Let it work its own way to the surface. Eileen switched her mind to the key that had been stolen from her.

Her subconscious must have been working on that problem too, for at once a picture came to her of an incident she had forgotten. She was having tea in Douglas's flat, when Douglas knocked over her hand-bag and the contents spilled on the floor. She could still see him on his knees picking them up and restoring them to the bag with withering comments on the objects a woman carried round with her. Her key ring was one of them, and Douglas had asked if the big one was the key to her chastity belt. The "big one" was in fact the key to the garden shed in the school.

An insignificant incident, except that Eileen had the strong impression that it took place on the very foggy day last November. And if that was so, it cleared Tom King, and it cleared the other teachers as well. They couldn't have stolen the key if she still had it after school that day. . . .

Angus Pratt came home at 6.30. He had left a note in the morning that he would be in for supper. It was, these days, a rare occasion.

It soon appeared that it was a special occasion too. He took his soup in his usual remote silence, but when Eileen brought in the main course, he said: "I didn't like to waken you this morning."

"That was nice of you," said Eileen dryly.

"I was wanting a talk with you all the same. I've been thinking over what we discussed last night."

"What was that?" She wasn't giving him any help.

"I thought I might—if it's not putting you about, mark you—move over to Edencraigs at the week-end."

"That suits me. Sooner if you like."

How she *hated* him. It was the timing that was so monstrous. A week after his son's funeral, ten days after his wife was admitted to a mental hospital.

"What about Mother. What if she recovers?"

He shrugged. "Your mother never needed me."

"You won't visit her, even?"

He looked at her in surprise. "Will you?"

So far they weren't allowing visitors. Later, Eileen had no doubt, she would go to the hospital regularly. She would do no good; her mother, even if she recovered sufficiently to recognise her, would take no solace from her visits. But Eileen would still go: it was her duty.

Angus Pratt was more realistic. Or more inhuman, depending on how you looked at it.

What did surprise Eileen was his willingness to face a scandal. He had always hitherto maintained a veneer of respectability: Janet Macdonald herself had commented on it. And what about his post in the Ministry of Labour? Surely the Civil Service would frown on this kind of behaviour?

She put the point to him. He told her he was giving up his job.

"You're going to let your mistress keep you, is that it?"

It wasn't often that Angus Pratt's imperturbability was penetrated; but Eileen achieved it now.

171

"That's a disgusting suggestion, Eileen. I bought that pub for Janet and I still own a share of it. I'll help her run it. . . . Anyway, I'm not a pauper, you know."

Yes, it was hard to adjust to that. All these years her mother had boasted it was her money that gave them a comfortable standard of living and that Angus's salary was barely enough to keep them in food and clothing.

"What about this house?" she said.

Pratt shrugged. "It's in Margaret's name. I've no interest. Do what you like with it."

The episode was closed. He turned to his food and began to eat with his usual relish.

Eileen watched him for a moment, then pushed her own plate aside untasted. She stood up.

"There's an apple-cake in the oven, Father," she said coldly, "and the coffee's in the percolator."

He looked up. "Oh aye. Not hungry, eh?"

She had to restrain herself from banging the door. She went slowly upstairs to her bedroom.

She was angry and hurt. Unreasonably so. Her father had never pretended to any feelings for her: why should he begin now? But even insincerity would have been preferable to this bleak indifference.

The telephone rang. She heard her father go out to the hall to answer it.

"That's Douglas for you," he called.

Her heart leapt. She had been wondering if she should phone him. She ran downstairs.

"I'm all alone, darling," he said. "Really alone to-night. And pining. Any offers?"

"I'm sorry, Douglas," she said. She was remembering Nicolson's warning to stay at home to-night.

He sighed heavily. "Oh, God! Still in the doghouse, am I?"

At least he sounded as if he cared. Douglas was selfish, but not self-sufficient like that automaton in there.

"I really am sorry," she said. "We'll have lunch to-morrow, shall we?" Already she was half-convinced that Janet must have got her facts wrong about Douglas.

"While you're there, though," she added, "I've something to ask you. Do you remember the day you upset my bag in your flat and tumbled all the stuff out on the carpet?"

A long pause, then: "Vaguely. Why?"

"When was it, Douglas? What was the date?"

"The *date?* Have a heart, Eileen. I didn't mark it off on my calendar . . . I'd say about Christmas—maybe a week or two earlier."

"No, it was long before that. I think it was the 25th November. The day of the fog. The day Ian was murdered."

"What's all this in aid of, Eileen?" he said.

"If I've got the date right, it means that the key Tom King is supposed to have taken before four o'clock was still in my bag at 4.30."

"You're wrong about the date, though."

"I'm almost sure I'm not," she said with conviction.

Another pause. Then he said: "Remember you told me there was something familiar about the man who pushed you into the water?"

"Yes."

"Did you ever discover what it was?"

"Yes," she said. "It was his footsteps. I recognised his footsteps."

"You *recognised* them?"

"At the time I did. It's gone now. But it'll come back."

"Darling, I do wish you'd relent. Can't you come along even for an hour or so? Or shall I come and see you?"

No, she didn't want him here with her father around. All the same she was tempted: she so much needed company.

"Are you using the car to-night, Father?" she called through the open dining-room door.

"I was thinking of going to Edencraigs later on," he replied. "But if you——"

"No, thank you," she snapped. She wasn't taking favours from him.

She turned back to the telephone.

"If you call for me, Douglas," she said, "and drive me there and drive me back——"

"I'm on my way," he replied, and hung up.

"Don't go out to-night for *anything*," Nicolson had said. But she couldn't come to any harm if she was chaperoned all the time by her fiancé. . . .

If Douglas had shown a little more remorse, a little less contempt for Eileen's principles, the quarrel might never have developed. But then he wouldn't have been Douglas. . . .

It had started off so well, too. Douglas seemed determined to obliterate the memory of last night's fiasco. He made a fuss of her; plied her with sherry and cigarettes. And talked.

He could be entertaining when he was in the mood, for he combined the artist's gift of observation with a satirical turn of phrase. To-night he was describing his experience in the Latin quarter of Paris, where he had spent six months after leaving school.

Gradually Eileen's tension relaxed. She smiled, she laughed at his anecdotes. She was almost happy. Douglas looked quite different when his face was animated like this: the petted lines of the mouth were not apparent. This was the man she had fallen in love with.

It seemed a pity to spoil the idyll. Eileen, as always, was tempted to put off the hour, to accept this unexpected interlude of happiness. But the matter between them was too serious: the record had to be straightened.

She waited until Douglas had made coffee and brought it through. Then she said: "Douglas, why didn't you tell me about Alison Wright?"

The light and sparkle drained from his face, as if a cloud had passed over the sun. His eyes became wary and calculating. In them she could read his thought: should he deny it or not?

He decided not. "It was all over, darling, before I met you. I swear it."

"You should have told me." Eileen's tone was reproachful.

"Perhaps. Only I wasn't sure how you'd take it." He was still mildly penitent, but with just a hint of irritation.

Eileen was watching and listening very closely. This was vital. She could accept the Alison Wright episode, which was before her era; but she must satisfy herself there had been nothing of the sort in the last three years.

"Jennifer Cowie seemed very much at home here," she remarked.

Now his patience was wearing thin. "I told you last night, Eileen, she's just a stupid bitch of a model, that's all. She's nothing to me. You said you believed me."

"I did then."

"If you're looking for a quarrel——"

"I'm not. I just want to know how we stand."

"I *swear* there's been nothing like that since I met you. There, does that satisfy you?"

"Yes." A tiny doubt remained, but she was prepared to suppress it.

They had reached the crisis: the right word now from Douglas and the breach would have been healed. But what he said took them beyond the point of no return.

"Eileen, can't you understand, being engaged to a virgin puts an unnatural strain on a man."

"Virginity's not a sin, is it?"

"It's nothing to be proud of, either. Not nowadays. Honestly, darling, you're fifty years behind the times. . . . I really believe you'd rather I murdered your brother than spent the night in bed with Jenny Cowie."

"That's a *filthy* thing to say, Douglas." And then something in his expression told her the case wasn't hypothetical. "Where *were* you that night?" she asked.

He didn't answer. He didn't have to. Jennifer had given the answer last night.

And Jennifer wasn't the only one either. She remembered that Rugby Club dance last October. Lucia Finghetti talking and laughing with Douglas. It was Tom King who brought her to the dance but Douglas was the one she gravitated to. She had known him before, Eileen was certain of that; yet he had denied it.

"Lucia Finghetti must have been very adequate in bed, too, I should think," Eileen said savagely.

He stared at her, then smiled. "Very satisfactory indeed," he said.

"How long did you know her?"

Apparently he had decided on a policy of frankness.

"Three months. We lived dangerously. Neither of us was anxious to make a parade of our—friendship. I think we were clever to keep it dark so long, don't you?"

"You know, Douglas," said Eileen soberly, "if the police got to hear of this, you'd be in a mess. Just as well your 'stupid bitch of a model' can vouch for you. You were with Jennifer all that night?"

"All that night." He misinterpreted her quietness and added: "I'm glad you're being sensible about this, darling. These little—indiscretions don't mean a thing. I don't want to *marry* these girls."

He was probably being sincere, Eileen reflected. He simply couldn't understand why she should attach importance to it. It wasn't Douglas's fault, it wasn't Eileen's: their values were different, that was all.

Eileen was on her feet now. It was all finished; no point in lingering over the obsequies. She took off her ring and handed it to him.

"Good-bye, Douglas," she said.

He was utterly astounded. Eileen could even feel sorry for him as she saw the droop of the mouth that was the prelude to one of his bouts of depression and self-pity. "Let me drive you home," he offered, but without conviction.

"No, thank you. My bike's across the road, in the school."

She closed the door behind her and went down the steps and out into the street.

Her feelings were numbed. "I'll cry to-morrow": it was the phrase Annette had taught her as a child to repeat when she was hurt or unhappy.

"I'll cry to-morrow," she said to herself now, straightening her shoulders as she crossed the street to the school. A solitary car with dipped headlights was disappearing towards the town centre. Behind her a door opened and closed.

The road was white with frost and her breath traced silver patterns in the moonlight. Eileen went through the school gate, her footsteps ringing out in the stillness. Far over to the right was a light from a window of the headmaster's house.

She was half-way across the car park towards the cycle shed, which loomed ahead, a ghostly grey, when something irregular in the rhythm of her footsteps became apparent to her ear. She stopped. And the footsteps continued. And now she recognised them.

Eileen screamed. . . .

PART V

The Inspector

ONE

CHIEF DETECTIVE Inspector Mearns drummed his fingers on the desk. "I hope you're right, Maurice," he said. "I hope to God you're right."

For the second time to-day they had let King go after questioning; on both occasions on Nicolson's advice.

Mearns himself believed King was guilty but he hadn't the confidence to back his judgment. His handling of the case had mercilessly exposed the flaws in his character: the weakness, the vacillation, the indecision. Whatever the outcome, he had failed to seize his opportunity; his last chance of promotion was gone. Nicolson knew it, the Chief Constable knew it, in his heart Mearns must know it too.

The King case was symptomatic. He had listened to Nicolson and to Allan Cameron, he had made a decision: King was released. At once came the reaction—the doubts and the tortured soul-searching.

"I mean," said the Chief Inspector, "why did he lie if he'd nothing to hide? That's what bothers me."

"Yes, sir," said Nicolson patiently. It was the third time in the last hour that Mearns had made the observation.

This morning King had denied that Ian Pratt ever called on him at the school at night. Later, faced with Eileen Pratt's evidence, he had admitted the boy was with him on five successive Wednesdays, helping him write his thesis. Confirmation, for Cameron and Mearns, of his guilt; whereas Nicolson saw it as a pointer to his innocence.

It was Nicolson himself who had first focused attention on Tom King. King had known Lucia Finghetti, there was some indication that he had been meeting Ian Pratt at night, he had the best opportunity to remove Eileen Pratt's key. When King's name was thrown up by the sorting machine as one of the four men in Silbridge who fitted the specifications of the murderer, Chief Inspector Mearns was convinced.

But Nicolson advised caution. Partly because there wasn't enough evidence yet, only suspicion. But partly also because he was impressed by Eileen's doubts: she didn't think it had been King who threw her in the harbour.

King's evasions and truculence and downright lies were now understandable: he had been unwilling to admit he'd needed help with his thesis. From his reading of King's character Nicolson believed he would have cracked under pressure if it had been murder he was concealing and not petty fraud.

The Chief Inspector looked at his watch. "What the hell are they doing with these cards?" he muttered. He put through a call.

It had been Nicolson's idea. Assume King was telling the truth, assume Ian Pratt had spent the Wednesday nights collaborating with him on a thesis and not visiting his blackmail victim. Then these nights were no longer relevant. Concentrate on three nights only: 20th October, when Lucia Finghetti was run over; 25th November, when Ian Pratt was murdered; and 16th January, when an attempt was made on Eileen Pratt's life. Run the cards through the machine again and pick out this time those with no alibi for these nights. The list would be longer, but it would mean something.

Mearns put down the phone. "Ten minutes yet," he said. Then he dialled again and spoke to Sergeant Cubitt: "Allan Cameron not back yet? Well, send him in as soon as he comes."

He still liked to have Cameron around as a sounding-board, though when it came to a difference between Cameron and Nicolson, he tended nowadays to place his faith in Nicolson. As over this business of King: Cameron had pressed for a charge of murder to be laid against King, but had been overruled.

Nicolson suspected that Allan Cameron was sulking. He had stalked off as soon as King was released; that was two hours ago and he wasn't back yet.

The Chief Inspector was pacing the room impatiently. As always when things weren't going well, he looked physically spent; haggard; on the verge of a break-down. Perhaps he was. But Nicolson had before seen evidence of his recuperative powers. It only needed a break in the clouds, a ray of sunshine. . . .

If only he weren't such a *vampire*. Battening on other people, robbing them of precious time. These interminable conferences—debating decisions it was already too late to alter; wondering what the chief constable would think of this, how the Press would react to that.

To-night for Nicolson it was especially frustrating. Exclude King and there were only two feasible suspects. With these two in mind re-examine every scrap of evidence and the vital clue would show up.

Somewhere along the line the murderer must have made a mistake; they all did. You might miss it if you had ten or twenty or a hundred suspects: with two you couldn't.

If only he could have peace to concentrate, if Mearns wouldn't talk so: he was still burbling on about Allan Cameron. . . .

Police Constable Gray knocked and brought in a foolscap sheet and handed it to the Chief Inspector. Mearns grabbed it eagerly.

"It's not so bad," he said, counting. "I make it twenty-three. And some of them——"

"Just a minute," Nicolson interrupted: the pieces had suddenly clicked into place. "Is that name on the list?"

He tore a sheet from the pad on Mearns's desk, scribbled on it and passed it across.

Mearns looked at it, consulted his list. "Yes," he said. "Yes, it is. . . . Why?"

Nicolson told him.

They hadn't proof. Nothing that would stand up in court. Not yet.

They would get it. But it would take time. And there was Eileen to consider.

Mearns was reassuring. "He'd have had another go by now," he said, "if he'd been worried. He must think he's safe."

"I wouldn't bet on it," said Nicolson grimly. "I'm going to speak to her." He lifted the telephone. The time was 9.15. . . .

TWO

As THE traffic lights turned to green the patrol car crept gingerly round from the High Street into Drumchapel Row.

"Faster, Craig," Nicolson called from the back seat.

"There's ice on the road, sir," said the driver reprovingly.

So there was. Anyway, what was the hurry? She had been home a week and had come to no harm. Why should to-night be so critical?

It was illogical, but now that he knew its source, the danger seemed to Nicolson more immediate and more menacing. He felt every minute might count.

If only she had stayed home to-night. He'd *warned* her not to go out. Inside she was comparatively safe; all the murderer's operations had been conducted in the anonymity of the open air.

They were on Greene Road now.

"About half-way up, is it?" said Craig.

"Yes. Almost opposite the school. Number 93."

The car pulled up outside the flat and Nicolson and the detective constable got out. At that moment they heard the scream.

"It's from the school," Nicolson shouted, and sprinted across the road, with Wood at his heels. Craig started up his engine again and swung the car round towards the gate.

A hundred yards ahead Nicolson could pick out in the moonlight two shadowy figures, running. A girl and a man. They were about forty yards apart and were heading left towards the main school building.

When she reached the school, the girl stopped. The gap rapidly closed. What the devil was she doing? Nicolson was running at full stretch but he was too far away, he'd never get there in time. Even the car, now sweeping in through the gate, was going to be too late.

Five seconds the girl must have stood. It seemed minutes: a nightmare in slow motion. Then a key clicked in a lock, the door opened, and the girl was inside. The man threw himself at the door to stop it closing, there was a brief struggle, then he too was through. And now the door slammed shut as the police car shrieked to a halt alongside. A moment later Nicolson and Wood were there too.

Inside there was the clatter of feet on stone steps. Lights went up, on the ground floor, then the first. The girl was screaming again.

Nicolson pulled himself up on a window sill, smashed a pane with his elbow, put a hand in and released the catch. Detective-Constable Wood followed him in. Wood switched on his torch and they picked their way between desks to the door.

This end of the corridor and the stair-well were a blaze of light. The man must be throwing on the switches as he passed. The screaming was above them now and muffled.

Nicolson took the stairs three at a time, then sprinted along the corridor to the gymnasium. He guessed that was where Eileen would make for, like a rabbit scuttling for its burrow.

The gymnasium itself was unlit. But as Nicolson thrust open the swing door he had a glimpse, in the borrowed light from the corridor, of ropes and wall-bars and the trampoline; and on the floor two panting, struggling figures, the girl on her back, the man straddling her, his hands on her throat. The screams were silenced now.

Nicolson launched himself in a rugby tackle. Behind him the door opened again as Constable Wood ran in; the light caught the look of surprise on the man's face as he jerked round.

The sudden movement almost caused Nicolson's tackle to miss. But as he slithered past, his knee cracked full into the man's chin and knocked him out cold.

"Put the lights on, Wood," he shouted as he dragged the man's body off the girl.

She was whimpering softly, her arms still feebly clawing the air.

"It's all right now, Eileen," he said, leaning over her. "Everything's all right now."

The lights went on. He saw her fingers stained crimson where her nails had clawed at the strangler's wrists. He saw her eyes dilate with terror, then gradually relax as she recognised who was now bending over her.

"Everything's all right now," Nicolson repeated gently.

Behind him there was a gasp from Wood. "God," he muttered, "it's her old man!"

Eileen heard him. "Yes," she whispered. "It's my father."

EPILOGUE

EILEEN CAME in nervously and shook his hand as if they were strangers. She wore a dark suit under her lemon raincoat.

"They told me at the police station it was your day off," she said.

"I hoped you'd get in touch." He had heard she was in Silbridge to see about selling the house. "It's been a long time."

"Eight weeks."

"You look fit," he said.

"Annette's been spoiling me. I've put on weight."

"Not so as you'd notice. Come and sit down. Sherry? Gin?"

"Sherry, please."

Nicolson wondered how long they could skate round the subject.

But Eileen took a deep breath and was launched. "Thank you for saving my life, Maurice."

"Forget it."

"I won't forget it ever. How did you know——"

"Don't let's talk about it, Eileen."

She frowned. "I'm sick of people protecting me. I'm not a child, and I'm not ill any more. There are things I don't understand. I want to *know*, Maurice." The knuckles of the hand that held the sherry glass were white.

"What do you want to know?" he asked.

"Why he did it, how he did it. And for a start, how you turned up that night just when I needed you."

It wasn't what he wanted to discuss with her. But he saw she was determined.

"We phoned your house," he said, "and got no reply. Our man reported you'd gone off in your fiancé's car and that your father left on your heels."

"What do you mean—'your man'?"

"The man we had watching your house."

"But I asked you——"

Nicolson grinned. "Yes, you asked us to take him away. Of course," he added, "his job was to keep unwelcome visitors *out*. We didn't know then where the real danger lay."

"When did you find out?"

"Much too late."

Ian Pratt's mysterious outings on Wednesday nights, he told her, had been the red herring. His diary—what Bradley saw of it—suggested that that was when he met his blackmail victim; Lenny Ferguson and others seemed to confirm it. But it was false.

Once Nicolson learned about King and his thesis, he was able to reconsider suspects who had been eliminated because they had an alibi for one or more of the Wednesday nights.

"Especially your father and your fiancé," he said.

"Why?"

"Because you didn't *want* to remember who had pushed you into the harbour. 'Your mind closed up,' you said. You were scared, that's why. You knew it was someone close."

Eileen nodded. "Yes," she agreed. "I think that's true."

"Troup seemed the better bet." He watched her but could detect no reaction. "As a master in the school he was more likely to think of burying a body in the grounds. Also—" he hesitated "—he did know Lucia Finghetti."

Eileen showed a flash of temper. "You don't need to be delicate," she said. "She was Douglas's mistress. I *know* all that."

"Yes. . . . But then one or two things came back to me. Little things. . . ."

"Give me a cigarette, Maurice, would you?" she interrupted.

"Of course." He looked at her anxiously. "Are you sure you want me to go on?"

She nodded impatiently as she lit her cigarette.

"Well, it was something your father said about the green suitcase. He told me he hadn't seen it for two years. It was too big, he said, and besides one of the locks was broken. That was why he'd stopped using it. But you told me you'd taken it on holiday last summer and it was only then that the lock got broken. How did he know it had a broken lock if he hadn't seen it for two years?"

"I see. . . . A bit tenuous, though, isn't it?"

"Perhaps. But it made me suspicious. And then . . . remember the phone call he said he'd had? From somebody pretending to be me?"

"Yes."

He smiled. "Well, listen carefully. This is an exercise in logic. Your father said he was in bed when the phone rang at 11.50. He put on a dressing-gown over his pyjamas and went downstairs. That's how he was dressed when you came in, wasn't it?"

"Yes."

"Your mother, on the other hand, said he'd just come upstairs and hadn't even his clothes off when the phone rang."

"But I *explained* that, Maurice. Mother would never admit she was asleep. Her insomnia was a matter of pride. She would pretend she'd heard the phone. And she'd just guess whether Father was dressed or not. That doesn't mean a thing."

"It wouldn't," he agreed, "except that *he said she was awake*. And that must have been a lie. Your mother couldn't have made a *mistake* about how he was dressed."

"He invented the phone call, then?"

"Yes. It was very odd when you think of it—to get a message that his son's body had been found, and to let *you* go down to identify it."

"That wasn't odd at all if you'd known Father."

"Perhaps not. Still, it was remarkable that the battery of his car happened to be flat that particular night."

"That wasn't true, I suppose?"

"Of course not. He needed the car to get to the harbour ahead of you."

Eileen shivered.

"This is upsetting you, Eileen," he said.

"No!" Her tone was fierce. "I must understand what made him do it. Tell me it from the beginning."

The beginning? Who was to say what was the beginning? The roots went far back.

For years Angus Pratt had been living a double life. His family meant nothing to him; less than nothing—they were an encumbrance. The one person he cared for was Janet Macdonald.

But Janet aged more rapidly than he, and in time he looked elsewhere for his physical fulfilment. To Lucia Finghetti. She was expensive but doubtless satisfactory.

But then Lucia became pregnant and sought to turn the situation to her advantage by a little mild blackmail. She did in fact squeeze money from one of her clients, but she was playing a dangerous game when she threatened Pratt.

On the night she died Lucia and Angus must have met and discussed it. He would drop her as usual outside The Boar's Head and she would turn up Potter Street towards home. Pratt followed her in the car . . .

"I don't think the murder was planned," said Nicolson. "It would be a sudden impulse, triggered off by seeing the girl in his headlights in the dark, empty street. In fact—who knows?—it might even have been an accident. Anyway, he didn't stop. . . . And the street wasn't quite empty after all."

"Ian?"

"Yes. I imagine he was up at the corner, on Crane Road. He probably had just come out of the café. He saw what happened and recognised the car. He went down through the slush to where the girl lay and saw she was dead. He didn't report it."

"It was his own father," said Eileen hotly. "And anyway I'm sure Ian didn't know the girl had been *murdered*."

"Probably not. It was still his duty to report it. Instead he put the squeeze on your father."

"You make that sound *horrible*," said Eileen. "You can't blame Ian for not turning in his own father."

"He extorted money from him, there's no getting away from that."

But seeing Eileen's distress, he added gently: "Perhaps 'extorted' is too strong. He probably thought your father owed it to him for the wrongs he'd done his family." Better leave her with some illusions; she had little enough to hold on to.

"And then?" said Eileen harshly. She was fumbling with another cigarette.

Ian and his father must have struck a bargain. Ian would go off and start a new life somewhere else—he had been hovering on the brink for months anyway—and would accept a lump sum in final payment.

"The £2,000?" said Eileen.

"We've only that one reference in the diary to the amount. But it must have been substantial; it must have been worth killing for."

Since Pratt's arrest they had found in his cheque book a blank among the counterfoils for 25th November. It was believed he had given Ian the cheque some time during that day and had recovered it later from his body.

Pratt knew Ian's plans. He knew he was going back to the school to complete his work with King before catching his train. And he lay in wait for him at the school. He struck him down, then strangled him, and recovered from his pockets the cheque and the left luggage counterfoil for the suitcase. He hid the body while he went to the station to pick up the case. He removed the diaries for later destruction, then dumped the case, with the rest of its contents, off Cradock Pier. He returned to the school late, and, using Eileen's key, took a spade and the gardener's boots from the toolshed and buried the body.

"That's largely conjecture," Nicolson added, "although he's admitted some of it."

"He was lucky it was so foggy," said Eileen.

"If the conditions hadn't been right, he wouldn't have gone through with the murder; he'd have accepted the loss of his money."

"Imagine him thinking of the toolshed! Of course, he knew it. He was a crony of the gardener."

"And it would be easy for him to get your key, I suppose?"

"He probably took it from my bag while I was making the supper. But why didn't he put it back on my ring when he got home?"

"No opportunity, perhaps. Or maybe he just forgot. If it was a mistake, it was almost his only one."

It had been a devilishly ingenious murder, because Pratt had taken advantage of—indeed, had probably *encouraged*—Ian's plan to disappear secretly. Afterwards the plan was allowed to leak out gradually. Pratt hadn't had to say much himself; others had done his work for him. And he had a gratuitous slice of luck when the boy Thomas was identified as Ian in Glasgow.

"He'd have got away with it," said Nicolson frankly, "if you hadn't been so persistent."

"I know why he attacked me," said Eileen.

"You knew too much?"

"He *thought* I knew too much. That night I came home from Glasgow, I was talking to Mother about Lucia. He was there. I mentioned the time I met her at the dance. 'You're not like him,' she said to me. She meant Ian. But I didn't make that clear when I was describing it to Mother. Father got up and went out of the room. He looked kind of funny. . . . That came back to me just the other night. I realised then *why* he'd been afraid of me."

"He thought you knew of his connection with Lucia?"

"Yes."

"And the second attack—I suppose he was still afraid you might blurt it out?"

"He may have been. . . . But something hastened it on. He overheard me speaking to Douglas on the phone about the footsteps. I said I was near to remembering whose they were."

"What was special about the footsteps?"

Eileen shivered. "It's the *deliberate* way he walked, sort of heel first. I've never known anyone else walk quite like that."

They fell silent. The real reason for Eileen's visit hadn't yet been touched on. Nicolson waited.

"Where's the photograph?" she asked abruptly.

"Of Ruth? I took it down." When she didn't answer he added: "I was never in love with Ruth, you know."

"I got your letter, Maurice," she said. Her face was white and strained. But she veered away again. Back to her father. "Do you think he's insane, Maurice?"

Nicolson was uneasily aware of where this was leading. He wondered if he should give a comforting answer; but he paid her the compliment of the truth.

"Certainly not in the legal sense," he said. Pratt was going to plead insanity; but it was a defence born of despair. "And not even medically insane either. Not unless every murderer is insane by definition."

No, Angus Pratt was simply a self-centred man who had given way to sudden and fatal temptation. A dark night, a girl who was a menace to him caught in his headlamps in a deserted street. . . . And after one murder, a second was all too easy.

"Douglas has had a lucky escape, hasn't he?" said Eileen.

"I don't understand," said Nicolson. But he did.

"Well, I returned his ring just in time, didn't I? Saved him the embarrassment of breaking it off."

"You're not still pining for Douglas, are you?"

She shook her head emphatically. "No, that's over. I've no regrets. . . . I've accepted a post in Liverpool, did you know that?"

"No."

"I'll stay with Annette and Peter for a bit." She stood up and held out her hand. "Well, Maurice——"

"You haven't given me an answer," he said quietly.

There was a hunted look on her face. "I hoped I wouldn't have to put it into words. The answer is 'No,' Maurice. I'm not going to marry. Not now, not ever. Not you, not anyone."

"Why not?" Again he knew the answer.

"There's such a thing as heredity. I've one parent in a mental hospital and the other awaiting trial for murder."

"It's not your parents I want to marry. It's *you*."

"They're part of me. I can't escape from them. Don't think I'm not grateful, Maurice. I've heard you're a sucker for lame dogs."

"Don't be a little fool! I'm not sorry for you: I love you. Don't you understand plain English?"

"Good-bye, Maurice," she said firmly. But she didn't look at him.

"I'll write," he said.

She hesitated. "If you like. . . . But don't expect——"

"I'll be patient," he said. "I can wait."

She turned away.

From his window Nicolson watched her cross the road, her lemon raincoat loose over her shoulders, her head held high.

THE END